AS THE TIDE TURNS

CHRISTINE HOLMES

AMBASSADOR

BELFAST, NORTHERN IRELAND
GREENVILLE, SOUTH CAROLINA

As The Tide Turns
© Copyright 2003 Christine Holmes

All rights reserved

ISBN 1 84030 148 1

Published by the Ambassador Group
Ambassador Publications
a division of
Ambassador Productions Ltd.
Providence House
Ardenlee Street,
Belfast,
BT6 8QJ
Northern Ireland
www.ambassador-productions.com
&
Ambassador Emerald International
427 Wade Hampton Blvd.
Greenville
SC 29609, USA
www.emeraldhouse.com

Contents

Acknowledgments

Writing a novel began as a dream in my heart a very long time ago and I would like to thank God that with Him all things are possible and dreams do come true.

I'd like to thank my husband and family for their support while I was writing this book and for their encouragement to keep going until the last chapter.

My parents have played an important role in my dream to become a writer. As a child they encouraged my dream to write and my love of reading. My dad gave me paper and pens and I declared to both my parents when I grew up I would write books! My dad is in heaven now but I'm sure he would be very happy for me. My mum is still with us and it is good that she can see the fulfilment of my dream.

Throughout my life God has brought people along who encouraged me and prayed with me and I would like to thank them that the seeds were planted in faith are now producing a harvest. There are too many to name but you all know who you are and from the bottom of my heart I thank you for your love and support. I thank God for your words of encouragement and your prayers for me that have been answered and I've discovered that writing a book doesn't just involve me but the people that God brings along the way just when I need it most.

My thanks to Pastor Lewis Smyth and his wife Gwen for their faithful ministry and to the family of Jordan Victory Church. We are continually being built up in the Lord and in His Word, to believe for our dreams, to know we have a purpose in God and to have vision for the future. I thank God I am part of the vision.

My thanks to the staff at Ambassador Productions, to Gillian, Linda and especially to Samuel Lowry who encouraged me along the way from the first few chapters of the book until the end, your support means so much to me. Thank you. To all the staff involved in producing and printing the book my thanks to you, it couldn't happen without you and I appreciate your work.

This book is the result of not one writer but many people and most of all to the One to whom I give all thanks, my Lord Jesus Christ.

Christine Holmes

1 IT HAD BEEN a long busy day and at 7:30pm Emily decided it was time to go home. As she tidied her desk she glanced at her diary for the next day. She sighed. Another busy day lay ahead yet the work load remained constant.

Suddenly the office door opened and Emily saw Steven in the half light. With only her desk lamp on the room was in semi-darkness. Emily felt uneasy inside as Steven approached her.

She stood up but stayed behind her desk. "What are you doing here Steven? I thought you had finished business for today."

He sat down opposite to were she was standing and Emily could smell whiskey on his breath. "What do you want Steven?"

He grinned. "What do I want? Emily, that isn't a nice welcome. It lacks warmth. Don't you think?"

Emily ignored his question and sat down behind her desk. "Steven I don't have any reason to be nice to you so why don't you say whatever it is you came to say and then you can go. I'm tired and I'd like to get home to my family."

He laughed in a mocking sort of way. "Oh yes. Home to your lovely husband and your nice children."

"Yes Steven I do appreciate my husband and children."

The smile disappeared from his face and Emily shivered as his eyes focused on her. She had always disliked the man because he couldn't be trusted but she knew that he hated her. Everything about Steven was so false.

"Emily there is no need to feel uncomfortable; I just want a little chat. Actually I wanted to put you straight on some things. My lovely wife Victoria had lunch with you today and although I'm not sure what it is you find to talk about I don't like the influence you seem to have on Victoria. She came home today full of silly nonsense, you know the kind I mean Emily."

"I'll stop you right there Steven. Victoria and I had a very enjoyable lunch and nothing I talk about to her is silly nonsense."

"Victoria came home today and I got the usual stuff about how she puts up with me and that she has dreams of her own that she would like to pursue. She only talks like this when she has been with you Emily and its' all nonsense." His voice slurred and Emily guessed he'd had several whiskies.

"Steven you already know how I feel about the way in which you treat Victoria but she is your wife and she is still with you. However, I simply encouraged her to take up painting again. I have seen her work and she is good Steven. Victoria is a very talented woman and she should be encouraged."

He laughed. "So now you are also an expert on talent. My brother must be so glad he married someone as clever as you. Now you listen to me Emily.

Victoria is my wife and when you encourage her she then becomes restless. I don't like that Emily because it leads to arguments. Victoria is usually quite happy to support me in managing the hotel and she looks after our daughter. She doesn't need you interfering in her life. Do you understand?"

"So you have come to warn me off?"

"Now Emily, you should be careful with your words."

Emily laughed. "Have you finished now? You have hardly paused for breath. You know Steven I'm not sure what it is with you. You seem to think Victoria shouldn't have any other interests in her life. What's your problem? Are you afraid she might become successful? Maybe you couldn't stand the competition." Emily tried not to get angry and in her heart she knew warning bells were ringing.

"Emily I don't have anything to be afraid of. My wife is supporting me in business and she is a mother. That is quite enough for her I think."

"Oh you think! Victoria can't think for herself now."

"I'll remind you that Victoria does not have time for stupid hobbies. The business which is part of the same hotel chain you work for is enough for both of us. Now I'd be grateful in future if you would get on with your own life and keep out of ours."

"Don't give me all that happy marriage stuff Steven. We both know how you really treat Victoria. Not exactly the loving husband, are you? More of a bully I should think. Then there are your hobbies, and you have quite a few. It's no wonder that Victoria had no time for anything else in her life."

Emily could see the tension in his face. "What are you implying?"

"I'm not implying anything. I know how deeply involved you are with gambling and then there are the free drinks from the private bar. Oh and we mustn't forget your other interests, outside of the happy marriage you have."

"I hope you are not telling these lies to Victoria. It's no wonder she seems unhappy at times. I want you to stay away from my wife Emily."

Emily knew she had hit a nerve. She stood up and walked around her desk. "Don't threaten me Steven. I'm not afraid of you and I don't have to put up with you like Victoria does. Regarding your outside interests, I think we both know that you would fail a lie detector test when it comes to faithfulness. Now I think it's time you left."

He stood up and walked toward the door. "Don't try to make trouble for me Emily because I give as good as I get."

"Steven I already know that there are no levels to which you would not sink, however, I would never do anything to hurt Victoria. I'll leave that one to you. One last thing Steven. One day you are going to slip up, you'll get over confident in thinking all your tracks are covered and when you do, Victoria will not want to know you."

He stood closer to Emily's face and the smell of whiskey turned her stomach. "Listen lady, you were nothing when you married into this family. Tread carefully or you could be nothing again."

"Are you threatening me Steven?"

"I don't threaten Emily. I'm just reminding you where you came from and that you never had it so good until Jack came along."

"You're wrong Steven. You think I married Jack because of the precious Dillon-Spence family name and the hotel chain. Jack and I love each other and everything else comes second to that, including the business."

He stepped back and clapped his hands. "Nice speech Emily. You really have it down to a fine art. I'm surprised you haven't mentioned the God bit. You know what I mean. You talk about this God who has blessed you and Jack. Well I don't believe that for a second. When you met Jack you saw an opportunity for a new life for you and your daughter. You grabbed on with both hands because not every man would take on someone else's child but then Jack always did have a big heart. You could never have let someone like him slip by."

"At least Jack has a heart, unlike you Steven."

Stop! I'm the only one who can change hearts.

Emily knew that the Holy Spirit wanted her out of that situation before it turned nasty.

Steven opened the door. "We go back to England soon but in the meantime, stay away from Victoria."

Emily held her breath. There was so much more she could have said but anger was not the way God sorted situations. "Lord I'm sorry that man annoys me so."

He's not your responsibility. Leave Victoria's needs to me.

The telephone rang and Emily jumped as she went to answer it. "Hello."

"Hi honey. Don't you think it's time you quit? Anna has prepared a meal for us so get out of that office before I send security for you."

Emily laughed as she breathed a sigh of relief. "I'll be there soon Jack. I'm just tidying my desk."

"You've got fifteen minutes and then I'm coming for you myself. Bye."

Emily replaced the receiver and suddenly she felt tears in her eyes. She wasn't sure why she was crying. Maybe it was hearing the love in Jacks voice after listening to such bitterness in Steven's tone. She took out her make up and tided her face. She didn't want Jack to know she'd been crying. "Lord, thank you for my husband and my family. I can almost feel sorry for Steven. He has never known such love but maybe one day you will be able to reach into his heart."

It's called grace and mercy. Leave Steven with me.

Emily smiled as she switched off the desk lamp and headed for home. She stepped into the elevator and felt relieved that she didn't have to travel far since they had the penthouse apartment in the hotel. One of the joys of managing a first class hotel was that they got to live there too!

The Cedar Lodge Hotel was located along the Antrim Coast in Northern Ireland. The back of the hotel faced towards the mountains displaying the most amazing shades of green. The gardens in the surrounding area were landscaped with trees and flowerbeds. The front of the building overlooked the sea and the vastness of the coastline. Golden sand, white rocks and the fresh sea air. It stretched for miles and the most magnificent sight was watching the rays of the sun shining down on the waves like shafts of light reflecting the glimmer of diamonds as they sparkled. The sun setting was another glorious sight as the day changed to amber light on the horizon that brought calmness to the soul. Emily loved to watch it as it reminded her of how awesome God is and that only her Creator could design such scenic perfection.

Jack and Emily had moved to Northern Ireland after they married. The Cedar Lodge was the first hotel bought over by the Dillon-Spence Group in Ireland. They owned the Royal Court in Kensington, London were Jacks parents resided and the Edgewater Hotel, in Bournemouth in the south of England which was managed by Steven and Victoria. The tourist industry had been their lives from when Jacks grandfather had died leaving a small bed and breakfast guesthouse to Jacks father. The family had worked hard to become the business empire that the Dillon-Spence Group were known as.

The Cedar Lodge was busy all year round, in the industry a lot of work was seasonal and promotions were targeted to each season. Jack and Emily worked hard to maintain their five star rating with the tourist board and they promoted the business at every opportunity. They catered for family holidays, business conferences and company residentials were an all round favourite. The location was good as it brought people out of the work place for business training. Wedding receptions were big business for the hotel and the bridal suite was furnished in romantic, soft colourings and subtle lighting.

Overall the hotel did everything possible to provide the best service for its guests and Jack and Emily took pride in the hard work that also brought rewards of career and financial satisfaction.

Emily opened the door to the penthouse suite and the smell of Anna's lovely cooking greeted her. She tended to forget to eat when she was busy but suddenly she realised she was starving.

"Hi everyone, I'm home."

Jack came out of the kitchen looking at his watch. "About time too. You are keeping long hour's lady and it's not allowed anymore."

Emily laughed as she then kissed him. "Yes sir! I know I was running late but now I'm really glad to be home."

"Mummy I missed you." Three year old Nathan came running down the hallway. Emily picked him up and hugged him. "Oh that feels good darling." She kissed his cheek and he laughed as he wrapped his chubby arms around her neck. Nathan looked so much like his dad with dark eyes and a smile that melted Emily's heart.

Anna came out of the dining room. "Dinner is ready now."

Emily gave Nathan to Jack. "Give me a few minutes to get changed out of this suit and into something more comfortable. Where's Rosa?"

"I'm in here mummy."

Emily followed the direction of her little voice and found her watching television in the lounge. "Hello sweetheart. How has your day been?"

"It's been good. I did well in school with my story for English class so I have no homework tonight."

Emily stroked her hair. "Maybe one day you will be a writer."

Rosa laughed. "Maybe I will but I still want to be a teacher too."

"Darling you can be anything you want to be. Now have you had dinner?"

"Yes. Anna made dinner for Nathan and I ages ago." Emily laughed. "I know I'm late back tonight but I had lots of work to do. I'm going to get changed and have dinner with daddy. Anna is going to get Nathan settled and you are going into the bath."

"When you have dinner will you come and read me a story?"

"Of course I will but for now I really need to get these shoes off. My feet are killing me."

Rosa laughed. "When I grow up can I have high heeled shoes like you and lots of make up? I might like a car too."

"I'm sure you can. Maybe daddy will buy you your first car." She teased.

Rosa's eyes grew bigger at the thought. "Mummy I think we will keep that one a secret until I'm grown."

"I think so too. We wouldn't want to surprise daddy to soon." They both giggled and Emily hugged her. Rosa was seven now and quite a determined little lady. Emily believed in encouraging and inspiring her children's dreams and building their confidence. They were being taught that with God all things are possible and that in him they have a destiny.

Emily changed out of her business suit and into casual trousers and a loose top. She slipped her feet in comfortable mules and glanced at herself in the mirror. She loved this part of the day when she dressed down for dinner instead of the other way round and she loved coming home to her family.

Anna looked after the children while Jack and Emily had dinner. She had been their live-in nanny since they had arrived in Ireland and Emily felt blessed in having someone she could trust with her children. After dinner Emily went into Nathan's room and found him lying in bed with his favourite teddy and looking very sleepy. Emily kissed his cheek. "Oh you smell so good. I bet you had lots of bubbles in your bath."

"Lots and lots." He sat up and hugged her. "I love you and daddy and Rosa and Anna."

"And we all love you. Nathan you are a special boy darling." He yawned and Emily settled him down in his bed. "I think it's time my little boy was asleep." She stroked his head as he closed his eyes and in a few minutes Nathan was sound asleep. Emily kissed his cheek and she thought her heart would burst with love for her son. The miracle of both her children was something she never took for granted.

Jack had begun to tell Rosa a story as Emily came in and sat down on the wicker chair.

"You have to be quiet mummy and let daddy read the story."

"I will. I'm sure daddy is very good at it."

Ten minutes into the story and Rosa's eyes were heavy. By the end of the chapter she was asleep.

Jack and Emily cuddled up on the sofa. The lamp gave off enough light to create a relaxing mood and Anna had lit a few candles.

Lying with her head on Jack's chest she could hear the sound of his heartbeat and feel the warmth of his body. She loved the secure feeling this gave her and being with Jack was something she looked forward to at the end of each day.

"You seemed quiet at dinner tonight Emily. Is there any problems at work I should know about?"

"No work is fine. I did have a visit from Steven just before I left the office."

Emily felt his body tense. "Why didn't you telephone me? I would have come down."

"I know you would but I can handle Steven. He's really just a weak insecure man and I think he sees me as a threat. He thinks I'm a bad influence on Victoria. I had lunch with her today and he doesn't like her spending time with me."

Jack laughed. "I suppose you told him what you thought of him."

"I did. Sometimes Steven makes me feel so angry and at other times I feel sorry for him. He tries to fill up his life with so many things that could ruin him. He can be smart in business yet reckless in gambling. Victoria is a lovely wife and a good mother, she is also his business partner yet he has to stroke his ego by seeing other women. I feel sorry for Victoria. She pretends she doesn't know about the other women but I think she just ignores it."

"Steven always had this self-centred side to his nature, even when we were children. He was always getting into trouble with dad. I think he just wants the best of both worlds. He wants a wife and family but still has ties with his single life."

"Maybe you're right but that doesn't excuse the way he treats Victoria. I know he has physically abused her. I saw the bruises."

"Then why does she put up with him?"

Emily laughed. "Think about it Jack. She has no family that she is close to and Steven is a powerful influence in her life which makes her afraid to go up against him. In public he is the loving husband and devoted daddy. That's the image he creates and people believe that's the person he is, including your parents. If Victoria left he would find a way to blame the break up on her. Steven is good at manipulating when it suits him."

"I suppose you're right but until Victoria decides to do anything about it there is nothing we can do. She must know we would help her."

"Yes she does but she's afraid of many things Jack. I'll always be her friend and that's one thing she is assured of."

"I do feel sorry for Victoria and I agree you should be a friend to her but I'll be glad when Steven goes back to England. I don't trust him, especially in business and I try to watch him at every turn."

Emily yawned. "Enough about him. I'm tired and I'm home where I belong. Why don't we go to bed?"

Jack kissed her head. "That sounds good to me. Let's go."

Lying next to Jack was all Emily needed to feel loved. His arms around her were like a security net that made her feel safe and warm. She felt nothing could ever harm her when she was with him. Closing her eyes she said a grateful prayer of thanks for her husband and children. God had blessed her life so much and yet she remembered a time when God hadn't meant anything to her.

She could hear the steady rhythm of Jack breathing and she closed her eyes. "I love you Jack." She whispered.

"I love you Emily, forever."

Sleep came like a peaceful blanket covering both of them, wrapped in the security that God was watching over them.

2

RECEPTION WAS ALWAYS a busy place early in the morning. Guests checking out and accounts to be made up, keys handed back and usually luggage all over the floor. The staff had been well trained in doing their job quickly and efficiently. As Emily passed through reception she smiled to herself as she remembered the years she had trained, first as a junior receptionist and finally head receptionist and then she had met Jack.

She went into her office to find Jack already checking the diary for that day.

"You have got off to an early start darling. We have a conference arriving this morning and then a meeting with the shareholders plus the routine stuff".

Jack grinned at her and Emily caught the twinkle in his eyes. "Emily you shouldn't be here. This is supposed to be your day off and you told me you were going to visit the children's home."

"Yes I know and I am. I just didn't realise how busy the hotel is today."

"Emily I don't want you here. I know the hotel is busy but it's busy every day. We can manage so go and enjoy your day. I promise I'll still be in one piece when you get back."

Emily laughed. "Ok, if you're sure. I'll see you for dinner tonight."

Jack kissed her. "I'll look forward to it. Now go and be back before dark."

"I'm a big girl Jack and I've stayed out late before."

"Well I want you back early, I'll miss you."

Emily hugged him. "That's kind of you. I don't know how I'd cope without you."

"I think you should go before I'm tempted to chain you to the office chair."

"Maybe I might like that." She teased.

"Not if I include the accounts for you to do."

"Fine I'm out of here. Bye."

Driving out of the hotel Emily admired the surrounding gardens and she made a mental note to mention it to the gardener. She always thought it important to tell someone they were doing a good job and to make them feel appreciated. She and Jack were good at building staff confidence in whatever role an employee worked. The hotel needed everyone working together in order for it to be the success it was and they had a good team when it came to staff.

Emily enjoyed the drive along the coast road as a cool breeze blew through the open window. The view of the ocean was breathtaking and its vastness reflected the God she loved. Only he could create the beauty that daily surrounded her. As she drove she sang a song of praise and she knew his voice in her heart.

I've loved you with an everlasting love.

His words brought joy to her spirit and her heart was full of thanks to him for the new life he had given her.

Emily's life hadn't always been happy, something her brother-in-law Steven liked to remind her about. He had been born into wealth and a powerful family name. He never had to struggle for anything and he took a lot for granted in his life.

Emily had been reborn when she had an experience with God that taught her what real love was about. At times she found herself praying for Steven even if she didn't get along with him!

Emily had a meeting with Iris Boyd who was the matron of Cedar Children's Home. She and Jack took an active part in fundraising for the home and they took an interest in the older children who were preparing to leave. Sometimes it was possible to let them have work experience at the hotel and if any of them showed an interest in either catering or hotel administration, Emily did whatever possible to help them begin their career.

Emily had grown up in a children's home in Kingsbridge, South Devon. The home was located not far from Kingsbridge in a place called Hope Cove which was a small fishing village with beautiful sandy beaches.

She knew every feeling and emotion that children in care experienced. She remembered as a little girl hoping someone would adopt her. She wanted so much to be part of a loving family. For some children it happened but there were those like herself who faced the disappointment of being left behind.

Emily had been placed in care when she was three months old. She went into foster care for awhile and her birth mother came to visit her several times. Just before her first birthday her mother made the decision to let her go and Emily remained in the children's home. Her mother never came back to visit her and because she was still a baby she had no memory of what her mother looked like.

Emily got on well with the matron of the home. Adele Adams was a kind compassionate woman whom all the children loved. Emily had been in the home the longest so she helped take care of the younger children and when one of them was placed for adoption she would help organise the farewell party. By the time she was in her teens she had stopped hoping that someone would want her. People tended to adopt younger children but Emily had discovered someone else in her life. A local pastor who came to visit the children had held a special service for them and he told the story about the lost sheep but Jesus the shepherd searched until he found it. Emily nearly cried when she thought of a little sheep lost and lonely then she realised she felt that way about herself. At the end of the meeting he asked if anyone would like to invite Jesus into their heart and she put her hand up. She was the only one but the pastor came and prayed with her and although she didn't know much about God, she knew her life had a purpose and she was loved.

When she was almost sixteen she began to ask more questions about her background. The matron told her that her mother was only fifteen when she had her and her family didn't want anything to do with her. Then it was something to be ashamed of and they gave her mother no choice but to put Emily into care. Her dad had been a lad helping out on one of the farms but when her mother became pregnant he left overnight and never came back.

Emily realised that letting her go must have been so difficult for her mother because had her family supported her she would have kept her baby. Now that Emily was nearing her sixteenth birthday she had hoped her mother would try to trace her but she never did and Emily still felt sad about that. She had often thought of her life as being one big mistake but after she accepted Jesus into her heart the pastor had given her a bible of her own. Her biggest breakthrough came when she opened at Jeremiah chapter one and verse five. *"Before I formed you in the womb I knew you, before you were born I set you apart…"*

Her heart leapt for joy because God had known her and her life was not a mistake. He had a purpose for her regardless of the circumstances of her birth.

The day before her birthday Adele called her into the office and handed her an envelope. This was something her birth mother had left years ago and matron thought it best to give it to her the day before her birthday rather than on the day. Adele always tried to be sensitive to the children's feelings. "Emily this is something personal from your mother to you. Now you can open it here and I'll stay with you or you can go to your room and open it in private."

"I'll go to my room but if I need you."

"I'm here for you Emily."

Emily had her own room being one of the longest staying children at the home. She remembered sitting on her bed and opening the envelope.

Her hands were shaking as she poured the contents onto the bed. There was a photograph of her mother with Emily in her arms. It had been taken in a garden and Emily was surprised how young her mother looked. She knew she was just fifteen when Emily was born but she looked even younger in the photo. There was a silver heart pendent which had tarnished over the years but Emily knew she could polish it up. Inside was a tiny photograph of Emily, taken when she was just a few weeks by the look of it. Lastly there was a letter and Emily sat back on her bed to read it.

My little Emily

I love you and I'm so sorry to have to let you go. When you are older I hope you will forgive me. It is impossible for me to keep you but that doesn't mean I don't want to. I will always love you and I pray you will have a good life. You are beautiful and you deserve only the best. Please don't think that I'm a bad person, I'm not, although right now it doesn't feel that way. You are a precious baby and I know and believe with all my heart that you will grow up to be someone special. God bless you and keep you safe always.

I love you forever

Mummy, xxxxxxxx

Emily cried for a long time and she read the letter over and over. In awhile the door knocked and Adele came in. There was no need for words. She sat down on Emily's bed and hugged her tightly as the years of built up raw emotion finally took their toll. Emily sobbed. "I want my mummy. I want to know her and to love her."

"I know child. It's hard to accept Emily but believe me when I tell you that I remember your mother and she really didn't want to let you go. Her family had threatened to disown her and shortly after you were placed here they moved away. Your mother was forbidden to have contact with you but it was not her fault and certainly not her choice.

Emily dried her tears. "I don't blame her at all. I just miss not knowing her and not having any memory of her. Maybe one day she might want to trace me."

"Emily you believe in God so trust him for your mother and leave the situation in his hands."

"Yes I will. He knows what is best for all of us."

The Seaford Inn owned by John and Renee White was located in Kingsbridge, South Devon. The area was great for tourists; it was near to the harbour and the beaches and had a large number of shops. The scenery was beautiful and it was a lovely place for a holiday or a weekend break.

Renee had no children of her own but she was a good friend of Adele Adams. She was a regular visitor to the children's home and was also on the board of directors. She took an interest in the children and attended special events and concerts put on by the children.

Adele knew that Emily's time with them would soon come to an end and she had to do something that would help secure a future for her.

She spoke to Renee and explained that Emily had ambition and wanted to do something with her life. Renee agreed to offer Emily a job as junior receptionist at the hotel and see how she got on. She could also go to college one day a week to be properly trained in hotel administration.

Emily remembered moving from the home to the hotel. There had been a party for her and some of the younger children had cried at her leaving. She was like a big sister to them and the final farewell was a very emotional one.

Renee had come to collect her and her few personal belongings and take her to the hotel. The job came with live-in accommodation and Emily looked on her room as her very own bed-sit. This was like her first place of her own and she was excited and frightened at the same time. One thing was certain, Emily had dreams and with hard work she believed she could make them happen. Having grown up in a children's home she was determined to make something of her life and things had to get better now that she was earning money.

Emily met the challenges of her new job with great enthusiasm. She worked hard at the hotel and studied her course work for college. Renee was very impressed with her and encouraged her to take more training the following year. By the time Emily was nineteen she was senior receptionist and studying hotel management.

Work had been her rock and she seldom socialised. She had one friend who worked as a waitress in the hotel and that was Sophie. She had also spent some time in the children's home but not as long as Emily. Sophie drifted from one job to the next and had a total lack of ambition. She would lie across Emily's bed reading a magazine while Emily prepared her next assignment.

"Sophie why don't you do a course and train to do something with your life. You don't always want to be a waitress. I think you could do so much better if you put your mind to it."

"Emily I'm not like you. I can't sit still long enough to plan for anything. Besides, I don't have your ambition. I'm alright with being a waitress. The truth is what I'm really looking for I can't find in the job market."

Emily frowned. "What do you mean?"

"Someone to love me Emily. I'd like the handsome prince, the fairytale wedding and living happy ever after."

"Sophie that is not real life. Wake up to yourself. You have to work for what you want in life. You can't just drift along hoping for the handsome prince."

Sophie laughed. "I know you're probably right but it's a lovely thought. I think I will meet him one day. You wait and see."

Emily sighed. She worried about Sophie because she seemed the sort of person who needed looking after but she could also attract the wrong kind of man to do it. Emily could understand her need to be loved. She felt that way about herself yet she knew she couldn't depend on other people for everything. Emily had learned to be independent but Sophie still looked to others to fulfil her needs.

"Emily don't look so serious. You need to have more fun in your life; after all it's to short to waste." She threw a pillow at Emily and they both laughed. "Sophie maybe one day you will grow up but I don't know when."

"Emily that college you go to. Is there a course on how to find Mr Right?"

"No that one hasn't been thought up yet although maybe you could design it."

"Maybe I could but I'll have to find him first."

Emily shook her head in despair. "Sophie I worry about you sometimes."

Sophie lay across the pillows. "I don't worry but I dream a lot."

3

"GOOD MORNING, MAY I help you?"

"I hope so. I've an appointment with Mrs White. I think I may be a little early so if she is busy I can wait. It's no problem."

Emily smiled at the attractive man and noticed he had lovely blue eyes. "I'll ring through to her office and let her know you are here. Can I have your name please?"

He laughed. "Only if I can have yours."

Emily blushed and before she could answer he read her name on her badge.

"I'm Trevor Briggs and you are Miss Emily Gibson."

She laughed. "Well its good you can read." Emily rang through and informed Renee that Mr Briggs was in reception.

"If you'd like to take a seat Mr Briggs she will be with you shortly. Is there anything you would like while you are waiting?"

"How about a date with you?"

"I thought you came to see Mrs White."

"Mrs White is the person I have a meeting with but you are the one I would like to have dinner with."

"I'm not sure. I don't usually date strangers."

"Miss Gibson, I'm staying at the hotel for a few days. We can have dinner here and after tonight I won't be a stranger. I promise

I'm just a normal guy and not Jack the ripper. I won't even try to get you to run off with me."

"You won't!" Emily teased.

Trevor laughed. "Ok I think you've teased enough. Do we have a date?"

"It just happens that I'm off tonight so I suppose the answer is yes."

"Great. I'll meet you in the bar at about 7:30pm."

"I'll reserve us a table for dinner. It's my job to look after the guests."

"It seems I'm come to the right place then."

Renee came out of her office and whisked Trevor away and Emily checked him into a room. She was surprised at herself accepting a dinner invitation from someone she hardly knew but what harm could it do?

Dinner with Trevor that night turned out to be a very enjoyable experience and Emily knew from that first date that she would be seeing more of him. It was late when she got back to her room but she was so excited she could hardly get to sleep. She kept replaying the evening over in her mind. Trevor had a great sense of humour and she couldn't remember the last time she had laughed so much. He paid her little compliments that made her blush and by the end of the evening he kissed her good-night.   There was something about that kiss that broke down a wall inside her that had been her protection for many years. She felt open with him and there was no need for barriers. It was time to love and she felt ready to give love back.

The next few months began a whirlwind romance that left Emily feeling she was on a roller coaster ride. Renee noticed the change in her and as they sat in her office going over the hotel bookings for the coming months she teased Emily. "I must say you seem to have a certain glow about you lately. I assume you and Trevor are still seeing each other."

"Oh yes. For the first time in my life I feel so relaxed and at ease with someone. I'm not afraid anymore and Trevor has helped me to feel more secure about myself. I know with his job we don't see each other as much as we'd like to but as you know he has to travel around the country quite a lot. We have looked at renting an apartment in town and the one we saw yesterday seemed perfect but we'll decide when he gets back."

"Do you mean you might be moving out soon? It will seem strange if you do. You have been with us for three years now and I hope it's been more of a home to you as well as work."

"Yes it is home and I have only one doubt about the apartment. With Trevor away at work I'm going to be spending time on my own that I'm not used to."

"Then why don't we keep your room here and you can stay if you wish."

"Thank you Renee. That sounds ideal. I wasn't looking forward to going back to an empty apartment especially after working a late shift."

"Well that won't be necessary. I suppose because I've known you from you were little you are like a daughter to me. I want only the best for you Emily."

"You have been so good to me over the years Renee and I want you to know I really appreciate you. Life would have been so much harder if I'd not known you."

"That's a lovely thing to say Emily. I'm glad I've been able to help you. I could never have children of my own and John was never that keen on having a family anyway. When he and I got married the business became our baby and I think we have done well in turning it into the success it is. We have a comfortable life that we have worked hard for but sometimes I used to wonder what it would be like to hold a baby of my own."

"What about your sister? She has two children."

"Yes but they live so far away and I don't see them nearly as much as I'd like. The children seem to grow up so quickly and I feel I missed on knowing them more."

Emily picked up the bridal promotion brochures. "Maybe when I get married and have children you can be their grandma. I don't know if I'll ever see my birth mother again and I'd want my children to have a grandmother."

Renee squeezed her hand. "I know life hasn't been easy for you but you have done well Emily. You work here is highly commendable and now you have met Trevor you are a lot happier. I'd also love to be a grandma one day so I'll hold you to that."

They both laughed. "Yes I'd really like that too."

The next few months were a frenzy of activity for Emily. The hotel was busy so when Trevor was away she would work extra shifts and then stay at her room there. When Trevor was home they stayed at the apartment. Emily enjoyed buying things for it to give it the personal touch and she loved it when Trevor sent her flowers which she then spent ages arranging in a vase.

Sophie was excited for her and they had agreed that when she and Trevor got married she would bridesmaid. She still came to Emily's room when she stayed at the hotel and she still lacked the ambition that Emily tried to encourage her with.

"Emily do you remember me telling you that I was waiting for my prince charming to come into my life?"

"Yes. I also remember telling you it wasn't going to happen."

"Well look at you. Trevor came into your life and you're happy."

"Yes that's true but I already had my career established before I met Trevor. I still want to maintain some independence Sophie."

"I suppose I do tend to drift a little through life."

Emily laughed. "Yes I think you do."

On her twentieth birthday Trevor cooked a beautiful meal at the apartment. The table was set with candles and soft music played in the background. Emily looked beautiful in a new black dress and her hair hung loosely curled on her shoulders.

Trevor poured the wine for a toast. "Happy birthday darling. I have been so happy with you Emily. I never thought a relationship could be as good as what we have. I do love you."

"Thank you Trevor. This has been a special time for me and in a way our relationship has taken down a lot of barriers I'd put up inside me over the years. I always felt I had to keep people at a distance because I was afraid. With you everything has been like a natural progression of getting rid of any barriers and I'm happy and I love you."

"I'm glad you feel that way. Now I have a special present so close your eyes. No looking until I say so."

Emily giggled like an excited child. "Hurry up I can hardly wait."

"Ok you can open them now."

Emily opened her eyes and saw a little black box in his hand. "Go on. Open it."

She opened it up and inside was a beautiful diamond pendant and earrings. They sparkled in the light and Emily drew in her breath. "Trevor they are so beautiful. Thank you for such a lovely present." She reached over and kissed him.

"Let me put them on you." He was pleased when he saw her wearing them. "Diamonds suit you Emily. They are lovely on you."

The gift was a generous one but somewhere in Emily's heart she had hoped for a diamond ring. She chided herself as it was probably too soon for such a commitment. Maybe next year they would both be ready for it.

Life settled into a routine of work, relationship and planning the future. Trevor had to tread carefully when they discussed the future because they were different in their opinions. Trevor was very much a here and now person and believed in taking life as it came. Emily wanted to feel more secure in knowing that one day she would have a husband, home and family.

She wasn't quite sure when it was that she began to feel unwell. She had been working longer hours and she seemed to always have a headache. When she wasn't working she just wanted to sleep. She had never been this tired in her life. During working hours she wore a little more make up so no one would notice the dark circles under her eyes.

When Trevor was out of town on business Emily went to the doctor to get checked over. There had been no point in saying anything to Trevor until she was able to find out if anything was physically wrong with her.

The doctor was a cheerful man and Emily felt like maybe she was wasting his time. He examined her and did a test and then Emily sat and waited feeling a bit puzzled.

"Well that was easy." He smiled.

"I still don't know what's wrong with me. What was easy?"

"Emily there is nothing wrong with you. You are not sick. You are pregnant."

Emily felt shock waves go through her. How could she have been so naïve?

It all made sense now. She began to laugh. "Oh doctor I feel so foolish. I never thought about being pregnant. What a nice surprise."

By the time Trevor got back Emily was so excited about the baby and she couldn't wait to tell him. On his first night home she planned a special meal. Trevor wouldn't suspect anything because they always did something special when he had been away. When he sat down at the table she had his plate covered with a napkin. "Now close your eyes and don't look until I tell you. This is special"

Trevor laughed. "Have you been taking cookery lessons? This is all very secret."

Emily sat down facing him. "Alright you can look now."

He opened his eyes and removed the napkin from is plate. Emily will never forget the expression on his face. He began to laugh and Emily felt so excited.

"What's this Emily? Some sort of joke?"

Emily was laughing. "Do you think I would joke about something like this? I wanted to surprise you."

Trevor's smile disappeared. His face frozen. Emily stopped laughing. Then there was silence.

"Trevor I thought you would like the surprise."

He looked down at his plate where Emily had placed a tiny pair of white baby bootees. Suddenly he picked them up and threw them at her. "This is one surprise I can do without. We didn't discuss babies and I thought we had been careful. Emily what were you thinking of?"

She felt herself go pale with shock and then the tears came. "Trevor why are you so angry? I didn't get pregnant on purpose. It did take two of us."

Hurt and confused Emily got up and went into the kitchen. Trevor came in behind her and tried to put his arms round her but she pulled away from him. She couldn't believe he had treated her the way he did.

"Emily I'm sorry I got angry. I don't want to hurt you. You know that I love you."

"Trevor I'm not sure I know you at all. I mean all this anger about a baby that's yours. I don't understand Trevor."

"I'll be honest with you Emily. I love you and I love what we have together but I don't want children, at least not for years. I just can't imagine myself in the parent role. I enjoy my job and I love to travel. I love my freedom and yet I love coming back to you. I'm not ready for that to change. I don't want any big commitments and I don't want to be tied down."

"Trevor I'm glad you're being honest even if it comes a little too late. You have to realise that this is no longer just about you and what you want. I'm pregnant with our child. You can still do the same job. Having a baby isn't going to interfere with your work and you can look forward to coming home to two of us instead of just me."

He smiled for a moment and there seemed to be softness in his expression. "Emily." He held her hands. "I don't want to play happy families and already I'm feeling trapped."

Emily shivered at the coldness in his voice. She found it hard to believe that Trevor could love her but not their baby. Maybe her relationship with Trevor had been a mistake. Maybe because she felt starved of love all her life she had a different view of relationship and commitment.

They talked long into the night but they just kept going around in circles.

"Trevor I'm trying to understand how you feel but the fact remains that I'm having our baby and I thought we were in this together."

"Emily, look what we have is good. I've never felt this way about anyone but you. We are both young and we don't have to keep the baby. There are other ways."

Emily went cold inside. "Trevor I grew up in a children's home and I know I could never give up my baby. I could never allow a child to go through the things I have gone through in my life."

"Emily I'm not saying that you carry this baby and then give it away. I have an idea so hear me out. I know of a clinic you could go to. A friend of mine took his girlfriend there and the problem was dealt with. She got over it and now they are happy although they make sure they are a lot more careful." He laughed.

Emily couldn't believe what she was hearing. "Trevor are you seriously asking me to consider an abortion? I'll tell you now that the answer is no. I'm not giving up my baby so forget the options."

Emily stormed off to bed in tears and cried herself to sleep. She left Trevor sitting on the sofa drinking a beer.

The next morning Emily woke up and at first she thought Trevor had fallen asleep on the sofa.

She went into the living room and there was a letter on the table beside the pair of baby bootees. With a heavy heart Emily sat down and opened the envelope.

"Dear Emily

I'm sorry it has to be this way but I'm not ready for the baby stuff. I'd probably be a terrible dad. I know you didn't get pregnant by yourself but it is your choice to stay pregnant. I love you but for me the choice is clear. It's either the baby or our relationship. You have chosen the baby over our relationship so I think it best if I get out of your life and stay out. I've left some money to help out but I'll not contact you again. There's no point in making things harder for both of us. I know this all sounds selfish on my part but I have to be honest with you even if it appears to have come too late. I do love you.

Good-bye,

Trevor."

Emily cried for a long time. Loving and losing Trevor was pain that was new to her. She felt lonely and scared but she had managed to protect the life growing inside her. Something inside her made her feel strong. It was the same kind of feeling she'd had when she first gave her heart to Jesus. Suddenly she knew that in the months ahead she would need to draw on that strength. Tears gave way to heart rending sobs. "Oh God I need your help."

I will never leave you or forsake you.

Emily realised she had heard his voice. It had been a long time yet it was unmistakable. "Thank you Lord. I know you are with me."

More tears poured from her until there weren't any left, yet she had to cry her feelings for Trevor out of her heart. When she stopped crying she felt as though a link had been severed from inside her. Now she had to think of the future.

4 EMILY WENT FOR a walk and the fresh air helped to clear her head. She wasn't due to start work until late that afternoon and that would give her time to calm the raw emotions inside her. As she walked through the park she felt as though every thing about her life was unreal. Yesterday she had been the happiest woman in the world with everything to look forward to. Today her future with Trevor and the baby had been snatched away from her and the rejection cut like a knife through her heart.

Emily walked until she was so tired she needed to sit down. She saw a church and as she walked towards it she could see the doors were open. Slipping quietly inside she saw that no one was about so she sat down to rest. On the altar candles burned giving a warm glow and she sighed as she suddenly felt at peace. Sitting in the stillness Emily felt reassured that God loved her and her baby. She also realised that during the time she had been building her career and falling in love with Trevor, God hadn't seemed to be important in her life like he once was. Maybe she had built too much of her security around the man she loved and for a time Trevor had met her needs, but not anymore. Tears flowed again as the well of emotions inside her burst. She had felt loved and rejected by Trevor and yet the deep love she felt for her baby was stronger than any pain Trevor had caused her.

"Can I help you?"

Emily looked up and the pastor was smiling at her. She felt embarrassed.

"I hope you don't mind but I just needed to come in and sit for awhile."

"Stay as long as like. Do you mind if I sit down for a moment. My name is Nigel, what's yours?"

Emily smiled at his friendly manner. "I'm Emily. I hope you don't mind me coming in. I saw the doors open and I needed to be here."

Emily found herself telling him about growing up in the children's home and meeting Trevor and now she was pregnant and he had left her. By the time she had finished she was in floods of tears again and she was surprised at herself for pouring out her life to a stranger. "I'm sorry I didn't mean to say all this. I'm sure you have other things to do."

Nigel had sat quietly listening, he hadn't spoken but yet he was there for her. He reached out and took her hand. "Emily I can assure you there is nothing I'd rather be doing right now than being here with you. It must have taken courage for you to share with me. God will love you through this and your baby. He won't reject you like Trevor did. He knows your heart and I want to pray with you if that's alright."

"Yes I'd like that. I feel as though I'd put God on hold in my life while I got on with other things and today I realised that I need him and while I'd stopped thinking of him, he never forgot about me. That's an incredible thought for me. I think I need to pray."

Nigel smiled. "Let's do that."

Emily held onto Nigel's hand as she took a deep breath. "Lord I know you love me and my baby. I know in my heart that you will help me through this and saying thanks doesn't seem enough yet I do thank you. I'm sorry that I put everyone and everything in front of what I once had with you.

Forgive me. Today is a new beginning and you have shown mercy and love to me. I know I can always depend on you. Thank you."

"Lord I'm grateful that you directed Emily here today. Thank you that she realises that you are the one who will meet all her needs and the needs of her child. God let love and truth guide her every decision in the coming months and that she knows there is a place here for her to come when she needs to. Amen."

They both sat in the stillness for a few moments and then Emily heard his voice again.

I'll go before you. Don't be afraid.

"Nigel I hear his voice. He has quietly spoken to my heart and I'm not to be afraid."

"Emily you will hear him as long as you keep your heart open to him."

"I have to go now. Thank you for listening Nigel and for praying with me. I'll come back again. I like it here."

Nigel laughed. "I'm glad. We aim to please. By the way, I do some work at the children's home you mentioned. My wife is also involved. Maybe you would like to meet her sometime and we could talk over some future projects we are planning."

"I'd like that Nigel. I'm always interested in helping out at the home. I remember that it was once my home."

When Emily left the church she felt a lightness in her spirit. She realised life as a single-parent wasn't going to be easy but yet her decision to keep her baby was the right one. She had an assurance in her heart that God was with her and in a way she felt sorry for Trevor. It was sad he would miss out on the happiness she believed this baby would bring.

Emily called at the hotel and went to Renee's office. She wanted to see her before it was time to start her shift later that afternoon.

"Hello Emily. What are you doing here at this time?"

"I need to talk to you. Are you busy?"

Renee could see Emily had been crying. "Come and sit down. It doesn't matter about business. You look like something is wrong Emily. Will I order tea for us?"

"Yes please. I've just realised I forgot to eat today. Could I have some toast?"

Renee picked up the telephone. "You can have anything you want."

Emily told Renee everything that had happened with Trevor as they had their tea. She told her about going to the church and meeting Nigel and how they had prayed.

"I feel I've let everyone down Renee although now I've prayed I believe God will help me through the coming months."

"Emily don't condemn yourself because God doesn't. I will help you in any way I can so be assured of that. If you want to give up the apartment and move back here you can that. I don't like to think of you on your own now."

"I think I will. The apartment won't be the same now after all that has happened and I wouldn't want to be on my own there. Thank you Renee for being so kind. You have always been a friend to me."

"We will get a room ready for you. Don't worry about anything Emily. You made the right decision and I know it took courage to stand up against Trevor. It was unfair of him to try to make you chose between him and the baby but it is his loss. I'm glad you called in at the church. I know Nigel and his wife Diane. He has also helped me through a few problems in my life." Emily looked puzzled. "I find it hard to imagine you having problems. You always seem to have everything so together."

Renee laughed. "Emily dear, all that glitters is not gold. I mean that not everything is what it appears to be. I've been a Christian for a few years now and my relationship with Jesus has sustained me through a lot. In case you didn't notice, John and I tend to lead separate lives. Our marriage is more like a business partnership and then we couldn't have children either. John doesn't share my faith. He doesn't believe in God and his life is this hotel, his friends in business and those he sees socially. To some our marriage seems perfect but only God sees the heart Emily. In a way this hotel has been my baby and my work at the children's home, where I first met you. Overall I think I've had a good life and the best is yet to come. Emily your baby is a new blessing."

Emily filled up with tears. "Renee when I got up this morning I thought this was going to be the worst day of my life, yet I have felt so loved today. I believe I'm going to get to know God like you and Nigel do. I remember in my teens when I was still living at the home I asked Jesus into my heart but then as I got older I didn't really put any commitment behind that decision. I think that's where things began to go wrong. I allowed everything to take the place of God in my life but not anymore."

As she was leaving the hotel Sophie was coming out of the dining room.

"Hi Emily. Are you alright? You seem upset."

"Oh Sophie it's a long story and I don't have time to give you the details. Let's just say that prince charming has lost his charm. Trevor has left me Sophie and I'm pregnant."

"Oh Emily I'm sorry. I didn't think he was the type to do something awful like this. Look I'm working the late shift. Maybe I'll see you then."

"Yes I'm working late too. Sophie now will you stop believing in prince charming. You might as well believe in Santa"

"Emily I'm so sorry. It's hard to take in what's happened."

"I have to go now but I'll catch you later."

Emily gave up the apartment and moved back to the hotel. In the months that followed she blossomed and Renee fussed over her like she was her own daughter. Sophie had changed her attitude a little and talked about getting her life together but she still wasn't sure how.

Emily met Nigel and his wife Diane and she visited the church where she met new people. It was like God was bringing new friendships and most of all, more of his love into her life.

Emily went into labour two days before her due date. Renee stayed with her as her birthing partner and after hours of sweat and hard work Emily gave birth to her baby. She gasped as she heard her baby cry for the first time.

"Emily you have a beautiful baby girl and she has a healthy pair of lungs." The nurse placed the baby in Emily's arms.

"Oh Renee, she's beautiful. Oh thank you Lord." She held her baby close to her heart and she and Renee both wept with joy.

"Here Renee, you hold her and say hello to your grand-daughter."

"Oh Emily, what a privilege." She took the baby and in her heart she praised God that at long last she knew what it felt like to hold a newborn child. "You are so beautiful and I think I've just fallen in love with you."

"I'm going to call her Rosa Louise. Do you like those names?"

"Emily my middle name is Louise. Thank you."

"I thought you would be pleased. I'm glad she will grow up having a grandmother. I missed out on all that being in the children's home but Rosa will have everything. Isn't she so precious Renee?"

"Yes Emily. She is a lovely blessing and she will want for nothing."

News soon got out that Emily had given birth to a baby girl. Soon visitors began to arrive and flowers came from Nigel and Diane. Friends from the hotel and the church brought presents for the baby and Emily was overcome by the love and kindness shown by everyone.

She brought the baby back to the hotel to live and Renee had arranged for her to have a small suite for her and Rosa. It felt like their own apartment within the hotel. Emily settled into motherhood and loved every minute with her baby. Renee was the doting grandmother although John remained distant. Babies were definitely not for him.

Emily had planned to return to work when Rosa was four months old but before that she arranged a service at the church with Nigel for Rosa Louise to be dedicated. Renee felt so proud holding the baby as they walked to the front of the church where Emily would promise before God to love and care for the precious gift he had given her.

Sometimes Emily wondered if Trevor ever thought about her as he must have realised the child would have been born. He never tried to contact Emily and she decided it was time to put the past behind her and move on.

Emily returned to work and concentrated on giving Rosa everything she needed. She returned to her studies gained a qualification in hotel management, with some encouragement from

Renee. She was then promoted at work and that meant more money coming to provide for Rosa.

Three years seem to fly by and Rosa had become a very lively talkative toddler. On Emily's birthday she was in the office sorting through the post when Renee called her to come to her sitting room.

Emily was surprised to find Rosa waiting with Renee. "Happy birthday mummy. We have a surprise for you."

"Don't be telling Rosa." Renee reminded her.

The door knocked and a waitress brought in a cake with candles lit. Rosa squealed with delight and burst into a chorus of happy birthday.

Emily laughed. "Thank you darling and you too Renee. The cake is beautiful."

"I hope you don't mind but I thought we could have lunch in here today."

"It's not lunch grandma. You said it was a birthday tea."

"Sorry Rosa. It is a birthday tea."

Emily laughed. "You never forget anything Rosa."

"Mummy we have presents too but you have to sit down and close your eyes."

Emily played along as Rosa had fun giving her presents. The waitress brought in the food and laid it out. "You have to cut our cake mummy."

"Oh I will and I'll remember and take a wish."

"But you can't tell anyone, not even grandma Renee."

"Oh I know. It must be a secret."

Rosa frowned and then whispered into Emily's ear. "Maybe you could tell me."

Emily laughed. "Not even you."

The door knocked and Renee answered it. "Oh Jack come in. I didn't realise it was time for our appointment. Come in and join us."

Emily looked up at the man and felt herself blush.

"Is it someone's birthday?"

"Yes it's my mummy's."

"Emily this is Jack Dillon-Spence. I hope you don't mind if he joins us for lunch."

"No not at all. Pleased to meet you Jack. I hope you like birthday cake."

Jack laughed. "I assume this is your birthday."

"Yes. My daughter Rosa and her grandma thought we would have a birthday tea."

Emily caught the smile on Rosa's face that she had said tea and not lunch.

"Can I call you Jack?" Rosa was over by his side.

"Of course you can but only if I can call you Rosa."

She giggled. "We have to sing happy birthday again to my mummy now you are here."

"Rosa I think you should leave Jack alone and eat some food."

Jack laughed and looked at Renee. "I don't mind a chorus of happy birthday."

Just as that the door opened and several of the staff came in smiling.

Emily blushed crimson as they all sang to her again.

The birthday party was the first time that Emily had met Jack but it was not to be the last. He made several visits to see Renee and then finally he asked Emily to dinner. Renee offered to baby-sit and Emily got the feeling that Jack really liked her. By the end of their first date she knew she liked him and any doubts she had about men were dismissed in her mind.

She discovered that Jack was a Christian, in his late twenties and still single despite his mother's attempts to have him marry.

His family were quite wealthy, powerful and had a lot of influence in the world of business. The Dillon-Spence Group owned several hotels and restaurants and they invested in the tourist industry. Jack was their eldest son and he was the heir to the Dillon-Spence Empire. There was a younger son, Steven who had married Victoria. They managed a small hotel in Bournemouth, in the south of England. Steven wasn't always responsible in making business decisions and he had caused his parents problems on a number of occasions.

When Jack introduced Emily to his family they were a little surprised at his choice. His father and Emily became instant friends but his mother remained slightly aloof. She liked Emily as a person but she hadn't imagined Jack wanting to marry a single parent who had been raised in a children's home herself and had no real family connections. Jack often teased his mother and told her she was a snob, something she denied of course. She had wanted Jack to fall in love with someone with a title to their name and have the society wedding of the year. Jacks choice of bride couldn't have been more opposite to his mother's idea, something his father found amusing.

One year after meeting Jack, Emily accepted his marriage proposal. They had a beautiful wedding with Rosa as flower girl. Renee was so proud of Emily and she acted as mother of the bride. Emily loved her like she was her mother and she knew Renee loved her and Rosa like they were her own.

Now that she was Mrs Jack Dillon-Spence, Jack planned to adopt Rosa. Life had taken a new turn and with her faith in God, Emily was ready for the challenges that lay ahead.

Within a year of their marriage Emily discovered she was pregnant and they had a son, Nathan Jack Dillon-Spence. Jack's mother had grown to love Emily, despite her background and when Nathan was born her happiness was complete.

Emily supported Jack in business and everything that Renee had taught her about hotel management certainly helped make her and Jack into a good working team. The Dillon-Spence Group got an invitation to look at a hotel on the Antrim coast of Ireland. Jack and Emily went over to view the hotel and they liked it. The setting along the coast road was one of the most beautiful places they had ever seen. The Cedar Lodge Hotel was situated in beautiful grounds with well maintained gardens. The mountains were to the back of the hotel and Emily had never seen so much beauty in the colour green. There were tall trees, immaculate lawns and the flower beds were a work of creation. To the front of the hotel was a fantastic view of the ocean that stretched for miles along the coast. It was like Irelands little piece of heaven. It was summer and as she looked at the view from the hotel balcony she saw shafts of sunlight shinning down onto the waves and they shimmered like diamonds on the water.

After dinner she and Jack walked along the beach hand in hand. "Jack just breathing in this fresh air is heaven. This place is beautiful."

"Yes I agree but we have to decide if it is beautiful for a holiday or beautiful enough for our group to buy the hotel."

Emily thought for a moment. "Jack when I look out at the vastness of the ocean it reminds me of our God who created it all. Something in my heart wants to be here. I think this would be a great investment."

"I'll sleep on it Emily but you could be right."

As they made their way back to the hotel the sun was setting and a huge red and amber glow settled over the sea. "Jack isn't God so creative? That sunset could only be his idea."

Jack hugged her. "Yes. He always knows how to do things great."

The next morning when Emily woke she found Jack standing on the balcony looking out to the sea.

"You are up early darling."

"Emily I didn't sleep much last night. I've prayed so more and in my heart I believe we should go ahead and put in an offer for this place."

"Oh Jack that's great. What happens if we get it?"

"That's what we need to talk about Emily. My father doesn't really trust Steven to manage a new venture like this and I'm not keen to bring in a stranger."

"Jack do you mean we would move to live in Ireland?"

"It looks that way but would you want to Emily?"

"Yes I would. I know we have heard negative news about this country but Jack it isn't all bad. The people we have met have been so friendly and the setting of this place is too good to pass up. Think of the potential here Jack. We would bring in our own ideas and turn this place into the best hotel on the coast."

"Emily I'm so glad I married you. We make a great team."

The offer made by the Dillon-Spence Group was the best and soon Jack and Emily with their children were on their way to Ireland. Plans had been drawn up to close the hotel for a few months while renovation work took place and a complete change of decoration. During this time Jack and Emily received invitations to various social events and soon they had built up a new social circle of friends. Emily found a church nearby and discovered there was a children's home not far from the hotel. She made it her business to introduce herself to the matron, Iris Boyd and offered her help to the home. They employed Anna who would be a live-in nanny to their children and they soon discovered she was a blessing to them. Rosa and Nathan loved her.

Emily believed God had a purpose in bringing her and Jack to Ireland and it wasn't just to run a new hotel, although that was part of it. They met with local counsellors and planned projects for the home that would help give the older children work at the hotel. Those who wanted to work within the industry would be encouraged either by training in catering or in administration and future management. Before long the business was up and running and Emily knew that God was going to bless this place. He had work for them to do and she and Jack walked in obedience to him.

5 THE PLANE LANDED at Heathrow at 7:30am. Emily had slept during the short trip but the sudden bump onto the runway startled her.

"Wake up honey. We have landed and you are in London."

She yawned. "I don't think I like these early morning flights Jack."

He gazed at her sleepy face and smiled. "You still look beautiful."

Emily laughed. "You are such a charmer, even at this time of the morning."

"I know and you love me with all your heart."

She squeezed his hand. "Yes I do."

"I think we'd better move off the plane. Everyone else seems to have gone."

Emily viewed the empty seats and the air stewardess was waiting at the door, smiling patiently.

"Jack, you're right. We need to go."

A limousine was waiting for them and the driver arranged for their luggage to be brought from the baggage area. Jack and Emily climbed into the limo and settled back in the soft leather seats for the journey to the Royal Court Hotel in Kensington.

"Wow, your dad sure knows how to travel in style. I thought we might have to take a taxi."

Jack laughed. "Emily how could you insult my father. He would never have the heir to his empire travel by taxi."

"Maybe we should do it sometime just for the experience."

"Emily you can be a bad influence on me, be careful or my mother will catch on to you."

They enjoyed teasing each other and it helped lighten the responsibilities they were facing. The journey to London had meant leaving the children behind and Jack knew how much Emily hated to be away from Rosa and Nathan.

"Why has your father called a family meeting Jack? You haven't really said much about this visit."

"Emily I'm not sure. He told me he is concerned about the way Steven is running the Edgewater Hotel and he needs to discuss it in detail in person."

"Well I don't know what he expects you to do. Steven doesn't like to take advice from anyone."

"Steven and Victoria will be arriving at lunch time today but I'm not sure if they are staying over."

"It will be good to see Victoria again. I worry about her at times. Steven isn't the best husband in the world."

No I agree with you but he has Victoria right where he wants her. Steven controls his own little empire and his wife is included. I'm not sure if Victoria could cope without Steven as she is so used to doing what he says. Maybe that's the reason she stays with him, who knows."

"I think you are right. Victoria doesn't know how to cope on her own because Steven has manipulated her for years. I think she would need a lot of support, however, I'd like to see her learn to stand up for herself a little."

Jack smiled. "Emily you are a strong woman and maybe Victoria would like to be more like you but the truth is, she is not anything like you."

"Jack I might appear to be a strong person to Victoria but you know that it is my relationship with the Lord that I draw strength from. Maybe Victoria needs to experience God in her life."

The car stopped at the entrance to the Royal Court Hotel. The hotel was sheer luxury and rated very highly as one of the top hotels in London. Jack and Emily walked through reception to the elevator. They smiled at the staff but didn't stop for conversation. Already they were curious about the family visit. Usually the family came together for board meetings or special family occasions but Jack sensed this visit was going to be different so he wanted no gossip.

Jack senior and his wife Sarah were waiting in the penthouse suite as Jack and Emily arrived.

"Hello dad." Jack hugged his father and shook his hand. "Mum, still looking as beautiful as ever." He kissed her cheek and hugged her.

Emily kissed her father-in-law. "Hi you, it's good to see you." He hugged her and his eyes had that twinkle Emily saw the first time she met Jack. She loved her father-in-law and felt very close to him. The first time she was introduced to him there had been an instant bond between them that had grown stronger with time. Having grown up in a children's home Emily had never known her father but God had blessed her with a wonderful father in Jack senior. She was like the daughter he never had although he loved his sons very much but Sarah didn't want anymore children after Steven was born. She had been a good mother although not the most maternal. Jack had spent a lot of time with the nanny as Sarah had a busy social circle and she was on endless committees.

"Emily, my dear welcome." Sarah kissed her daughter-in-law lightly on the cheek. Sarah lacked warmth but Emily had realised a long time ago that she simply wasn't the type of person for showing affection.

"Your baggage will be in suite one for you and Steven and Victoria will be across the hall in suite two. I don't know if they will be staying over and I suppose Steven will decide when they get here."

Jack and Emily relaxed on the sofa and just then a waitress arrived with a breakfast trolley.

"We didn't think you would have eaten so early so I arranged a variety for you."

Emily laughed. "Thank you mum. You must have ordered everything on the menu. We are starving because we had such an early flight."

They sat down at the dining table and helped themselves to eggs, bacon and toast. Emily and Sarah preferred tea while Jack and his father got through a large pot of coffee in no time.

"Dad can you tell me anymore about this meeting. You didn't give too much away on the telephone. Is there problems with the business?"

"Jack I wanted you and Emily to arrive early so as we could talk. The business as a whole is doing very well, our hotels and restaurants are providing an excellent income and your mother is still being kept in a style to which she has grown accustomed to." He looked at his wife and that familiar twinkle made her blush a little.

"But there is a problem dad?"

"Yes Jack. I've had a few complaints about the way in which Steven is running the Edgewater. The hotel is showing a profit but not as good as it used to. I sent a few people down there to check in as paying guests and the reports I got back were not good. There is a lack of staff, bad service and some other areas of neglect. Now I don't want the health authorities down on us so we need to get these problems sorted out."

"And you have talked to Steven?"

"Oh yes. I went down there myself and I didn't tell him I was arriving. He was out all morning. The assistant manager seems to do most of the work although he got into a right flap when I walked in."

Jack smiled. "I bet he did. You can be so smart dad."

"Yes I can. Anyway, Steven arrived later and came out with some story to explain his whereabouts but I'm not stupid. I know he is spending to much time in the gambling casino's and Victoria leads an unhappy existence with him. He is careful not to allow her to become too involved in the business because he doesn't want her to see too much. We had words in his private office and he admitted that things had become slack so I left him to sort out the business and his marriage."

"So why call us here today?"

"Stories are reaching me that I don't like. Steven is spending more time out of the hotel than in it and I have it on good authority that there is another woman in his life. I've spoke to Victoria on the telephone but she seems to be scared of Steven and I don't like that either. No woman should live like that, especially my daughter-in-law. Jack I need you with me today when I confront Steven. A few members of the board are listening to gossip and they are getting nervous. Good people have invested money in the Dillon-Spence Group and I don't want Steven to ruin it for them or the family. I also have the reputation of the Group as a whole to protect and that is why I need you there when I confront Steven. It is time I spelt out a few home truths to him and I need a witness."

Jack had an anxious look on his face that Emily recognised. "Sure dad. I'll support anything you say. There are two ways it can go. Steven will have to see that he needs to be more responsible or he will resent you for interfering in his life. You know he doesn't have the sweetest nature."

"Oh I know he might rant and rave a little but he has to understand that I won't allow him to ruin the Edgewater Hotel and maybe do untold damage to our reputation. I won't stand for it Jack."

"I agree with you dad. We'll talk with him and try to sort things out."

"Emily I want you to spend some time with Victoria today. Try to find out how things are between her and Steven. I'm concerned for her welfare."

"We thought it would be better you talking to her rather than me. I wouldn't want her to see me as the interfering mother-in-law."

Emily smiled at Sarah. She knew that when it came to family matters Sarah left her husband to sort things out. "I'll talk to her. If she is frightened of Steven she will need some family reassurance."

"Emily you let me know how she is. Tell her the family will always support her and little Chloe."

Later when Emily was alone in her suite she lay on the bed having a rest. Her body was tired but her mind wouldn't switch off. She was trying to think of what she would say to Victoria and how she would even begin a conversation about her marriage to Steven. She got off the bed and fetched her bible. She began to look over several scriptures but she still felt restless inside. Turning to the book of Proverbs she read the verses that had helped her so much in her own life.

"Trust in the Lord with all your heart and lean not on your own understanding. In all your ways acknowledge Him, and He shall direct your paths." Proverbs 3:5-6.

Emily breathed a sigh of relief. "Oh Lord thank you for your word. I really don't know what to say to Victoria but I trust you with this situation and I believe you have prepared the way."

"Emily I am the way. Just be still and listen for my voice."

"Thank you Lord, my heart feels lighter now." Emily was aware of a lovely stillness inside her and she felt so peaceful. She lay down on the bed and fell into a deep sleep.

"Hi wake up sleepy head. I've ordered some tea for you."

Emily stirred. "How long have I been asleep?"

"Just over an hour."

"Goodness I must have needed the rest. I certainly feel better for it. Have Steven and Victoria arrived yet?"

"Yes. They are in their suite now. Dad has arranged a business lunch for our meeting and you can have lunch with Victoria."

"And what will your mother be doing this afternoon?"

"Oh you know mum. She has some charity lunch to attend."

Emily laughed. "Your mother really has style. I'm sure she must be on dozens of committees and each time she goes to a function it must cost your father another new outfit."

"Yes and I can just hear her tell him that her social engagements are really a networking exercise. She is doing the job of maintaining the Dillon-Spence reputation."

"I think I will invite Victoria here this afternoon. I can order lunch and maybe she will feel more relaxed in our suite. The restaurant is to public and I wouldn't dream of discussing anything with her there. You never know who might be listening."

"That's a good idea. Now I need to go and speak to dad before this meeting. I can't say I'm looking forward to it."

"Jack have you prayed?"

"I haven't stopped but I have the feeling I will have the right words to say when the time comes. I know I don't have them now."

Emily laughed. "Jack I read Proverbs three earlier. I think God is trying to tell us something."

"I know the scripture you are referring to. I'm glad you reminded me. I'll see you later." He kissed her and she held him close. "Emily I'd better go before you make me want to stay."

She kissed him again and he knew she was teasing.

"I'll see you later and I won't forget this."

Emily telephoned Victoria and arranged lunch in her suite. They both wanted to shower and freshen up so lunch in one hour was agreed. Emily had her shower and then decided on a blue silk shirt and cream trousers. She applied her make-up and some silver jewellery and a final touch of perfume. "Now Lord we are ready for whatever." She was convinced that God had a great sense of humour and he laughed along with her.

In the conference room Jack and his father sat at the conference table checking the accounts from the Edgewater Hotel. Profits were down but not enough to cause any major concern.

"Dad what are you looking for? I know the hotel could be doing better but there is still a healthy profit margin."

"Jack it isn't the amount that bothers me. If you look closely, the hotel has been loosing a steady amount over six months. It isn't one large sum of money but finances are being drained away slowly. That concerns me Jack."

"What do you see as the problem?"

"Only Steven will know the answer to that one. He may try to make excuses that business is slow but that won't wash with me. No, I think Steven could be gambling and he is getting in too deep."

Jack could feel the tension inside him. It hurt him to think that Steven would gamble away a business his father had worked so hard to establish.

Lunch arrived and the waiters brought in a trolley with a selection of meat, salad and bread.

"Just leave it there gentlemen and we will help ourselves."

"Yes sir."

Steven arrived with his usual show of friendliness. "Hello Jack, I thought you might be here." He shook Jack's hand but there was no sincerity in his tone or the handshake.

"If you two would like to help yourselves to food then we can begin the meeting." There was a serious tone to their father's voice and he seemed anxious to get started.

The three of them sat down to lunch and Jack senior poured glasses of water.

"Dad we usually have wine with lunch."

"Not today Steven, this is business. You can have a drink later."

Jack had a feeling that Steven might just need a drink later but this was not the time for any jokes. The smile had disappeared from his fathers face and it looked like the meeting was now in session.

"Dad I thought we had covered several issues so if there are any other problems I'm not aware of them."

"Steven I will outline the reasons we are all here today. I would like you both to listen carefully to the things that have been brought to my attention.

This business not only concerns our families but the shareholders that have invested good money in the Dillon-Spence Group."

Steven sat quietly, feeling uncomfortable. He sensed his father was about to deal with issues that he preferred to keep to himself.

6 VICTORIA ARRIVED ON time for lunch with Emily although she was feeling a little nervous. She liked Emily a lot but because they didn't see each other often she felt a little uneasy in her company.

"Come in Victoria, it's good to see you again." Emily hugged her and sensed the tension in her. "Come through to the sitting room. I have ordered lunch. I thought soup to start with and then a chicken salad. I'm sure there will be some desert too."

Victoria smiled. "Yes we are always spoiled for choice."

Emily noticed how pale Victoria looked although she had make-up on it didn't cover up the dark circles under her eyes. She seemed to be tired and the strain was showing. She wore a black trouser suite and she was very slim but Emily knew she never had a problem with her weight. She seemed naturally slim.

"Sit down and make yourself comfortable. Kick off your shoes, I'm going to."

Victoria laughed as she slid her feet out of her shoes and relaxed on the sofa. "I wish I could be more like you Emily. You always seem so full of life."

Emily laughed. "You wouldn't have said that if you had seen me earlier. I had to have a sleep after we arrived. I don't like early morning flights."

Lunch arrived and Emily and Victoria helped themselves. Emily enjoyed everything but she noticed Victoria seemed to struggle to eat at all. "Are you alright Victoria?"

"Yes I'm fine. Sometimes I skip out lunch altogether."

"You don't want to get to thin. You have to look after your health."

Victoria smiled. "I'm fine Emily. Chloe keeps me fit as she gets into all kinds of mischief. I really would have liked to have brought her today but Steven doesn't like her routine disrupted."

"Then you won't be staying tonight?"

"I don't think so. We hadn't planned to but I suppose it depends how long the business meeting goes on for."

"Yes I suppose it does. How is business at the Edgewater?"

"It's good. The hotel is always busy so I hope Steven's father is pleased. I know he likes to look at the accounts from time to time."

"Yes well he does have a vested interest as do the other share-holders. However if Steven has everything running smoothly then his father will be very pleased."

"Yes he will."

Victoria lapsed into silence. Emily couldn't help but notice how defensive her conversation had been and her attitude was fearful. The black trouser suite seemed to hide the real Victoria and this thin, anxious woman was trying hard to pretend that everything was alright. Her shoulder length blonde hair framed her face and she was an attractive woman although she seemed to wear too much make-up. Emily was sure she would be even more beautiful if she wore less, she had lovely blue eyes but they lacked sparkle.

"Victoria how are you? I know that Steven isn't the easiest person in the world to get on with."

"I'm fine. I've already told you."

Emily was finding this more difficult than she imagined. She seemed to be coming up against a brick wall with her questions and now there was an awkward silence.

"Oh God help? I'm not sure what to say next."

"Emily do you know what the meeting is about between Steven, Jack and his dad?"

Emily knew this wasn't going to be easy but suddenly she remembered the peace she had felt earlier when she had read Proverbs three. She knew that now was the time to trust God.

"Victoria there are concerns about the Edgewater Hotel. Steven's father needs to discuss it and he wants Jack there also."

Victoria looked puzzled. "I've just told you the hotel is busy and if my observations are anything to go by then the accounts should be showing a healthy profit."

"Your observations are not in question but I know the accounts are. Does Steven not discuss business with you? Surely you must have some idea of how much money the hotel should be making."

Victoria laughed. "Forgive me Emily but you know Steven well enough to realise he considers me to be his wife, the mother of his child and the woman who does what she is told."

Emily suddenly felt hurt inside and then she realised that she was feeling the pain Victoria felt about her marriage.

"Victoria you know I'm your friend and we have discussed many issues in the past yet today there seems to be a barrier between us. Am I right or is this my imagination?"

Victoria began to cry. "Oh Emily you know me to well. There has been a barrier between us and I'm afraid I created it. I don't know what to do and Steven warned me to be careful what I said to anyone."

Emily went and sat down beside her on the sofa. She gave her a tissue and they both sat quite for a few minutes. Emily sensed in her spirit that Victoria needed to cry and to feel safe although she was very vulnerable.

"I'm sorry Emily. I feel under such strain lately." She tried to compose herself.

"Victoria I want you to understand that I am your friend and I'm concerned about you. You don't need to put up any barriers with me. I know Steven can be difficult but you are the only one who sees that side of him, the side that his family and business partners don't see."

"Emily, Steven and I have grown so far apart that I'm surprised he hasn't left me. When he is not working he is out of the hotel and

I know he visits the casino and I don't believe for a moment that he is faithful to me.

I feel trapped in a loveless marriage and everything about our lives is one big deception, one lie after another and I don't know what to do about it."

"Have you thought of leaving?"

"Everyday Emily. I imagine a new life for Chloe and I and for a little while I escape into my dreams. The reality is, I wouldn't know how to leave. Steven has the bank account in his name and I get a monthly allowance for myself and Chloe. I also have to tell him what Chloe needs and how much I spend. He knows I have no family in England as my parents and brother live in New Zealand. I don't have any close friends and Stevens friends are the sort of men who treat their wives like Steven treats me. The sad thing is that some of these women don't mind the way they are treated."

"What do you mean?"

"I know a few women whose husbands treat them badly in private. In pubic they play the role of devoted husband and wife and they smile all the time. It is all so false and I know these people are miserable. They stay because of the lifestyle and they like to mix in social circles and attend endless dinner parties. They enjoy the wealth, the clothes and the jewellery and then there are the holidays abroad regardless of the price they have to pay by way of self respect and self worth."

"I can't begin to imagine what that must be like."

"Emily these women don't know how to think for themselves anymore. They do what they are told and stand by their men.

They accept that nothing in life is perfect so they simply make the best of what they have and they learn to use it to their advantage."

"How shallow is that."

"It's sad Emily and none of these women will admit to being unhappy."

"Victoria I don't know the outcome of this meeting but there could be changes."

"That frightens me because I know if Steven gets on the wrong side of his father he is going to be very hard for me to live with. He might even cut my allowance!"

"Would he do such a thing?"

Victoria laughed. "Emily I am not high on Stevens's list of priorities and I may not be on his list at all. Nothing he does surprises me anymore."

"Do you think he is gambling too much?"

"It's not just that. Steven had his own social circle of friends, men as well as women. They enjoy late nights, drinking, gambling and going to nightclubs. I've never wanted to be part of all that although Steven has never invited me. There are some things a wife doesn't get to see but eventually she hears the whispers.

Emily drew in her breath; she had a feeling of dread inside.

"Let me explain. I know that Steven hasn't always been faithful to me. He knows that I know but it doesn't seem to bother him. I'm his wife, I know my place and in return Steven provides for us. I always know when he is seeing someone else; it's as if I sense it. I don't think he will ever leave me because he would never give up the business and I come with the package so I accept that Steven leads a double life. At the Edgewater he is professional in his work, deals with the running of the hotel and in public he treats me politely. Outside of working hours and playing the role of loving husband he has a different life. He plays hard Emily and I wonder how long he expects to get away with it."

"Is he seeing someone at present?"

"Yes I believe he is. He always becomes distant with me and he never looks me in the eye when we talk. Chloe tends to become very possessive about him and I sometimes think she is picking up the tension that exists at home.

She is only four but she seems to sense it when Steven withdraws from us. Anyway there is a girl who I've seen in the hotel bar a few times although she doesn't work at the hotel. She works as a cocktail waitress at the casino and she's very attractive, blonde, lovely figure. I've suspected for a long time that she and Steven are seeing each other and she hasn't been the first."

"Do you know anything else about her?"

"A friend of mine and I use the term friend loosely. She has been to this casino and saw Steven all over this woman. She has also seen them in a restaurant having dinner and then there was the weekend Steven was supposed to be playing golf except he couldn't have been because his golf clubs were at home. Emily I've caught him out in so many lies yet I think Steven actually believes what he is telling me. Anyway this girl he is seeing, I've found out her name is Sophie and she's single. She has been in hotel work and casino's all her working life. She doesn't appear to have family and she seems a bit of a loner. I'm more worried this time, it's as though she has a hold over Steven that no one else had and she doesn't seem to be just another fling."

"Victoria I'm so sorry. I didn't realise that your life was so unhappy or that Steven treats you in this way. Victoria you know that I'm a Christian and I have come through some hard times in my own life but through it all I learned to trust God. Have you ever thought of trusting God for your own life?"

"I don't know Emily. I feel very insecure right now and I'm almost afraid to step out in any direction. If Steven thought for a minute I was interested in Christianity he would laugh. He doesn't believe in anyone but himself."

"I realise how difficult he could make your life but I do believe that God wants to help you. Your choice is whether you will allow him to but until then I will be praying for you. I know with Jack and I living in Northern Ireland we don't see each other very often but we can still keep in contact with each other by telephone."

"Yes I'd like that. I know I can trust you and Jack."

"Victoria I believe the Lord will bring you through this. I don't know how but I know you can depend on him. He knows Steven better than anyone of us and there is nothing or no one impossible for him."

Victoria laughed. "Does that mean he might hit Steven with a bolt of lightning?"

"No I don't think that is the way he works. God is full of grace and mercy and by accepting his Son Jesus as Lord in our lives we freely give him the opportunity to change us into what he wants us to be. His blessings are the best but he does ask for our obedience. God is faithful and he will never let anyone down who puts their trust in him."

"So you are saying that God has given us the choice to accept him and invite him into our lives?"

"Yes and I can assure you that he is the best choice you will ever make."

"I will think about all you've said Emily and I'm so glad that I told you everything. I feel so much lighter inside now that I've shared with you. There is one thing that worries me though."

Emily looked puzzled. "And what would that be?"

"If my marriage to Steven ended, especially now that I know there is another woman. How would his parents react? They might want to disown me. You know what his mother is like about the Dillon-Spence reputation."

Emily smiled. "Believe me; his parents will never disown you. They love you and Chloe is their granddaughter and they won't want to loose either of you. They may want to disown Steven because they do have strong values when it comes to family life so I don't think you need to be anxious about that. Why don't you think about coming over to Northern Ireland for a holiday? It would be good for you and Chloe and give you a break from Steven. With some space between you both you will be able to think much clearer."

Victoria's face beamed. That is a good idea. I would love to come. I'll make plans after today and be in touch with you."

The door opened and Jack came in. Emily noticed he looked strained.

"Victoria it is lovely to see you again." He hugged her and sat down beside her. "How are you?"

"Jack I'll leave Emily to answer that question but it is good to see you again. Tell me, is the meeting over yet?"

"Steven and dad are still talking but they shouldn't be long now."

"I think I'll get back to our suite. Emily thank you for today and maybe I will see you both later."

Emily left her to the door and hugged her. "Victoria I meant every word I said today. You are no longer alone in this."

"I know that now and that feels good. I'm glad of your support and I appreciate your friendship. Bye for now."

7   EMILY SAT BESIDE Jack on the sofa and he took her hand. "Jack what happened at the meeting? You look so tired."

"Steven is in big trouble Emily and there is no way he will be able to talk his way out of this one. How is Victoria? Did you two talk about their problems?"

"Jack there is so much pain in that woman's life she needs God to heal her. She is so wounded inside. She knows that Steven is being unfaithful to her and she feels so rejected by him. She needs our support Jack."

"She has that already and the family will stand by any decisions she makes for herself and Chloe."

"Tell me about the meeting."

"My father did most of the talking. He showed Steven the accounts and asked him what had been going on. At first Steven tried every excuse he could come up with but eventually he admitted he had been gambling and drinking more than usual. He didn't say anything about the other woman although my father isn't stupid, he knows Steven better than he realises."

"What will happen now?"

"Dad has talked about putting in a new manager at the Edgewater. Steven will remain there but not with the same authority. The new manager will report directly to my father. Steven has messed up the accounts and I don't think he knows himself what he has done with the money. The hotel is going to take a loss in the next quarter but at least now that dad knows what the problem is he can do something about it."

"If I know your dad he will have that hotel running smoothly in no time and Steven will have to learn to obey orders from your dad. I think this is the last chance he will get to sort himself out."

"He and Victoria will not be staying over tonight. Steven can't wait to get out of here."

"I hope I see Victoria before she leaves."

It was late afternoon and Emily went for a walk in the hotel gardens. The smell of the flowers and the freshness in the air helped to clear her head. Emily's concern for Victoria had felt like a dark cloud over her and she felt annoyed at Steven for the way in which he was treating her. Victoria had always depended on him a lot and he had used her dependence on him to control her life.

Emily sat on the garden swing deep in thought. "God it is at times like this when my mind seems clogged up with concerns that I don't know what to pray for. I find it hard to watch the pain in the lives of those I care for."

In the stillness of the afternoon she struggled to find answers but her mind couldn't see past the problems. Suddenly she was aware of the still small voice in her heart.

"Trust me. I know the end from the beginning. I see your heart is distressed but don't be anxious. Daily surrender to me the circumstances that you can't change."

Emily felt such thankfulness in her spirit. "Oh Lord you are going to change all this mess." Then she felt a tug in her heart.

"No, I said to trust me for what you can't change and release those you love to my care."

Emily understood. Looking back over her own life there had been times when she had experienced difficult circumstances and she depended on the Lord to bring her through them. He didn't always change the circumstances but he changed her heart and her attitude in the process.

As Emily returned to the hotel she saw Victoria at the reception having coffee. "Hi, mind if I join you?"

"Oh please do. I'd be glad of your company."

A waitress brought Emily another cup of coffee.

"How has Steven been from the meeting with his father?"

"Not good. He is sulking and he says his father is now undermining his authority and treating him like a child. Now he is behaving like one."

Emily laughed. "I'm sorry Victoria I know the situation is serious but Steven is quite good at sulking when he can't get his own way."

"Tell me about it. I live with the man. Our daughter is four and she has more sense than her father. Steven should be here soon. He is saying good-bye to his mother and then we are off home."

"How will the new changes at the hotel affect you?"

"I don't think they will. Steven always takes everything to do with management and I just do what I'm told. I think the worst thing is putting up with Steven and his attitude. His mood swings are like the male version of P.MT." They both laughed.

"I'm so glad you have a sense of humour Victoria and you can find something to smile about."

"I find it easy to smile when I'm around you. I don't have to pretend when I'm in your company. Before I came downstairs I heard Steven on the telephone and I think he was talking to his mistress. I suppose when we get back she will shower him with sympathy and whatever else."

"I'm sorry you are going back to all that but whatever decision you make about your future, Jack and I will support you. You are sure about this woman?"

"Oh yes Emily I'm sure. He met her at a conference. She was the waitress in the hotel he stayed at. Then she changed jobs to a very exclusive casino where the clientele come recommended. Everything in her life has changed from she met him and she isn't going to let him go if she can help it."

"Victoria she must know that he is married and he has a daughter."

"Emily this woman wants to maintain her lifestyle so I don't think those other facts come into it."

Just then Steven came into reception looking for Victoria. He walked towards them and Emily could tell that he wasn't a happy man and his dislike of her was obvious.

"We are ready to go now Victoria so I'll see you out front."

He walked outside to the waiting limo. He never spoke to Emily at all.

Victoria hugged Emily and they parted company promising to stay in contact with each other. Steven had an impatient look on his face as a smiling Victoria walked away from Emily.

"When you are ready dear, I would like to get home."

"Yes darling." She smiled at him although her heart ached.

As Emily headed for the elevator she heard Steven's name being paged from reception. She walked over to the desk. "Lisa, Mr Steven Dillon-Spence has left the hotel."

The receptionist looked a little flustered. "Oh dear this caller was insisting on talking to him."

"Give me the telephone."

The receptionist handed her the receiver. "Hello. I'm sorry but the person you wish to speak to is no longer here. He has left the hotel."

"Can you tell me where I can reach him?"

Emily listened closely to the woman's voice. "Who is calling please?"

"I'm a friend. Sophie Howard."

Emily couldn't speak. She felt sick inside.

"Look could you tell me how I can contact Mr Dillon-Spence?"

"He has left with his wife and cannot be contacted. Good-bye."

"Are you alright? You look a bit pale."

Emily stared at the receptionist. "Oh I'm fine. I thought that caller might become nasty. I don't think she will bother you again."

Emily went up to her suite and Jack was working at the desk.

"Hi darling. Did you get to say good-bye to Victoria?"

"Yes we had coffee downstairs while she waited for Steven. They have gone home now. Jack something strange happened to me in reception. I took a call that came in just after Steven had gone and it was from a woman. I thought I knew her voice and then she said her name was Sophie Howard."

"We don't know anyone by that name."

"Jack we don't but I do. When I was growing up in the home my friend was called Sophie Howard. I'm sure she is the same woman who is involved with Steven."

"Emily this must be a shock for you but there is nothing you can do about it and until Victoria has more proof we just have to wait."

Emily sighed. "I know. Jack I have a headache so I think I'll have a rest before dinner."

Jack kissed her. "You do that and I'll finish my paperwork."

8

EMILY WAS GLAD to get back to Ireland and to her children. She felt subdued regarding the family business and she couldn't get Sophie Howard out of her mind. She decided to wait until she heard from Victoria and then she would try to find out more about this other woman.

The Cedar Lodge was entering a busy season. The autumn/ winter theme brought a new buzz to the place. Emily had begun to take bookings for Christmas for lunches and dinners and tourists were making provisional bookings. The chef had new ideas for the Christmas menu and in between they still had a Halloween Dance and the Fireworks displays.

Emily checked the bookings for autumn/winter weddings and they had several receptions booked between now and Christmas. She closed the books feeling quite satisfied that business should run smoothly between September and New Year. The telephone rang and Emily was surprised to hear from Victoria. "How are you and Chloe?"

"We are fine. Nothing has changed here though and Steven is still sulking everyday. His father has two other people working here and Steven feels he is being watched all the time."

"I can understand that. Steven always likes to do things his own way. How is he treating you?"

"He goes out more than ever now and I feel so lonely at times. When he is here he doesn't really talk to me much. We are like two strangers Emily. I tried to discuss our marriage with him but he just stared at me and never spoke. I asked him if he wanted a divorce and he laughed in my face. I really don't know what to think anymore."

"Victoria I don't think Steven would want a divorce. With you and Chloe there no one else suspects there is another woman. He stills needs you but not for the right reasons."

"I know that is true. In front of other people he still plays the attentive husband and doting daddy to Chloe but in private he withdraws from us. I found out a little more about the woman. She has always worked in hotels because she had somewhere to live. She doesn't appear to have family and she seems to have a bit of a loner. She is in her thirties but has never married although there doesn't seem to have been any shortage of boyfriends."

"Victoria how did you find this out? Is it gossip or a reliable source?"

"Emily when we returned from London I hired a private detective and he has a file on the girl."

Emily felt uneasy. "She must have family somewhere. What did he get on her background?"

"Not very much. She was in care for a number of years and there is no trace of her mother now. She must have left the children's home and went into hotel work. Anyway I'm not really interested in her early life, it's now I need to know about."

"Yes you are right. Have you made any plans or given any thought to the future?"

"I'm not sure. I know I can't continue to live this way but it's not a good time to make changes. The hotel is busy and should continue to be through to the New Year. Chloe is already becoming excited about Christmas every time she sees a new toy on television."

Emily laughed. "I know what that's like; our children are exactly the same."

"Maybe I'll think about coming over for a holiday. I'll let you know. Give my love to Jack and the children. Bye for now."

"God bless, bye." Emily replaced the receiver and sat down at her desk. She knew inside her heart that the woman Steven was involved with and the girl she grew up with were the same people. She also had a feeling deep down that one day she would come face to face with her.

Making her way to reception Emily was still deep in thought. "Tracey there are the bookings diaries, I'll put them under the desk. We are going to be very busy in the next few months."

"Good. I love the hotel when it is busy. There a certain buzz about the place."

Emily laughed. "Yes I feel that too. I'm glad you are happy Tracey. You do a good job and you have worked hard to achieve so much."

"And that is all down to you and your husband. You gave me the opportunity to do something with my life and I'm grateful to you."

"That's a lovely thing to say Tracey but you did work hard at college and you deserve the credit."

"I'll not argue with my boss." Tracey teased.

"I should think not."

"Excuse me but could I have some service here please."

Emily turned quickly towards the person at the desk. "Oh goodness, Renee what a surprise. Why didn't you let us know you were coming and I could have met you at the airport?"

"Not a chance. Surprises are much more fun and besides you should have seen the look on both your faces a few minutes ago."

Emily shook her head. "You are such a joker. Tracey I'd like you to meet my special friend Renee White. We have known each other a long time."

"Hello Mrs White, I'm pleased to meet you. You will be staying here?"

"I hope so dear."

"Tracey, Mrs White will have our special guest suite."

"Of course Mrs Dillon-Spence."

"Have you got luggage Renee?"

"Oh yes. I've lots and lots. You know me. I pack everything I need and everything I don't need and a few just in case items."

They all laughed.

"Mrs White I'll arrange for your luggage to be taken to your suite."

"Thank you Tracey and may I say you are doing a very good job. Someone must have trained you well." She winked at Tracey and laughed.

"Tracey if you could arrange for coffee and scones to be sent into the sitting room."

"Right away madam."

Renee relaxed on the comfortable sofa and Emily sat facing her with a grin on her face. "This is such a surprise. Just wait until Jack sees you. You are a minx for not telling us though."

"I know. I had my reasons for not telephoning first. I suppose I didn't want to have to give explanations over the phone."

Emily frowned. "Is there something wrong?"

Before Renee could answer the door knocked and in came a waitress with a trolley.

"Oh Emily fresh scones with jam and cream. These are my favourite and I would never dream of counting the calories."

"No and I won't either, so just eat up and enjoy."

They helped themselves and for a few minutes there was silence as they indulged in the forbidden calories.

"I'm so glad you are here Renee. It has been such a long time since we got together."

"I know. Life can be so busy that you don't realise how quickly it is passing you by. One day you wake up and wonder what happened to the last ten years."

"I find in the hotel business everything revolves around seasons. I tend to think of time when I'm looking at the bookings ledger but then you would know all about that."

"I do and I think I taught you well Emily. You are a successful business woman, a wife and mother and you have come so far. I thank God for the way he has directed your life."

"I'm not superwoman Renee. I actually get lots of help from other people so that I can do the work I have to do. Tell me, why the unexpected visit? I don't think you are here on holiday."

"Well I did need a holiday but it isn't the only reason. Emily many years ago when you lived at the Seaford Inn I'm sure you were aware of the different lifestyles John and I led. We had no children and the business became our baby in a way. That was then but now that we are older our lives have changed. I'm still committed in my relationship with the Lord and I'm still working hard. It is different for John. He decided some time ago that he wanted out of the business and our marriage. Emily, he left me two months ago and I've been running the hotel myself."

"Renee I'm so sorry. I never thought you and John would break up although you did lead different lives. Why didn't you contact me?"

"I needed time to accept that it was over. John wanted his share of the business partnership and once the money was sorted out he left for New Zealand. He has family there and he wanted to travel. You know I didn't see the signs of the break-up. I suppose I had gotten so used to the way things were that I thought we would just continue like that forever. I felt foolish when it all ended."

"Oh Renee I wish I could have been there for you. If you gave John his share of the business how are you managing now?"

"Well it has been difficult and that's one of the reasons for my visit here. I had some capital of my own and I borrowed the rest from the bank. Financially I am coping but if some crisis were to happen in the business I would be in trouble. Emily I have a proposition I would like to discuss with you and Jack and you both can be thinking about it while I'm here."

Emily refilled the cups. "Tell me what your plan is."

"I enjoy my work and the Seaford Inn has been my home for many years and I wouldn't want it any other way. I don't want to lose my home should business suddenly become slow and I can't repay the bank loan and in this business there are times when it is slack."

"Yes it happens. Do go on."

"I was wondering if the Dillon-Spence Group would like to buy over the Seaford Inn and allow me to remain as manager. That way I will have some capital from the sale and I can repay the bank and still get to live and work in the hotel."

"You are a very smart lady. I think it is a great idea and we can talk it through with Jack tonight when we have dinner."

"I'd like that very much. I realise that even if Jack likes the idea he will have to present the proposal to the Dillon-Spence Group but I wanted you and he to think about my plan first. I'd appreciate your opinion."

"I'm glad you came Renee. We will have dinner in our apartment tonight and the children will love having you. I won't tell them you are here and you can surprise them."

"Just like I surprised you."

"Yes. I enjoy surprises when they are for someone else."

"Well if you don't mind I'd like to have a rest. Travelling can be very tiring and I will need my energy for tonight!"

"Of course. I'll take you to our guest suite. Dinner will be at 7:30 and by that time the children should be tired and ready for bed."

"If I don't rest now then I'll be joining them." She laughed.

"I'll send Jack to escort you about 6:45pm."

"Oh that would be lovely."

"Well a lady like you should have an escort."

"You flatter me Emily and I like it."

Emily returned to her office. She had lots of work to catch up on but just then Jack came in. "Emily where have you been? I've been looking for you."

"Jack I had such a surprise earlier." She kissed him and sat against his desk.

"Well tell me. You have a big grin all over your face."

"I was in reception earlier and Renee White walked in. I couldn't believe it. One minute I was talking to Tracey and then I heard the voice, turned around and there she was. She really enjoyed the look on my face."

"I bet she did. Wow this is a surprise. What brings her to Ireland and why didn't she let us know and we could have met her at the airport?"

"She wanted it to be a surprise."

Jack sat back in his chair with a smile across his face and then a frown. Emily knew that look. She loved his intense dark eyes and his attractive smile. Jack wasn't just her husband, he was her soul mate.

He reached out for her hand and she knew he was teasing her. "I get the feeling that there is more to this visit than just a surprise. Am I right?"

"You could be. What's it worth for me to tell you?"

He pulled her down onto his knee. "I could torture you, tickle you or worse."

He suddenly kissed her. "Start talking."

Emily laughed as she stroked his hair. "I love you Jack so very much."

"I know and it's a good feeling to know I'm loved. Of course I always knew you couldn't resist me."

"You couldn't stay away from me. It was love at first sight and you fell head over heels."

"Maybe I did. Now tell me about Renee's visit."

"You are right that there is more to it than just a holiday."

"Hold on I think I need a coffee." He picked the telephone and arranged for a light lunch to be sent through.

"Let's sit over on the sofa and then you have my attention."

"First of all, Renee's visit isn't the only surprise. John has left her. He wanted out of the business and the marriage."

"You mean he has actually left?"

"Yes and he is in New Zealand."

"But what about the hotel? It has been Renee's home for so many years and she has run that place so well."

"Before the marriage ended John asked Renee to buy him out. She had some capital and she took out a bank loan for the rest. Once the money was sorted out John left for New Zealand."

"Renee must be devastated. Ending a marriage and a business partnership must have had a huge effect on her."

"It has. I don't think she thought it would ever come to this."

"When did it happen?"

"Two months ago. She told me she needed time on her own just to accept it. Anyway she has come here with a very interesting business proposal."

"Go on, I'm listening."

"Renee loves the hotel but she is concerned about repaying the loan. She is just about breaking even. She thought if the Dillon-Spence Group bought over the hotel she could remain as manager and she would have some capital from the sale to pay off the bank."

"It's worth thinking about. Our Group doesn't have any hotels in South Devon. It's a good tourist area and it could be a profitable venture. When does Renee need to know?"

"I've invited her to dinner tonight in our apartment to discuss it. She realises that you would need to discuss the plan with your father and the proposal would have to be put before the Dillon-Spence board. So I suppose as soon as possible."

"I'll ring my father this afternoon and talk with him first. I like the idea of buying the Seaford Inn. It would be completely refurbished to the Dillon-Spence standard which would update the place. Yes it sounds good to me."

"And what about Renee staying on as manager?"

"That shouldn't be a problem. She is excellent at her job and I believe she would be a great asset to our company. I'll get things moving today."

Emily sipped her coffee feeling quite happy about it all. "Oh before I forget to tell you, I had a call from Victoria this morning. The situation between her and Steven seems to be getting worse. She also hired a private detective and she knows all about the other woman. One thing is bothering me that I couldn't tell Victoria."

"What's troubling you?"

"Jack I know this other woman and I'm sure she is the same Sophie Howard I told you about. I have a feeling I'm going to meet her someday. I don't know how or when, it's just a feeling."

"Be careful Emily how far you get involved. How sure are you about this woman?"

"Victoria told me her name was Sophie and she had worked in hotels. The detective couldn't find out to much about her early life because there doesn't seem to be any trace of her family. Jack I grew up with a girl called Sophie in the children's home and I helped to get her the first job she ever did as a waitress."

"Emily even if you met with this woman nothing you will say is going to change the way she feels about Steven. You be careful honey and don't do anything until we talk more about it."

"I know and I promise I won't rush into anything."

"Good. Now I'm going to get hold of my father and see what I can do for Renee this afternoon. Maybe I'll have something to tell her tonight."

9 SOPHIE HOWARD PUT the finishing touches to her make-up. She liked the effect. Diamond drop earrings added the finishing touch and she was ready to meet the man who had captured her heart. Sophie took a final look at herself in the full length mirror. She worked hard to stay slim and the short fitted red dress hugged her figure like a second skin. Sophie liked the style of the dress, off the shoulders but not to revealing, just enough to get the right attention. Her shoulder length blonde hair graced her shoulders neatly and she admired the perfect styling. Stepping into sliver high heels she picked up the evening bag off the dressing table, excitement had begun to bubble up inside her and she thrived on it.

At 9pm Sophie sat in the casino bar sipping a cocktail. It was quiet mid week and Sophie loved the relaxing atmosphere, the dim lighting and the warmth she felt inside. She looked towards the entrance watching for Steven to arrive. She liked to see him as he came in looking around for her. His smile sent shivers down her spine and no one had ever had that effect on her. Steven was the only man who had released emotions within her that she never knew existed. Sophie knew that he had a wife and a daughter but she never felt she was a threat to his marriage. She knew the kind of relationship she had with Steven and as long as they both played by the rules then everything was fine.

Sophie had met Steven when he attended a conference in the hotel were she was a waitress. There was an instant attraction between them and before long they had their first date. Sophie saw Steven as the tall, dark, handsome type. He was wealthy and that was a bonus but he had something else that had attracted her to him. It was like there was an aura about him and when he entered a room she would know he was there without having to look. He was a man who liked to be in control and to do things his way and she liked that. She wanted him to care for her and eventually he did. She fell in love with him right from the start and he treated her so well she would have done just about anything for him.

When they had met Sophie had lived in a small flat on the cheap side of town and Steven hated it. One day he called unexpectedly and she was embarrassed because she had on her old dressing gown and no make-up.

He had laughed at her and then he held her in his arms and everything else was forgotten. He pretended he was taking her for lunch but instead he drove to a new apartment and surprised her by handing her the key. It was now hers and all she had to do was move into it. At first she had doubts. Sophie liked her independence. Just for a moment she thought he might leave his wife and move in with her but it was just for a moment.

She loved the place. It was big and had beautiful furniture and it was hers.

"Oh Steven thank you but it is further to work from here."

"I have another surprise for you. I have got a new job for you which has a bit more class to it. A friend of mine owns a casino and it is the kind of place where the clients have to come recommended before they get inside the door. The salary is good and it's for you if you want it."

"Of course I want it." She kissed him.

"Steven I'm so happy with you but we need to talk before I move in here and change jobs. I need to know what is happening with us."

"Sophie I'll be honest with you. I want you to have the apartment and I know you like to be independent so it is now in your name. I just think you are beautiful and deserve to be surrounded by lovely things. I have deep feelings for you and I think I love you Sophie."

Sophie heart had begun to beat a little faster.

"Honey I need you be clear about us. I want to be with you but because of other commitments I can't leave Victoria and I have a daughter. There's also the family business and I can't complicate things there."

"So I am your mistress and that is why you have given me this apartment but no promises of a future together."

"Don't say it like that. I don't know about the future. Maybe we will be together but I can't give you anymore than we have right now. It's your choice."

"You know I want this and I am happy with you; just sometimes I wish our situation could be different."

Later when Sophie was alone in her new apartment there was something that had taken the edge of the excitement. She knew in her heart she was settling for second best and that she would always be the one who would have to wait until Steven had the time to spend with her. She would always have to stay in the background and play by his rules.

All her life she had felt second best and unwanted. Her mother couldn't cope with her so she was placed in care and her father was someone she saw maybe three times a year. After she turned thirteen she never saw him again. As an adult the rejection and the loneliness were still the greatest problems she faced in her life. When Steven had taken an interest in her she thought all her dreams had come true and although he had a wife he made her feel special and there was no way she wanted to lose that feeling.

A few more people had come into the cocktail bar and Sophie watched every time the door opened. She saw him the second he came in. He looked in her direction and she smiled.

"Hello lovely lady. I've missed you."

"Hi. It's good to see you again."

The waiter brought their drinks and they sat down at a table. "I thought maybe we could go somewhere for a meal and then back to your apartment for coffee. You do have coffee?"

She smiled. Oh yes and you can even have cream."

"Maybe we should skip the meal and go for coffee."

She loved it when he teased her. "Or we could order a take away meal and eat at my place."

"That's sound good to me. Drink up and let's go."

10

THE DILLON-SPENCE board of directors were always eager for new business ventures especially one that was as solid as the Seaford Inn. Jack had drawn up a business proposal and faxed it through to the Royal Court for his father to read. Now he had to wait but he was confident that it would be approved.

At 6:45pm Jack knocked on the door of the guest suite. A smiling Renee welcomed him in. Jack hugged her. "It is so good to see you again even if you did surprise us."

Renee crossed the room to get her bag. "I did enjoy doing that."

"Your arrival wasn't the only surprise."

"I suppose Emily has told you that John and I are separated."

He took her hand. "I'm so sorry Renee. I never thought this would happen and it must have been hard for you to accept."

"Jack at first I just drifted along not quite believing it myself but eventually I had to face up to it. I did a lot of praying and in my heart I didn't want my marriage to end but a relationship takes two people and John didn't want to stay."

"Your faith in God has remained strong."

Renee smiled. "I'm not sure that strong is the word I would use but my relationship with the Lord has sustained me through it all. I feel that I couldn't have come through this without those quiet times with him when he strengthened me."

"I know what that intimate relationship is like with him. I could never imagine trying to live my life without him."

"Neither would I. When you have something good you hold on tight."

Jack laughed. "Renee I faxed through a proposal to my father late this afternoon. I have recommended buying your hotel and keeping you on as manager."

"Do you think the board will be interested?"

"I would hope so. The hotel chain doesn't have any properties in that area and it would be a good investment. They would want to refurbish the place but that's to be expected."

"Oh I understand. The Dillon-Spence crest would be put on just about everything but I can live with that. My hope is that I can reap back the capital I've invested but remain as manager."

"Renee I believe that God will work this out for you and you know that Emily and I will support you. Now allow me to escort you to dinner."

"Thank you sir." She took his arm.

The evening was wonderful. Good company, good food and the children Renee adored. She put them to bed and read them a bedtime story, they tried to get her to read another one but Jack came to her rescue.

After dinner Emily lit some candles and dimmed the lamps in the lounge. She and Renee relaxed on the sofas and Jack came through with a tray of coffee and chocolate mints.

"I feel I have been really loved tonight. You two spoil me and those children are adorable."

"We must send them over to you for a week. I think you will soon change your mind."

"Jack you don't mean that. Our children are adorable, when they're asleep."

"Renee do you want cream and sugar."

"Yes please and a few of those chocolate mints."

Emily laughed. "More forbidden calories!"

"Honestly the way you women complain about calories and then eat them anyway."

Renee laughed. "We just like to indulge ourselves sometimes."

"Well I'll never understand you. It not like either of you is overweight."

"Jack darling, I'd quit while you're ahead. You might just say the wrong thing."

"A sensitive guy like me never says the wrong thing. Now Renee you are sure about the chocolate mints." He teased.

"Renee how long are you planning on staying? There are some beautiful places around here you could visit."

"Only a few days Emily. I really need to be back by the weekend. I would like to visit some shops though. Besides eating Jack, shopping is my other hobby."

"I'm not getting into this one. My wife also loves shopping."

"Actually I have to visit the children's home tomorrow if you would like to come with me and then we could have some retail therapy on the way back. We could drive to Coleraine where there are lots of shops in The Diamond Centre in Bridge Street and I'd like to go to Next in Church Street and there is a lovely restaurant in Queen Street."

"As you can tell Renee, my wife knows Coleraine quite well and so does our cheque book!"

Renee laughed. "I'd love that Emily. I'd like to do some shopping and take a few things back home with me. Now tell me about the children's home because it doesn't surprise me that you are involved with children."

Jack refilled her coffee cup. "We have several work projects in the hotel for the older children coming out of care. Emily also visits the younger children at the home and she is on the committee there."

"Jack that doesn't surprise me. Emily you have a good heart and I'm sure these children appreciate you taking an interest in them."

"My own childhood in care left quite an impression on me and I really do feel I need to help other children. We encourage the older ones to go on to further education and we employ them in the hotel while they are training.

I remember so well the time you came to the home Renee and asked me if I would like a job in your hotel. I felt like I'd been offered the world on a silver plate. It meant so much to me and because I remember that feeling I try to do the same for other children."

"At Christmas we bring them all here for a huge party. We have the large conference room decorated and a stage built for their play. They have a wonderful time and of course there is lots of food and at the end we have a Santa handing out presents."

"Jack is usually the Santa. We give them a good day but for me it's bittersweet because no matter how much we do, it can't fill their deepest need."

"I understand what you are trying to say Emily. You feel that no matter how much you do it doesn't take the place of being tucked up in bed at night by loving parents."

"Yes Renee that is exactly how I feel. I remember the first time I ever saw you. I was in the home and I was watching from the window. You parked your car and I watched you walk across to the entrance. I thought you had lovely clothes and make-up and you had a briefcase. That puzzled me because I only saw the social workers with a briefcase and I knew you weren't one of them. I liked you and something inside me wished I was just like you."

Renee felt a tear fall from her cheek. "Emily I never realised you felt that way."

"Oh yes although my childish imagination didn't always get it right. I thought you lived in a big house and were very wealthy and had lots of children. I was really shocked when I found out you worked in a hotel and there were no children. Of course I didn't know then that you owned the hotel. I was shocked though."

Renee laughed. "It's strange how first impressions can form all sorts of images in our minds and because we do it as children those images can stay with us for a long time."

Jack held Emily's hand. "Renee my darling wife would bring all the children here to live if she could."

"I do feel like that sometimes but in reality I know it's better for me to help give them get a good start in life. After they leave the home they can be so vulnerable and that concerns me more."

"I remember you at the home Emily. All the other children got to know me and would come and talk to me but you used to keep a safe distance. You were very good at looking after the younger children and you were like a big sister to them."

"I always felt more like their mummy. I had this over-whelming desire to protect them yet by the time a child goes into care a lot of damage has already been done."

"Although by the time Renee took you from the home you had already the desire within you to help other children."

"You're right Jack. Renee you have been my mentor in life in many ways."

"Well I hope I did something right."

"Of course you did Renee. If it wasn't for you Emily would not have met me and just think what she would have missed out on."

Emily laughed. "Listen to him. You got the best when you got me."

Renee yawned. "You two are made for each other. Now I'm tired and if you'll excuse me I need to be in bed."

"I'll walk you back to your suite."

"It's alright Jack. I'm a big girl and I've been finding my way around hotels for a long time."

"I know Renee and it's been years longer than me."

"Watch it Jack." She threw a cushion at him. "I'm not that old."

The next few days went quickly for Renee and Emily. They visited the home and Renee was very impressed. They went shopping and Renee bought gifts of Irish linen to take back with her and more clothes that she didn't need. The short holiday had been refreshing for her and in a way a healing experience emotionally. The view from the Cedar Lodge was beautiful and although it was quite cold Renee couldn't resist a walk along the beach. As she passed through reception on her way out Emily was behind the desk. "Where do you think you are going, the North Pole?"

"Very funny Emily. I want to walk along the beach and clear my head."

"You certainly seem to have enough clothes on so I don't think you'll get blown away. Enjoy your walk."

"I will." She walked briskly out the door.

Renee stood on the beach gazing at the view of the ocean. It was so vast and the roar of the waves so powerful she wanted to burst into song and praise God for his greatness. She breathed in the clean air as she walked along the damp sand. She stopped a few times and picked up some shells and threw them into the water. She felt as free as a child again. She came to some large rocks and sat down. She sensed a quietness in her spirit despite the roar of the sea and she worshiped in her heart the God of creation who had given her so much love. Tears flowed down her face as she felt a release in her spirit. The months of stress had taken there toll. "Oh Lord I love you more than life itself but how do I go on from here? Part of me looks back and there feels like something has been amputated from my life and it has hurt so much. John had been part of my life for thirty years and I've experienced the loss. Lord I don't want to become bitter, I want the rest of my life to count for something but I need your help. I can't do anything without you."

Renee walked on further down the beach and came to a small rock pool where she saw a little crab swimming around trying to find its way out. It waited until the next wave came in and gently it was carried back out to sea. Renee watched and then she heard the still small voice in her heart.

"You have felt like the crab in the rock pool. Swimming around, trying to find your way out. I'll be the wave that carries you. You don't need to struggle or fret. Relax and allow me to gently carry you through this time. I'll keep you safe, learn to let go now. Seasons come and go in your life, circumstances change but I am your Lord and your Rock and I never change. I am stable and unmoving. Trust me and depend on me. I have the way prepared."

The tears stopped and in her heart Renee felt such a cleansing that seemed to go right through her. She began to walk back the way she had come but inside she was different. "Oh thank you Lord. Your love is so tender and your healing within me has set me free to get on with my life for you. I believe we are entering a new season in my life and I want to embrace it."

Renee wrapped her scarf around her and walked back to the hotel. At the top of the pathway she stopped and looked out at the ocean and the view of the coast, it was amazing. Renee felt good inside and she was glad she had made this trip to Ireland. It had been a haven for her and a place of healing. God had helped her to put her life into his perspective and her future was secure in him. "Lord thank you again. This time has been precious to me and I'm ready to return to my responsibilities and face them with a new joy in my heart."

11

EMILY HAD SPENT a busy morning in the office and she had letters for Amy to type. She rang through for her and decided now was a good time for a coffee. "Amy I have some typing for you and I'm going to order coffee would you like to join me?"

"Yes thank you. I'll come in now."

Emily liked Amy and she knew the girl had worked hard to get this far in her work. Amy had come from the children's home and began working in the hotel on the reception desk. She also attended college and had gained qualifications in business administration and office practice. She went on to improve on her typing skills and learned shorthand. Since then she had worked as Emily's personal secretary.

The door opened and a waitress brought in coffee. Amy was right behind her. She poured out the coffee for Emily and herself but Emily noticed she was quiet. Usually Amy was all chat and full of smiles.

"Amy are you alright? You look a bit pale and you have been quiet this morning."

Amy smiled. "No. I'm not alright. Can I talk to you?"

"You know you can. Come and sit down."

Amy sat on the chair opposite. She was just twenty years old but she seemed so mature for her age.

"What's the problem Amy? You don't need to keep it to yourself."

"I don't know about anything anymore. I thought Nigel and I were happy and we had begun to make plans for our wedding. Last night he broke off our engagement. I can't believe it."

"Amy I'm so sorry. Did he explain why?"

"I suppose I should have seen the signs. Over these last few weeks, every time I tried to talk about the wedding he would go quiet and not say very much. Once he got impatient with me when I was reading another bridal magazine. The other night I asked him if we could settle on a date as I wanted to have the reception here and needed to book it. I rambled on a bit about a lovely dress I'd saw in town and what colour I wanted my bridesmaid in. He waited until I'd finished and then calmly told me he didn't want to get married and he thought we were both making a big mistake. At first I though maybe he wanted a longer engagement but he said he didn't want to marry me so there was no point going on with the engagement. He has decided he would like to travel and see the world before he settles down. Why on earth did he propose to me in the first place if he wants to travel the world?"

"He hasn't found someone else then?"

"No. He said there is no one else and that he really does want to travel. He says he loves me but he doesn't feel the time is right for him to marry and it wouldn't be fair to either of us if he continued with the engagement.

Mrs Dillon-Spence I am devastated. I imagined us having a lovely wedding and buying our first home. I suppose it is hard for Nigel to understand that I grew up in a children's home and I want all the things I never had before and I wanted to share them with him." Tears flowed and Emily fetched the tissues.

"Amy I'm so sorry and I do understand how you feel. I grew up in care and quite a few people here know that. I can understand how let down you feel but you need to look at this another way."

"I don't think there is another way. Nigel has dumped me and that's it."

"No listen to me. If Nigel had allowed this engagement to continue he would have saw you becoming more excited about the wedding and looking at houses. If he had gone through with the wedding but inside he was feeling trapped then eventually he would have begun to resent you. I know it is hard for you now but if Nigel doesn't feel ready to get married then you are better off without him."

"Yes I can see that but why bother get engaged in the first place?"

"Only Nigel can answer that. Has he any other family?"

"No he is an only child and I suppose he is used to getting his own way."

His parents are lovely people and they have a beautiful home and I suppose I wanted to feel part of it all."

"Amy I know how important family would mean to you but if this wasn't to be you must learn to let it go. I know people personally who have what you want. They are married and have a nice home and a family but as people they are unhappy in their lives."

"I know that happens but when you grow up in a home you just want to appreciate having a partner and a home of your own."

"I'm sure you will meet someone more worthy of you but if Nigel had gone ahead with this he would have been living a lie and that could have brought you a lot more pain later in life."

"I know he couldn't have been committed to me or this wouldn't have happened but it still hurts though. I loved him and I thought he loved me."

"Did you really love him or did you love the idea of being in love and having the beautiful wedding?" Amy looked puzzled. "I'm not sure now. I know I feel very insecure at times whereas Nigel was always so confident. Maybe that is why I was attracted to him. He seemed to be everything I wasn't yet I wanted to be like him."

"Amy I don't like to give advice because I believe this is something you need to work through. However I do think that you need to realise that you are everything. You don't need to compare yourself to anyone. You are attractive, intelligent and you have such a warm personality. Try to focus in on yourself and what you are and don't be selling yourself short. You grew up in a children's home but that hasn't made you into a weak person it has helped to develop your character and you are a stronger person because of it. Don't rush into anything because you feel you need to try and make yourself a better person. Learn to love who you are now and then meeting someone special later on will be a bonus."

"I never thought of it that way. You mean that I need to see myself as a whole person and not as someone who is incomplete?"

"That's exactly right. Learn to live your life for you and believe me it's when you are not looking for a man one will come along."

Amy smiled. "Thank you so much. You always seem to know exactly how the other person feels. I like that. Today is going to be the start of the rest of my life and I'm going to make it good."

Emily laughed. "That's a good attitude to begin with. Be confident about yourself. You are young and then tell yourself the best is yet to come."

"Thank you for listening. I'll get back to work now and I suppose I could make a start on your letters."

Emily was working at her desk when Jack came in. "Have you time for a coffee in the sitting room? I've asked Renee to join us."

"Have you had news from London?"

"Wait and see my darling."

Emily mused. "You so love to sound mysterious."

"I know and it adds to my charm."

Emily sighed. "Sitting room now Jack."

"Yes madam."

Renee was already waiting for them and the waitress had arrived with scones just baked by the lovely smell of them.

"I'm glad to see you two. I just couldn't hold back from these scones for much longer."

"And don't forget the jam and cream and the forbidden calories!"

"Shut up Jack. I'm entitled to a few luxuries in life."

"Oh I agree but I know you two women. You will enjoy the food now and complain the rest of the day."

Emily reached for a scone. "Shut up Jack and pour the coffee."

"Yes madam."

Over coffee Jack opened up the file which contained the business proposal for the Seaford Inn. "Renee as promised I've been in contact with my father regarding your proposal for our group to buy over the hotel. Dad liked the idea instantly. He has sound judgement and he knows a good deal when he is presented with one. He arranged a meeting last night with board members and they also agreed it would be a sound investment. They want to buy the hotel and retain you as manger with your own private apartment. They will want to make some changes to the hotel but we had already discussed that and I've told my father you are alright with it."

"Jack this is wonderful news. The hotel does need a major make over which I could never have afforded to do myself but this way makes it even better."

"I have some financial details for you to go through but I think you will be pleased the sale will be a generous one for you and one you won't regret."

Renee glanced at the paper. "Jack this is even more than I'd hoped for. Now I can pay off the bank loan and still have some capital plus a job and a new apartment."

"Renee while you manage the hotel you will be on an excellent salary. My father knows you have years of experience and the board agreed you should have a good financial package as part of the deal. There also are pension and other benefits included and I'm sure you will be happy."

"Jack and Emily this is so wonderful. I'm so glad I came to see you. You have been so good to me."

"Renee someone as special as you deserves the best blessings. I've never forgotten how well you treated me when I needed someone. I will always appreciate what you did for me especially when I had Rosa."

Renee felt tears in her eyes. "That's a lovely thing to say. I suppose I looked on you as my own daughter and when you had Rosa I felt like a real grandmother. Jack thank you for the way you have handled everything for me. I know in business there isn't always room for emotions but I am grateful to you and your family."

"Renee you know how much we care for you. The hotel will be a fresh challenge for you and that will be good for you."

"I realise that Jack. I feel that God is making all things new for me again and I won't let him or any of you down."

"I have no doubts on that one Renee. Now that you have agreed to the proposal a final draft will be faxed through from London for you to sign. Emily and I will be witnesses and the papers go back to London. In the next few weeks you will be contacted regarding the upgrading of the hotel."

"Sounds very exciting Renee."

"I know Emily and I'm very happy. Now I can plan to return home."

Jack left with the file and the two women sat on for awhile.

"I've just been thinking of all the years I've lived at the Inn. I never imagined life would one day take the turn it has. Still I know God well enough to trust him and he has worked everything in my favour."

Two days later Renee had packed everything and a car was waiting to take her to Belfast International Airport. The deal with the Dillon-Spence board had been signed and Renee had a new future to look forward to.

Jack and Emily walked with Renee to the car. Emily felt a little sad that she had to leave so soon but life in the hotel business never stopped or took holidays.

"I'll miss you Renee but I'm happy for you too."

"I'll stay in touch with you both. I'll miss you but we all have work to do."

Jack hugged her. "Jack thank you for everything. Give the children my love. Goodbye now."

Jack and Emily walked back into the hotel holding hands. "Jack isn't is great the way in which God can take painful situations and bring healing where it's needed and then he turns the situation into a blessing."

"It all down to trusting him Emily and wanting him to work out our problems. I wouldn't want to try and run a business without him."

"We have made some of our wisest decisions after we have prayed so you're right. We wouldn't want to be without him."

"My father is really looking forward to this new venture. He will be like a child with a new toy and he will have that place refurbished in no time."

Emily laughed. "I can almost hear him barking out his orders."

"Mrs Dillon-Spence a call for you."

"Put it through to the office Tracey."

The telephone was ringing when she opened the office door and she rushed to answer it. "Hello."

"Hi Emily its Victoria. I really need to talk to you."

"Alright, calm down and tell me what is wrong."

"Emily I've decided I can't do this anymore. I can't go on pretending that everything will be alright. I'm beginning to resent Steven so much I can hardly stay in the same room as him."

"I'm sorry it has come to this. The stress isn't good for you or Chloe."

"I'm worried about her too. She is becoming so fretful and cries if I'm out of her sight. She senses there is something wrong but she is too young to understand what it is."

"Victoria it is only a few weeks to Christmas so why don't you bring Chloe over here for the holiday. Stay until after New Year and give yourself time to think. At least you will be able to relax."

"That sounds like a good idea but the hotel is very busy now."

"Jack can get his father to send extra staff if needed. The hotel will not come to a stand still just because you need a holiday."

"Alright I'll come. I haven't bought any gifts for Chloe yet so we could go shopping together."

"I like that idea. I still have lots to buy so we will have a great time. Victoria would you like me to come over and help you pack. You will have a lot to sort out before you leave."

"Emily I would love that. I hate travelling as I get anxious over everything."

"I'll arrange a time with Jack and ring you tonight. Bye for now."

As Emily replaced the receiver another idea crossed her mind. While she was in England she hoped to fit in a visit to Sophie. She needed to know if it was the same person that she knew and if it was then she wanted to talk to her.

12

EMILY ARRIVED AT the Edgewater Hotel on a cold crisp December morning. Victoria was waiting for her and looked relieved as she walked through the door. They hugged each other.

"Emily I'm so happy you are here. Come through to the sitting room for coffee. I'll arrange for your luggage to be taken up to your suite."

Emily noticed how pale and strained Victoria looked and although her make-up was perfect there was no hiding the sadness in her eyes.

They sipped hot coffee and Emily relaxed in the warmth of the sitting room. "Tell me Victoria. What did Steven say when you told him you were going to the Antrim Coast for Christmas?"

"Well I was expecting a huge argument but it didn't happen. He said it was my decision. He is acting very strange lately. He is cold towards me in private, polite in public yet he seems pre-occupied with something else. He no longer talks about the business with me and I don't think he has forgiven his father for confronting him like he did. I know he is still seeing his girlfriend as he stays out of the hotel as much as he can."

"He is a strange man. Anyway let's talk about happier things. I've told Jack and the children you and Chloe are coming over and we will be back for the weekend. The children are very excited and

I know the holiday will be so good for you and Chloe. You need some space from Steven to think through what you want for your life and what's best for Chloe."

"I know you are right Emily. I've told Chloe we are going away for Christmas and I had to explain that daddy is very busy with work and has to stay behind. She accepted it and was especially happy at the thought of seeing Rosa and Nathan again."

"It will be such a good Christmas and I'm looking forward to it. Now I'd like to freshen up so tell me where to go."

"Of course and I'll be in the office if you are looking for me later."

"I might take a walk in the gardens. I know it's cold but I think better when I walk."

Emily unpacked her case and telephoned Jack just to let him know she had arrived. She felt tired but then she always did after travelling. Just as she was deciding on a rest there was a knock at the door. Emily opened it to find Steven standing there.

"Hello Steven."

"Well aren't you going to invite me in? I just thought I'd come along and welcome you."

"Come in then." She stepped aside and he brushed past her and suddenly she was aware of sharpness in her spirit. This was one man not to be trusted.

Steven sat down and for a moment appeared to be anxious then he smiled and had that confident look he wore. "Now Emily I know we haven't always agreed on things but I want to thank you."

Emily looked puzzled. "Thank me for what?"

"When Victoria told me she was going to Ireland I was annoyed at first. I mean, who wants to be apart from his wife and daughter at Christmas?"

"Exactly."

"However, I believe a holiday is just what my wife needs. She looks tired all the time and a change of scenery will be good for her. Chloe is looking forward to seeing Rosa and little Nathan again. So thank you for being concerned enough to do something like this."

Emily really wanted to throw up over him. He was acting so insincere yet he really tried to sound like a man who cared.

"Steven not so long ago you were telling me to stay away from your wife. You resented my friendship with Victoria and you only tolerate me because I am Jacks wife."

"Emily I know I've made mistakes in the past and I'm sure you are aware that I've mismanaged the business. My father is keeping a close eye on me and that is painful for me Emily. I hate being treated like a naughty schoolboy who needs to be punished."

"Except you are not a schoolboy Steven. You are a grown man. I know anyone can make mistakes but I'm not sure you ever learn by yours."

"Emily I'm trying. Well enjoy your stay; I need to get back to work now. I'm sure I'll see you before you leave."

After he had gone Emily lay down on the bed and tried to rest. She knew Steven had lied to her and he only wanted to deceive her into thinking he loved his wife. "Oh Lord I hate lies and deception. How can I help in a situation like this? Steven is so cold in his heart and so hard in his attitude that the only one he is deceiving is himself."

Emily closed her eyes and in her heart surrendered Steven over to God and then she fell asleep.

When she wakened she felt refreshed and there was stillness in her spirit. "God thank you for that rest and the peace inside. There is no more turmoil like I felt earlier."

"Emily be still and remember that I am God. I will quicken your spirit to hear me. Be open to my voice. I am the way for you and Victoria. I know the end from the beginning."

"Lord I'm open to hear you and I praise you because of who you are."

Emily changed into a trouser suite and put on a warm coat and her boots. She felt like a walk around the hotel gardens. She needed to think about how she could get to talk to Sophie and without Victoria finding out.

Suddenly she felt cold inside. "Oh God what am I doing? I am being just as deceptive as Steven and trying to feel right before you about it. Forgive me Lord and work out your plan for me in this situation. I surrender my will to you."

"Emily the truth will set you free. Leave all to me."

Emily breathed a sigh of relief and left her suite to enjoy her walk.

The Edgewater Hotel now had that touch of class that the Dillon-Spence Group imprinted on their businesses. At times she wondered what it would be like to live in a house rather than a hotel but she had to admit they did have certain benefits living and working on the premises.

Emily walked through some wooded area until she came to the wishing well and the garden swing. This place was perfect for wedding photographs and the gardens were landscaped. Emily sat down on the swing enjoying the stillness and the crisp fresh air. Suddenly a woman turned the corner and Emily assumed it was another guest out for a walk. The woman turned up the collar of her coat but Emily could see she had blonde hair. As she stared she felt her heartbeat quicken. "Oh Lord she reminds me of Sophie but surely she wouldn't come to the hotel."

The woman sat down on a nearby seat and a few times she looked across at Emily. "Lord I know it is her."

Emily got of the swing and walked towards the woman. "Lord if I have this wrong then I can just apologise and say I made a mistake."

"Hello. I think I know you. Are you Sophie?"

The girl blushed. She wanted to say no but she knew Emily the minute she spoke.

"Hello Emily. It's been a long time. I often wondered where you had moved on to."

"Well it's been a few years but it's good to see you again. Why are you here?"

"I was supposed to meet someone but I think I've been stood up. I see you wear a wedding ring, did you have any other children?"

"Well you know about Rosa and now I have a son, Nathan. Is there anyone special in your life Sophie? Have you met that handsome prince yet?"

Sophie shrugged her shoulders. "I haven't changed much Emily. I haven't settled down so there's no husband or children. I might have met the prince but I don't feel like the princess."

"Sophie whatever you are doing in your life just be happy. Anyone who has grown up in care like we did should be happy."

"Oh I don't know. I think we spend our adult lives getting over our childhood. My life has always seemed like second best and I've watched good things pass me by."

"Sophie I'm a Christian and I have found my purpose in God. He meets all my needs and he is my best friend that I can trust with everything."

"You make it sound so good."

"It is Sophie and it could also be yours. It's your choice."

Sophie took a pack of cigarettes from her bag and lit one. "I remember when we were growing up in the home I used to look up to you and when we started work I knew you would do well. I always seem to lack whatever it takes to be successful. I remember you used to try and talk sense into me but I just drifted along from one job to the next."

"I also remember you telling me you would wait for your handsome prince and the fairytale wedding and then you would live happy ever after. So what happened Sophie?"

"My prince already has a princess and I feel more like the maid."

"You were to meet him here today?"

"Yes but I've been stood up. I can only see him when he has the time for me. He has other commitments."

Emily looked at her and saw the same sadness in her face that she remembered from years ago. She felt compassion for this woman who has wasted years of her life looking for love in the wrong people.

"Sophie I need to be honest with you. I know who you are involved with and I know the reasons why you can't go into the hotel. You are in love with Steven and we both know he is already married."

Sophie was shocked. "I'm not going to deny it. I do love Steven but I'm not naïve enough to think that he is going to leave his wife.

Maybe I'll just have to settle for what I've got. I live in a nice apartment and he sees me whenever he can. How do you know Emily?"

"I'm married to Steven's brother Jack and I have a close friendship with Victoria."

"Oh no this is like my worst dream. Does she know about me?"

"She knows her husband is involved with someone but she doesn't know much about you. She found out a little about you but she was puzzled that there wasn't much information on your background. I figured out a lot for myself."

"Will she ever divorce him?"

"I honestly don't know. She has been holding on hoping that things might get better. She is involved in the running of the business and then there is their little girl to think of. Divorce isn't something she's thinking of now but then she feels rejected by the man that once loved her and the hurt is hard to take."

"I know how it feels to hurt Emily. Tell me about you?"

"Jack and I moved to Ireland to manage a hotel on the coast. We are happy and so are the children. Jack is a Christian and God has blessed us Sophie."

"Well at least one of us got something right. You got the handsome prince and I'm sure the beautiful wedding and living happy ever after."

"Sophie you don't have to settle for second best. Since I've known you I know you believed that someone would come along and make things alright for you. You wanted that someone to fill a vital gap inside your heart. Sophie that isn't the way it is."

"I know being with Steven isn't right but what else can I do. If I stop seeing him I have no one and nothing. My apartment was his idea and although he had my name put on it that means nothing. Without him I couldn't afford to live there. I'm sorry Victoria is hurting but I don't think that he loves her anymore and I'm not really sure if he loves me. Steven is a very complex person."

"I can understand how you see him that way but I see something different. Steven uses people to suit his purpose and he doesn't commit to one person. I think in his own selfish way he still wants to be with Victoria but not for herself but more for what she can do for him. She is good at business and she is a good wife and mother. He still needs her. You are the person he fits into the other side of his life. You are the distraction from responsibility and his marriage and from the image Steven has tried to establish with those in his family circle. What happens if he gets tired of you? Where do you see yourself in a year from now? Sophie you need to break away from this man because he will hurt you in the end."

Sophie stood up. "I know what you are saying and it makes sense but I'm not strong enough right now. I can't live without him in my life. I know I have no security with him but I don't allow myself to think to far ahead. Look I must go. I'm glad you are happy in your life. Maybe one day we will meet again."

"Sophie please don't allow this man to hurt you. You are worth so much more. Do you want my telephone number in case you need to talk?"

"No that is not a good idea. If I need you I will find you. Goodbye."

Emily watched her walk away and she felt sad that the affair would one day end in tears for Sophie and Victoria. Steven would look after himself while other people's lives would be left devastated. Sophie had made her choice and all Emily could do now was pray.

Emily walked around the garden trying to make sense of it all. She was relieved that she had met Sophie without having to deceive Victoria but she was annoyed at the games Steven played with other people's lives. Jack and Steven couldn't be more different and yet they were brothers. Jack was committed in his relationship with God and to his marriage yet Steven seemed committed to no one but himself. Emily was aware of her peace being disturbed and she realised she was simply comparing and judging Steven with Jack. "Lord forgive me I'm sorry. Cleanse my heart God. I know you are the only one who can change a person's heart."

"Emily each person has a free will and they choose."

Emily headed back towards the entrance to the hotel just as Steven turned the corner.

"Hi did you enjoy your walk?"

"Yes Steven I did."

"I just needed some fresh air myself so I'll go on."

"Steven she has left."

"No Victoria is in the office."

"Stop telling lies and playing games. I saw her and I spoke to her. I know Sophie."

"Then there is no point in denying it anymore. How do you know her?"

"I won't discuss that with you. Sophie will tell you if she wants you to know. I don't understand why you are doing this to Victoria. You have everything here Steven why ruin it?"

"I suppose you are going to tell Victoria?"

"Do you really think she doesn't know already? Why are you so intent on destroying everything?"

"Maybe I just like to get as much as I can out of life, after all it is to short to waste."

"Steven she still loves you. You could put a stop to all this."

"Emily I need to work this out for myself. I'm glad you are taking Victoria away for Christmas, it will give us both time to think."

"Well I hope you make the right decisions. See you later."

Victoria was chatting to a guest as Emily walked through reception. She looked happy when she was helping someone in some way. Emily prayed that she would be spared from any more heartache. She didn't deserve what Steven was doing to her."

13

SOPHIE ADMIRED THE lounge that she had spent hours arranging with candles and setting a romantic atmosphere for dinner. She had cooked a meal and everything was going according to plan and she was happy.

She sipped at a glass of wine and her thoughts were of Emily and how she hadn't seen her for years until today. It felt strange knowing she was married to Steven's brother. Emily seemed happy with being a Christian but Sophie had always been doubtful about that stuff. She remembered when they were younger Emily used to read the children bible stories in the home. Anyway she and Emily were different people and there was nothing that could change that.

The doorbell rang and Sophie glanced at herself in the mirror before she opened it.

"Hello darling. You look beautiful."

She kissed him. "Thank you. I missed you today."

"I missed you too. Something smells good in the kitchen and I have some wine."

For awhile over dinner they talked about everything except the issues that were on both their minds. They had their meal and moved to the sofa and they had more wine.

"Sophie what happened today that you didn't wait for me in the garden?"

"I waited a long time and it was cold."

"I'm sorry but I got delayed. It happens."

"It's alright Steven I understand. Forget about it, you are here now and that's what matters."

Steven sat up straight and Sophie tensed. "I know you look forward to our nights here but there is something I need to clear up with you. I know who you were talking to today."

Sophie felt her heart beat a little faster but she remained quiet.

"I want to know how you two know each other. What's going on Sophie?"

"Nothing is going on. What did Emily tell you?"

"The usual, that I should sort out my marriage and that would you tell me anything else. So talk to me."

"I knew Emily when I was younger. We grew up together and got our first jobs together but over the years we lost contact. She saw me in the garden and she knew who I was."

"Did you discuss our relationship?"

"Steven she already knew and I'm not going to lie about it. She told me to stay away from you but she knows I won't. I have accepted from the beginning that you are married and it has to be this way."

"You don't sound too happy about it. If you accept everything how come I'm getting the impression you feel cheated."

"That's because I do. I feel like I'm second best but that's my problem not yours."

"Sophie I don't treat you like second best. Just look around this apartment. You have everything you need."

"I know that and I appreciate it all but I still don't have you. I know there is no point talking about the future with you because you have always made it clear that you will not leave Victoria. What we have now is as good as it gets."

"Sophie I do love you. We both know my marriage is a sham but it's a good business asset besides, I'm not my father's favourite person at the moment. Divorce is out of the question plus my parents' rate marriage very highly and there are certain advantages in maintaining it."

Sophie could hear how cold he sounded and she wondered if he would ever feel that way about her.

"Sophie I asked you earlier how you knew Emily."

"And I told you we grew up together."

"I know that Emily grew up in a children's home but when we met you told me you had been brought up by an aunt."

"I know. I didn't want you to know the truth."

"But why?"

"I've always felt ashamed of my background so I covered it up. I couldn't wait to get out of that place but Emily did help me a lot when we were younger. I used to pretend she was my big sister. Emily was good to me."

"Well we have two differing opinions. I always thought that she married my brother because she was a single parent and Jack was a good catch."

"No Steven. Emily is not like that, she is not an opportunist in the way you see her. She is a good person who deserves her happiness."

"Sophie she got a whole new life when she married into my family."

"So you think she is not good enough?"

Steven laughed. "I just feel Jack could have met someone from within our circle of friends. Someone with a little more breeding."

"If you feel that way about Emily then how do you feel about me? I come from a similar background and it isn't good breeding."

"Sophie come on now. It doesn't matter to me what your background is. What we have now is important."

"Steven what we have now is me living as your mistress in your nice apartment and it will never be any different."

"Look I don't want to argue so I'll go. Maybe we both need an early night. Remember one thing. I put you here and you knew the rules from the start so I don't think you should be complaining now. Don't get greedy Sophie. Without me you could never afford this place. I'll leave you to think about it."

For the first time Sophie felt frightened by him. Later as she lay in bed alone she felt cheap and worthless. She realised some of her choices had not been good ones but she didn't know how to change. Without Steven she had no one. She tried to sleep but couldn't. After a restless night she got up and had a shower and made fresh coffee.

She thought of Emily and her faith in God and she so wished her life could be different. She decided to try and stay on the right side of Steven for a time just until she had thought more about her future. Somehow her life had to change. She didn't want to spend the rest of her life living this way and although she didn't know how to change things somewhere deep inside her she believed that the time would come when she no longer felt second best to anyone.

14

Victoria dressed Chloe in her new winter clothes. "Oh I love my coat mummy. It's all furry and soft and warm."

"You look beautiful darling. Now say good-bye to daddy and Aunt Emily will take you to wait in reception. I'll be along in a few minutes."

Steven picked her up in his arms. "Now you have a lovely time in Ireland and have a great Christmas."

"Daddy I want you to be there too. You won't see my new toys."

"I know darling and if daddy can get away for Christmas then maybe I'll get to be with you. It is very busy at work now but I will talk to you on the phone. Now you go with Emily."

Victoria stood along with Steven. She picked up her coat and her bag and went to walk past him but he caught her arm. "Victoria please wait a minute. I know it's my fault the way things have been between us so maybe I'll try to come to Ireland for Christmas and we can talk. Our marriage has got to be worth saving."

"Steven it is difficult to save a marriage when there is still another woman in it. I suggest you think about what you want from this marriage and what you are prepared to give in order to maintain it. I know I can't continue to be with someone who lies to me and is unfaithful. I have loved you so much but our relationship doesn't seem to be enough for you and I'm not prepared to ignore what you do outside our home."

"Victoria I know how I've messed things up but I do still love you and I'm sorry I've been so distant with you."

"How do I know you are just being sorry for yourself because you have been caught? Think about it. A few months ago you were spending money that was not yours to spend and you got involved with another woman. Now that everything is out in the open you are making promises I'm not sure you will keep. How can I trust you again?"

"I know how much I've hurt you but when you are away take some time to relax and think about the future. I'll ring you. Maybe we can sort things out."

"I don't know Steven; I'm not making you any promises. Have a nice Christmas"

He kissed her cheek but her heart felt cold and she wasn't sure they had a future.

As soon as they boarded the plane for Belfast, Victoria felt such relief inside. She loved flying. There was something about being surrounded by white clouds and blue sky that made her feel wonderful. There had been so much turmoil in her life but for awhile she was leaving it behind her and she felt free.

"I'm so glad you decided to come for Christmas. It will be so good for you."

"Emily I know and it has been my best decision in a long time."

"You will never regret it. The scenery is beautiful and the environment will be stress free for you."

Just before the plane landed Victoria looked out of the window and gasped with delight. "Emily I have never seen so many shades of green. This is amazing."

"Wait until you have seen the coastline and the ocean. Victoria you will love it here."

She smiled. "I might want to stay."

15

CHRISTMAS AT THE Cedar Lodge was a magical time. The hotel had been decorated and everyday and night business was steady. There was the lovely festive Christmas atmosphere and the guests were in holiday spirit.

Emily and Victoria had made several shopping trips to Coleraine and they had lots of gifts for the children. They had shopped at The Diamond, had lunch at the restaurant in Queen Street and Victoria felt happy and refreshed. They loaded up the car with all their Christmas gifts and Victoria couldn't wait to get back and begin to write cards and wrap up presents.

The day after the shopping trip the children from the home came for their Christmas party and carol singing at the hotel and it was a very special time for each one of them.

Steven had rang several times but Victoria kept the conversation brief. She needed time to think without any pressure.

Christmas Day was a beautiful family day and the children were excited all day. There were lots of presents and they had exhausted themselves by bedtime.

Victoria and Emily went for a walk on the beach leaving Jack with the children. It was cold but the sea breeze was fresh.

"Oh Emily I love this place. Miles of beach and a huge big ocean. No wonder you and Jack moved here, its lovely."

Emily laughed. "Yes the view is breathtaking but then so is the wind."

They watched as the waves crashed against the rocks further along the beach. "This is where I come when I want to walk and talk to God at the same time. Even through the roar of the waves I can still hear his voice."

"Maybe one day I'll be able to talk with him too. I'm beginning to understand more about your relationship with God. I think in my thoughts I am searching for him. I believe he has the answers for my life."

"I believe he has too and he won't rush you. Keep searching your heart for him, accept him into your life and he will be there."

"I know. Right now I'm freezing so can we go back?"

"I think we need a hot drink."

16

STEVEN HAD SPENT some of the holiday with Sophie and some of the time wallowing in self pity. Sophie was annoyed with him for not being more excited about Christmas and being together. She felt he had withdrawn from her at a time when she was expecting him to be closer to her. Something seemed to be reaching crisis point and she didn't like it.

Sitting at her dressing table putting on her make-up she wondered if Steven would remember they were going out tonight and she hoped he would stay with her. After all he didn't have a wife to rush home to.

He was late in arriving and Sophie was annoyed.

"I'm sorry I got delayed." He kissed her and she could smell whiskey of him.

"Steven it's too late to go out now. I telephoned and cancelled our table."

"You shouldn't have did that."

"Oh get real will you. It would take ages to drive out there and they weren't going to hold the table all night. Look we can stay here."

He sat down. "Do whatever you like. I've had a long day and since you have spoilt my night I might just as well go home again but I'll have a drink first."

"Steven I thought you were staying the night."

"No I didn't say that."

"So what are your plans then? I'm tired of you messing me around."

"Sophie I see you when I can. The hotel is busy and my wife is not here to help."

"Well at least she has her uses."

"Don't get nasty now. You know the rules."

"Yes I do but I also know your wife is away for a few weeks and I'm seeing less of you instead of more."

"Sophie I think this relationship is getting to complicated so maybe we need a break. I need time to think."

"Steven I don't believe you are saying this. You don't seem to know what you want."

"Victoria knows about us and I don't want to lose my wife and daughter."

"And your parents may not want you to manage their hotel without the respectable wife by your side. Maybe you are afraid you will lose the business and the money which pays for the lifestyle you like to lead."

"I don't want to lose anything." He sipped at his drink.

"Maybe it's just me you don't mind losing. I'm not really an asset."

He slammed the glass down. "Maybe I'm tired listening to you."

"Then go. Tonight could have been so good. I thought we would have a meal and come back here for the night but you're not interested anymore. Things are fine when we play the game without Victoria finding out but it's not much fun when you get caught."

"I'm going and I'll ring you sometime. I'm beginning to wonder if you're just another opportunist like Emily. Did you grow up in that home planning your futures? You know, meet some wealthy guy and get him to fall for you."

"Stop it Steven. Emily is whiter than white compared to you. She is a strong woman who has a loving husband and together they make a great team. Are you jealous Steven? Jack has so much compared to you and your pride can't stand it."

Sophie heard the slap but she didn't feel a thing until she had hit the floor. She felt him pull her to her feet but before she could speak he hit her again and pushed her away from him. She fell again but her instincts told her to stay still. She felt terrified as the pain began to register in her brain and sweat poured down her body.

"I'm going and I want you to think carefully about what you said. Victoria would never speak to me like that but then she has class."

"Then go back to her Steven. You may not think I'm good enough for you but it's the other way around. A bully like you is no longer good enough for me."

He bent down and grabbed her hair.

"Go on Steven be a real man and hit me again."

He let her go. "Goodbye Sophie."

She heard the door shut but she stayed on the floor. She cried in disbelief that Steven had hurt her physically and inside her heart was breaking.

She got up and went into the kitchen and poured a drink and then quickly had another. It numbed all the pain and she prayed that soon she would fell asleep.

Steven drove in the opposite direction of the hotel. He was angry and drunk so he kept the window down to let fresh air in. He couldn't believe he had hit Sophie and even if he wanted to finish with her this wasn't the way to do it. He had to calm down before he went home. He had become so quick with his temper lately. Tomorrow he would ring Sophie, even if she never saw him again. His mind was in turmoil and his thoughts all over the place. He didn't realise how fast he was driving, at least not until he came to a narrow bend.

The car hit a hedge on the opposite side of the road as it skidded across.

At 90mph it carried on through the hedge and down a steep ditch. Steven had lost control and with no seatbelt on he went through the windscreen as the car turned over onto the roof. The last thing he shouted was, "Oh God no." Then came the blackness. In a cold dark place Steven lay alone and unconscious.

It was daylight when a passing car driver noticed the hole in the hedge and stopped. He saw Steven's car overturned and he telephoned for help. Making his way towards the car he could see Steven underneath the bonnet.

Soon the area was sealed off and the police and ambulance people moved in.

They managed to get Steven out and put him on a stretcher. They checked for vital signs of life. There weren't any. They put a sheet over his face. Steven was dead.

17

Sophie had a restless night and although she was tired, sleep was impossible so she got up and made coffee. Her body hurt all over and she stared at herself in the mirror at the bruises that covered her. She still found it hard to believe that Steven had did this to her. In all the time she had known him there had never been a hint of aggression in his behaviour towards her.

Steven had been the one man who had made her feel special and when she was in his company he treated her like she was a lady. It had been so easy to fall in love with him and she felt almost privileged to be with him.

After her coffee Sophie had a shower to help wash away the pain and ease the tiredness from her body. The one thing the shower could not do was wash away the feeling of cheapness that she felt about herself. Steven had succeeded in making her feel worthless and now it seemed her relationship with him was a sham. She had been deceived into thinking that someone like Steven could have real feelings of love for her but now he had showed his true nature and he was a bully who had abused her in order to make him the one who made the rules in the relationship and when she had rebelled she had paid the price and now had the bruises to prove it.

After her shower Sophie felt a little better as the warm water washed away the tiredness from her body and she felt refreshed. She put on her bathrobe and dried her hair and applied a little make-up. Her pain had eased on the outside but on the inside her emotions felt raw. Her thoughts were confused as to why things had gone wrong between her and Steven at this particular time. When Steven had told her that Victoria was going away for Christmas she had hoped that they would be able to spend more time together and that he would be able to relax and enjoy the Christmas holiday. Instead Steven seemed to be more tense and had distanced himself from her and he found fault with just about everything. When he had become violent towards her she was shocked that this same man was the person she had fallen in love with and she believed that he loved her.

Sophie knew in her heart that she could no longer continue in the relationship with Steven. She knew that she was not entirely blameless. She had reacted in anger towards Steven and he had responded in anger and aggression. Sophie decided that if Steven did not contact her today then she would telephone him. She couldn't just leave the situation as it was so she had to end it. She wondered what had gone wrong between them as her feelings for him had not changed and she had been looking forward to spending more time with him. Thinking back over the weeks she realised that Steven had felt under pressure from the time his father had began to check out the way in which he was running the hotel. She knew that Victoria had also found out about her and that would have made things more difficult for Steven and he had talked with Emily and found out that she had grown up in the same children's home as her. When they had argued Steven has accused her of being an opportunist because that was the way in which he saw Emily. Maybe he was right and she had been selling herself short!

Sophie spent the day in her apartment trying to think things through. By late afternoon she thought about telephoning Steven but she knew if he was busy at the hotel he would be annoyed at her so she dialled his mobile number. She was surprised that there was no ringing tone. Steven never switched off his mobile.

She tried again because the answer service should have come on but there was nothing, it was as if the phone was broken. Sophie decided to wait until 7pm and then she would telephone the hotel. As the hours went by Sophie felt annoyed that Steven hadn't bothered to get in contact with her and apologize for his behaviour but she was still willing to talk with him and give him the opportunity to explain why he reacted the way he did. Sophie couldn't continue with him because she wouldn't risk his temper again and she wondered just how much his wife had to put up with. She wasn't his wife so she could make her own rules and the worst that could happen is that she would lose the apartment that he had given her. She had moved lots of times in her life so she would manage again if she had to.

At 6:15 Sophie made coffee and sat down on the sofa and picked up the remote control. She flicked through the television channels but there was nothing of interest. She picked up the mug of coffee and took a sip and then suddenly her attention was drawn to the television. She turned up the volume as the picture showed a silver car lying on its roof in a ditch. Her heart started beating faster as she listened to the report.

"Early this morning a passing motorist discovered the car in a ditch. The driver had been thrown clear but sustained severe injuries. Police and paramedics were quickly on the scene and have confirmed that the driver was the only person in the car. Police are not revealing any details until the next of kin has been informed."

Sophie felt physically sick inside. She knew that the car was Stevens but she didn't know if he was alive or dead. Her instinct told her that the accident had been fatal, why else would the police withhold information? Sophie paced up and down the living room, she didn't know what to do and her thoughts were racing. She thought of telephoning the hotel but if Steven had been in an accident then the staff would have prepared a statement to be realised should anyone inquire about Steven.

At 7:15pm Sophie could stand the waiting no longer so she got into her car and went for a drive. As she approached the stretch of road where the silver car had gone through the hedge she parked her car in a lay by. It was dark and cold as Sophie walked towards the gap in the hedge. The drop down the ditch was steep and as it had rained earlier the bank was wet and slippery. The police had sealed off the area with yellow tape but Sophie was able to get underneath it and taking her flashlight she made her way down the bank as far she could and shone the light towards the silver car. The BMW was still on its roof and it was hard to make out any detail. The number plate was upside down and was difficult to read but she was able to make out the letters, SD-S. A cry came from within her as she struggled up the bank again, she felt like she was going to throw up and she kept taking deep breaths. Sophie knew that Stevens family had personalised number plates and those letters she had just seen stood for, 'Steven Dillon-Spence.'

When Sophie arrived home she went through to her bedroom. She didn't turn on any lights but lay on the bed and sobbed until she thought her heart would break. She had loved that man no matter what he had done and she tried to imagine what it had been like for him as he drove away from her in anger and then the crash. She worried that he had been there all night before someone had found him. She wondered what his thoughts had been. Did he have time to think about his wife or his daughter or maybe even her? How was she going to live with the knowledge that their last night together had been nothing more than an aggressive row that had ended everything they had ever shared.

Sophie turned the television on to check the latest news report. The first one had said the driver of the car had serious injuries and somewhere in her heart she hoped that he was still alive. Other people had survived worse accidents and had to be cut from the wreckage so just maybe Steven had a chance of pulling through this. The worst part was she did not know if he was dead or alive and she felt in a strange kind of limbo. There was no point in contacting the hotel or the hospital because she was not close family and they would not give her any information so she decided to wait until morning and by then the news reports should give more detail and the local newspaper would report it also. Everyone locally knew of the Dillon-Spence family and the Edgewater Hotel and any news connected with them would make the headlines.

Sophie went to bed feeling exhausted but her sleep was restless and her dreams vivid. She dreamt of her and Steven being together and they were happy and she felt loved by him. In the next scene they were having an argument and she could hear his voice shouting at her yet she couldn't wake herself up from the dream. She saw him raise his hand and she felt the hard slap across her face and the shock as she hit the floor.

"No Steven." She shouted and the sound of her own voice woke her from the nightmare. Sophie sat up in bed and her hair was damp and her face soaked in sweat. She took deep breaths as she assured herself it was a dream although the reality of Steven hitting her was not her imagination. She looked at the clock and it said 4:20am. "I might as well have a shower because I can't sleep anyway."

The shower was refreshing because her body still hurt from the bruises Steven had given her and inside she felt emotionally drained and she just wanted the shower to wash all the pain away. The hot water helped to ease her tense muscles and washing her hair cleared the tension in her head.

After having coffee and toast Sophie cleaned the apartment and put fresh linen on the bed. She felt she was cleaning out a part of her life and when she had finished every room smelt fresh and she felt good about herself.

Sitting at her dressing table Sophie applied a little make-up and lip gloss and the consealer helped to cover the bruises. Just as she had finished she heard the doorbell ring. She wondered who would be calling on her so early and she was annoyed she hadn't left a few minutes ago to buy the morning paper.

Sophie kept the chain on the door and opened it slightly. "Hello."

She was surprised to see two police officers on the doorstep.

"Good morning Miss Howard. May we come in and talk to you?"

Somewhere inside Sophie was tempted to say no but thought better off it and opened the door instead. "Come in."

They went through to the lounge. "Sit down please and tell me why you are here."

The policewoman glanced at her colleague and he nodded his head.

"Miss Howard we have reason to believe that you are a friend of Mr Steven Dillon-Spence."

"Yes I am."

"When was the last time you saw him?"

Sophie didn't answer right away. Her memory flashed at the last picture she remembered of Steven, a man angry and aggressive who had left her lying on the floor and walked away.

"Miss Howard are you alright? We need to ask you a few questions."

"Yes I'm fine and call me Sophie."

18

VICTORIA STOOD AT the window looking out at the view. Snow had fallen during the night and the hotel gardens looked beautiful. The trees stripped of their leaves for winter stood tall, gracefully covered in snow and proud of their decoration. The lawns were covered in a blanket of pure white and the hedgerows hidden as they glistened with the rays of winter sun.

In the distance Victoria could see the ocean, the waves coloured dark winter grey yet as they crashed against the rocks white foam sprayed several feet into the air. She decided she would wrap up warm and go for a walk later. She wanted to feel what she was seeing as it inspired her artistic talent.

Opening up the desk drawer she took out the sketch pad and pencils that had been a gift from Emily at Christmas. Victoria loved the feeling she got when she could take a blank page and create something beautiful from the images in her mind. It had been such a long time from she had drawn anything and her paints were long since put away. Steven did not encourage her hobby as he thought it to be frivolous and work at the hotel was much more important.

Being in Ireland and surrounded by such beautiful scenery had awakened the desire within Victoria to sketch again. Her environment was relaxing and Emily saw to it that she had plenty of time to rest and to begin to think of herself. Her desire to pursue her own interests was new and exciting and as she looked out of the window at the scene before her she began to draw and she was surprised at how easily it all came back to her.

Victoria knew that while she was here to think about how she was going to sort out the problems she had left behind in England she had also realised that her life didn't have to revolve around Steven and the hotel, there was room for other interests.

As she sketched the scene of the gardens she could feel the images in her mind being transferred onto the page. She felt so at peace inside and the recent anxiety that had existed in her heart had gone.

As her pencilled lines began to form a picture on the page Victoria felt that this is what she was meant to be doing with her life, creating something beautiful. She loved this place so much she already felt as though she belonged here. Jack and Emily had shown that they cared about her and Chloe and they accepted her and encouraged her in every way possible. There was no one to ignore her or treat her like Steven did and she realised now just how much damage he had done mentally to her. So much of her personality had been submerged below the business life she led back home and her lack of confidence in herself and everyday put downs from her husband had almost destroyed the talent she kept hidden.

In her new environment she was treated with respect and she was discovering that part of her that she had kept hidden for a long time, the real Victoria was beginning to heal and her desires were beginning to surface

At 2:15pm the telephone rang and Victoria felt annoyed as she was almost finished her sketch and her next thought was to go for a walk before dark.

"Hello."

"Hi Victoria, its Emily. I need to come up and talk to you. I'll have coffee sent up to."

Before Victoria could answer Emily had hung up and she was puzzled. She returned to the sketch pad and she was pleased with her work. She promised herself that this drawing would be the first of many and soon she would paint again too.

The door knocked and Victoria put the pad into the desk drawer, for now she wanted to keep her desires to herself. "Come in, the door is open."

Emily and Jack came in followed by a waitress with coffee. They sat down on the sofa and Jack poured out coffee as the waitress left.

"Victoria we need to talk with you."

There was an uneasy tension that disturbed the peace Victoria had felt earlier.

"You look very serious Emily, whatever is wrong?"

Jack sat facing her and Emily beside her. "Victoria there is no easy way to tell you this so I'll get straight to the point. My father telephoned a while ago and Steven has been involved in an accident."

"Is he badly hurt? Have they said what his condition is?"

"Victoria it was a bad accident and Steven did not survive. I'm sorry but he is dead."

Victoria felt sick as the room began to spin around her. She could hear Emily's voice but it seemed so far away. She was aware of a cry that sounded like a wounded animal and then she realised it was coming from her.

"Victoria have some water." A glass was pressed into her hand and she sipped at the water. Tears were pouring down her face and Emily held her as Jack knelt in front of her holding her hands.

"Oh Jack I can't believe it. I never wanted it to end this way. I'd hoped this time apart would give him time to think and then we could talk when I got back. How do I tell Chloe that her daddy is dead and she will never see him again?"

"Victoria we don't need to tell her just yet. You need to give yourself time to accept it and at the moment you are in shock."

"Jack this is the worst thing that could have happened. Steven and I had been so unhappy and now I will never have the opportunity to put things right."

"Victoria don't be blaming yourself for the way things were. Steven made his own choices in life and you are not responsible for his decisions."

Emily passed her a cup of coffee. "Here drink this."

"Thanks, I have a dreadful headache."

"You have had a terrible shock and you should rest for awhile before we decide what to do next."

Victoria looked startled. "I don't know what I'm supposed to do next. I know I need to go back to England."

"Victoria don't worry about anything now. Jack and I and the family will give you all the support you need. We will be going to England with you. You are not alone and you never will be."

She began to cry again. "Jack how is your mum and dad? They have lost a son and they must be devastated."

"Mum is very distressed and my dad is trying to come to terms with the news and be strong for mum. I suppose this is a parents worst nightmare come true and I don't know how they will cope."

"I can only imagine the pain they are going through and I'm truly sorry."

"I know you are and they are concerned about you and Chloe and what lies ahead. I suggest you try and rest awhile and then we will make arrangements to return to England."

"Jack was Steven the only one in the car?"

"Yes he was. The police have said he had been drinking and he approached a bend in the road to fast. The car went out of control and ended in a ditch."

"Then who got help?"

"A passing motorist stopped and telephoned for help but it was too late. Steven died before anyone could get to him. The impact would have put him unconscious and he had severe head injuries so he would have died quickly."

Fresh tears poured down her face. "I can't bear to think of him dying alone. What if he had regained consciousness? He might have been lying in pain and no one to help him."

"Victoria listen to me. Steven had been drinking so he would have known nothing."

"But where is he now?"

Emily held her hand. "What do you mean? Tell me what you are thinking?"

"I mean, Steven wasn't like you and Jack. He wasn't a Christian; he lived his life for himself. We know he was involved with another woman and I don't think I've ever heard him speak about God. I believe in life after death but where is Steven?"

"Victoria it would be easy to look at situations in Stevens's life and judge the circumstances as we saw them to be but it isn't that simple."

"Emily you know the sort of person Steven was. I loved him and he knew I did but that didn't stop him from hurting me. How does someone like him fit with everything you have told me about God? You see, if Steven had been a Christian before he died then you would be assuring me now that he was in heaven and that would be a comfort. Steven wasn't a Christian so is he is hell?"

Jack could see the turmoil Victoria was in and it saddened him even more that this was his brother they were talking about.

"Victoria I know that you loved Steven even though he did not treat you with the love and respect you deserve but you still loved him. I loved him as a brother although our lifestyles were so opposite but I still loved him. You want to know if he is in hell, Victoria I don't know. The only one who knew Steven's heart was God and when he lay dying and there was no human help available after the accident, only God knows what his last thoughts were and if he cried out for help."

"Jack does that mean we have to spend the rest of our lives wondering and hoping that Steven made the right decision in the end?"

"No Victoria we don't spend our lives wondering. We settle it in our hearts once and for all that in this life we don't always have all the right answers. Sometimes we have to trust God for the things that we don't know. It says in the bible that, "the truth will set you free." Victoria the truth is, we are accountable to God for our own lives and the choices we make. We don't know what choice Steven made in the end but I'm prepared to trust God for him and not spend my life wondering where he is."

"Thank you Jack. You have given me a clearer perspective. I'm still trying to settle issues in my own life with God and I couldn't deal with the anxiety about Steven."

"Victoria it is time for you to rest. I'll keep Chloe in our apartment and Jack can begin to make the travel arrangements."

"Thank you both. I'm so glad I have your support."

When Victoria was alone she was aware of calmness inside her. She lay down on the sofa and closed her eyes. She knew that Steven was dead yet the reality of life without him hadn't registered in her head. She tried to think of her and Chloe and hotel with no Steven there and it just didn't seem real. She knew her own life would change but she wasn't sure what those changes would be. Steven had been manager of the hotel and now a new management would have to be instated but what would happen to her and Chloe. She wasn't sure she would want to continue to live at the Edgewater Hotel.

Suddenly she remembered there was another woman in Steven's life and she wondered if Sophie had heard the news of Stevens's death. Was she also grieving for the man she loved? In a way Victoria felt sorry for the woman because all she would have would be her memories. She would not have the family support and she would always be in the background because the family would never acknowledge her. It was easy to judge and think this woman deserved nothing less yet she had paid the price of her relationship with Steven. She now grieved for a man she loved alone, and her memories would be of Steven and whatever time he was able to spend with her.

Victoria could feel herself drift into sleep and as she did the grief inside seemed to slide away from her. She nestled into the cushions and surrendered to the rest that her body and mind needed.

19

SOPHIE FELT LIKE everything was closing in around her, she found it difficult to breathe and she needed air. Picking up her car keys and her bag she rushed out slamming the door behind her. She stood outside in the cold air taking deep breaths and fighting off the sick feeling in her stomach. Tears ran down her face as she got into her car and drove off in the direction where Steven's car had crashed.

The police had questioned her about her relationship with Steven and she hated having to tell them. They had got her name from the casino and they were trying to piece together Steven's last movements before the accident. She had to tell them that he was with her and they had a row before he left. When they confirmed that Steven had died she had tried to remain calm in front of them but she thought she was going to pass out and the policewoman had to get her a glass of water. Hearing herself talk about their last row made it sound worse now and she felt so guilty. If they had not argued he may not have had that last whiskey and maybe he would have stayed with her or got a taxi back to the hotel. Sophie's thoughts were racing and her mind full of doubts. She realised that nothing would change the facts but she was finding this grief hard to deal with and she felt so alone. She had no family and few friends and she wondered how she was going to get through her life now that Steven was gone.

Sophie stopped at a shop and bought flowers and a newspaper. The accident had made headline news and she sat in the car gazing at the picture of Steven on the front page and there was also a picture of the hotel. The headline was almost brutal.

'Hotel Owner Killed In Crash'.

The owner of the Edgewater Hotel, Mr Steven Dillon-Spence was killed when his car left the road and ended in a ditch. The silver car overturned onto the roof and the driver was thrown through the windscreen. He died of injuries sustained in the crash. Mr Dillon-Spence is the son of Jack Dillon-Spence Senior, owner of a group of hotels. He also leaves a wife and young daughter. Police said there had been a high level of alcohol in Mr Dillon-Spence's blood which would have contributed to the accident. A statement on behalf of the family said they were shocked and saddened and that funeral arrangements would be made at a later date.

Sophie drove to the scene of the accident and parked her car in a lay-by. She took the flowers and made her way down the road to where the police had sealed off the area with tape across the road. Sophie crept under the tape and edged her way along the hedge until she could see the car below in the ditch but she knew she couldn't go any further down as the ground was muddy and she could see the skid marks of the car before it had overturned. Sophie placed the flowers as near as she could but she didn't write any message on the card. This moment was private, something she wanted to do for Steven and what was in her heart was too precious to write on a card that would be on public display. She didn't linger at the scene in case other people arrived and the car would be removed now that the police were gone.

Sophie drove to the casino as George would be there getting the bar ready for opening time. She went in through the staff entrance and saw he was behind the bar.

"Sophie I've heard the news. How are you?"

She burst into tears and George put his arms around her. "It's alright honey, just cry if you need to."

"George what I'm I going to do? How am I going to live without him?"

"Come and sit down and I'll get some coffee."

Sophie sat in the semi-darkness of the casino and so many memories flooded her mind of how she had first met Steven here. She cried until her head hurt and her eyes were swollen. "George he is gone and I feel so lost."

George sat down and passed her the coffee. "Sophie you are a strong person and with time you will get over him. You are still in shock now and it's hard to take in."

"I know you are right George and I'll have to get over him but it doesn't change the way I feel about him inside. I really loved him even though I knew that there was no future for us because he was married. Steven wanted our relationship on his terms and we had to play by the rules."

"Sophie, the night of the accident, were you with Steven before it happened?"

"He was in my apartment." She began to cry. "George I feel so guilty."

He got up and wrapped his arms around her. "Come on girl, let it all out."

She sobbed and her body trembled as she poured out all the grief and pain that was tearing her apart. George held her until the tears stopped and then he cupped her face in his hands. "Sophie you don't have anything to feel guilty about. You loved him more than he deserved, you see, I know the type of person Steven was."

Sophie walked towards the bar. "I need a cold drink, my throat hurts and it is so dry." She poured tonic water with ice and lemon into a tall glass. George went behind the bar as she sat on a stool. She looked at him and for the first time she saw kindness in his eyes and she wondered how she'd never noticed before.

"George the night of the accident, Steven and I had a row, a very big row. I thought with his wife being away he and I would spend more time together. Steven seemed to distance himself from me and I didn't understand why. He arrived at my place but he seemed annoyed and he was short tempered with me. He had been drinking and I could smell whiskey on his breath. We were supposed to go out but because he was late I cancelled the table and thought it might be a better idea to eat at my place. I thought he would want to stay over and then he could have a few drinks. Anyway, Steven was angry with me as he wanted to go out. One word led to another and he said some awful things. I shouted back at him because I couldn't believe he was speaking to me with such anger in his voice. I remember hearing the slap, I hit the floor and then I felt the pain. I think I was in shock because I couldn't understand how Steven would want to hurt me when he loved me. I lay on the floor and the last thing he said was good-bye and then he walked out."

"I'm so sorry Sophie. He shouldn't have treated you so badly, believe me you deserve better that Steven. I don't know why you are feeling guilty."

"George if I hadn't cancelled dinner or had the argument with him then he wouldn't have stormed off like he did. He would be alive today and I can't help but feel responsible for the way things happened."

"No Sophie. Steven did what Steven wanted to do. It was his choice to hit you and it was his choice to leave, get into his car after drinking and drive away. All of this was Steven's choices, not yours so get off the guilt trip Sophie because you or anyone else could not have made Steven do anything differently."

Fresh tears came as she struggled to believe what George was saying to her. "I know what you've said is true but I loved him George and the bit that hurts is that when he hit me he made me feel cheap. I wish he hadn't done that."

George held her hands. "Sophie you are not cheap. You are a beautiful woman who fell in love with someone who wanted the best of both worlds. He wasn't willing to give up anything for you and it made him feel good having so much going on in his life. While he felt in control everything was fine but then he had his father checking up on him and then his wife found out about you. Steven didn't feel in control anymore and he couldn't handle it."

"How do you know all this George?"

"He used to come in here when there was no one around and after a few drinks he would talk. Sophie you would be surprised the things a bar man gets to hear. It's part of my job to be a good listener but say little."

Sophie kissed his cheek and hugged him. "Thank you for listening to me George and for being a friend today."

"I'll always be here for you Sophie."

"George why is a lovely man like you not married? Is there someone special in your life?"

"No. A long time ago there was someone but that's another story."

"You're not going to tell me?"

"Not today, maybe some other time. Remember I listen to others but I don't talk much."

"George I need a few days off from work. I've got to think about things."

"The casino can manage for a few days without you. Now go home and rest."

"I will and thank you George."

"If you need anything you just ring me. You are not on your own in this."

"I know that now. Bye."

Sophie drove past the scene of the accident on the way home. There were men preparing to move the car and she watched for a few minutes and then drove on.

When she arrived home the apartment seemed strangely quiet. She went through to the kitchen and put the kettle on then put two mugs on the counter.

As she spooned coffee into them she suddenly remembered that it was just her now and she was alone. "Oh God how am I going to live without him? I'll never make anything for him again or cuddle up on the sofa with him and it's to late take back the awful things we said to each other."

She went into the bedroom to rest and she looked at the photograph on the cupboard of Steven and her together, laughing. They had been to a restaurant that night and he had taken her out onto the terrace were it was cooler when the photographer took the picture. There were so many times when he had made her feel so special and that night was one of them. Nothing could ever take those memories from her now and she would treasure them in her heart.

20

THE DILLON-SPENCE family met at the Edgewater Hotel. Steven's parents had arrived from London and his mother was quickly taken to the private guest suite. She was finding it difficult to stay composed even in public and her grief for her son was evident.

Victoria, Chloe, Emily and Jack arrived from Ireland later that morning and the atmosphere in the hotel was depressing. The staff were finding the news hard to deal with as it was only a few days ago everyone was celebrating Christmas and the holiday spirit was in full swing. Now the staff went about their work quietly and waited to be told of the arrangements for the funeral of their boss.

Victoria was alone with Chloe in her bedroom and they arranged her new toys she had received at Christmas. Victoria decided she had to tell Chloe what had happed to Steven before she heard it from someone else. She had kept putting it off and just as she was about to pick up her courage Chloe asked. "Mummy when is daddy coming home? I though he might meet us coming off the airplane."

"Darling I need to talk to you. Come and sit beside me."

Chloe sat on the bed with her new doll on her lap. "Mummy why did I see Grandad and Nana here? Did they come for Christmas and we were in Ireland?"

"No darling they didn't come for Christmas. They got here this morning and Nana is having a rest so you can see them later."

"I saw Nana crying but why would she be sad at Christmas? I thought she would be happy that Uncle Jack and Aunt Emily are here and we will all be together when daddy comes home."

"Darling I have some sad news to tell you. While we were in Ireland and daddy stayed here to work, well he had an accident in the car."

Chloe eyes were fearful. "Did daddy get hurt in the car?"

"Yes he got hurt very badly and the doctors weren't able to make him better again."

"Do you mean that he is still hurt?" She frowned.

"No darling not anymore. Chloe daddy died because he had a very bad accident. He won't be coming home because he is in heaven now."

"Do you mean with Jesus and the angels? I know that they live there."

"Yes darling that's where daddy is."

Suddenly her little face crumpled and she began to cry. "I want daddy home and I don't want him to be in heaven."

Victoria hugged her daughter. "Chloe your daddy was very sick and in pain and the doctors couldn't do anymore to help him. I know this must be so hard for you and I'm sorry that daddy won't be here anymore. He loved you very much and he wouldn't want you to be sad Chloe but I'm sure he understands the reason you are."

"If daddy is in heaven then he won't be able to kiss me good night or read me any stories. Mummy I don't like this."

"I know and I don't like it either but we can't change what has happened darling so we have to be brave."

"I don't feel brave. I know now why Nana was crying and now we are sad too."

"Chloe it is sad that daddy isn't with us anymore but he wouldn't want us to be sad all the time. We should be glad that daddy was such a big part of our lives and we can learn to think happy thoughts about him and that will help us."

"Like the time we went on holiday and daddy and I played on the beach?"

"Yes that was a happy time."

"I think I will have lots of happy thoughts about daddy."

"That's the idea. Now I need to go and talk with Nana but Tina is going to come and stay with you."

"Ok. I can show her my new toys and talk about happy times with daddy."

"Good girl. I'll see you later."

Victoria met with the family in the living room. Steven's parents were devastated and his mother couldn't stop crying. His father was trying to be composed but he was quiet and in a state of unbelief.

"Victoria can I get you anything?"

"Just coffee Emily. I've just told Chloe about her daddy and she was very upset but I've tried to explain to her that if she thinks about the happy times with him it will help her."

Emily passed her the coffee and Victoria took a few sips. She sensed an uneasy silence and although she was with family she felt out of place.

"Is there something that I'm not aware off? Everyone seems to have become quiet since I walked in."

"Sorry Victoria. I think the news is beginning to sink in now that we are all together. There's nothing you are not aware off."

"Thank you Jack. Look I know how hard this is but we need to think about the funeral arrangements and I'm depending on your support. I'd appreciate any suggestions because I really don't know what to do."

"Victoria unless you have a preference as to where you want Steven buried we thought that you would consider a short service here and then the funeral would take place in London. Afterwards we could have people back to the Royal Court."

Victoria knew how hard those words had been for her father-in-law to say.

"I think that is a good idea. Although Steven worked here, the core of the family business took place in London so it seems fitting that he should be buried there. Jack if you could meet with the staff here and tell them about the arrangements, I know they are waiting for news."

"Yes leave that to me."

By mid-afternoon the arrangements were under way and Victoria had a headache again.

"Emily would you check on Chloe for me. I'd really like to take a walk and get some air."

"Of course I will. You have had a shock and you need time to absorb it. Go and have your walk and clear your head."

Victoria walked around the hotel gardens to the back where it was quiet. She sat down on the swing, gently swaying in the cool air. It was hard to believe that a few days before had been Christmas and she was in Ireland looking forward to the New Year. Steven had died on the 27 December and Jack was arranging the funeral for the 30th. It upset her to think that it wasn't that long ago she had said good-bye to him. She never thought it would end this way and she had hoped that the time apart from each other would help their marriage and their ability to communicate with each other. She wasn't sure how she would cope in the days ahead and her future seemed so uncertain.

There would be other decisions to be made in the next few weeks but right now she wondered how she would get through the next few days.

Victoria got off the swing and walked through the gardens. She and Steven used to walk together but that now seemed a long time ago. Looking back, she wasn't sure when their relationship began to go wrong. There wasn't one particular thing that had sparked off a major row. That was something that could have been talked through. They just seemed to drift apart and the changes began after Chloe was born. Steven was a good father but he seemed to distance himself from their marriage and take on more work. When Victoria tried to talk to him he used his work as the excuse for neglecting their relationship. She didn't know when it was that he developed interests outside the home but their seemed to be a side to Steven that she never knew and now it was to late.

Walking back towards the hotel she wondered how Sophie was taking the news. Being the other woman in Steven's life she would stay in the background but maybe she was with him before the accident. Steven had been alone in the car but he had been driving in the opposite direction of the hotel so the other woman must live in that area. In a way Victoria felt sorry for her because she would probably be grieving alone. She didn't know how deep the relationship went between Sophie and Steven so she would never know the extent of the grief Sophie would be experiencing.

Victoria tried to dismiss any thoughts of Sophie. She had to stay focussed to get through the next few days. By the 30th the funeral would be over and Steven would be buried. It seemed strange having a funeral between Christmas and New Year but then she never planned on something like this happening.

Victoria was cold when she arrived back from her walk so she stopped at reception and ordered tea and coffee to be send through to the living room.

Jack and his father were going over the arrangements when she got in. "Hi you two, I've order refreshments to be sent through."

"Victoria we have made arrangements with the undertaker but we need to go through it with you in case you want to change anything."

"Dad I'm sure everything will be fine."

Jack sat beside her. "Victoria we need to go through this with you. You are Steven's wife and this has to meet your approval."

"Alright then, let me see."

Jack had a list for her to look over. "Victoria if you want to see Steven, his body will be in the chapel of rest. We can take you tomorrow."

"I need to think about that. I wouldn't want Chloe to go; she's too young to understand."

"The funeral on the 30th will begin with a service at the chapel of rest here. Steven's body will then be taken to London for a second service and then the burial."

"Jack that is all fine with me. Thank you both; I couldn't do all this without you."

Her father-in-law came and sat beside her and she rested her head on his shoulder. She loved this man and he had been a real dad to her. There were times she wished that Steven was more like his father and she had seen some of those qualities in him but Steven liked the best of both worlds and he was never content with any less.

"Victoria you need to know that when the funeral is over and you will have time to think about the future, whatever you decide the family will support you in any way. We know that Steven didn't always treat you right and I'm sorry about that. He's my son and I love him but I can't deny his behaviour. You and Chloe will be financially provided for so money will never be an issue and you are not to worry about a thing. There will also be a trust fund set up for Chloe and you will both be looked after, you are family dear."

Victoria squeezed his hand. "I know this is my family and thank you for looking after Chloe and me. The time will come when I have to think about where we want to live and what I want to do with my life but right now it's important to get through the next few days and I know I have your love and support for that. I'm finding it hard to come to terms with what can happen between Christmas and New Year."

"I know. This year has been made different for everyone. Now I must go and check on Sarah."

"Mum is taking this really badly."

"Yes she is. She has lost her son and she just can't accept she is not going to see him again. Sarah has never appeared to be the most maternal person but her feelings run deep. We take it for granted that as parents we will die before our children. No parent wants to outlive their child. Sarah is heartbroken that her son has died before her and I'm concerned how we are going to get her through the next few days."

"Maybe we should call the doctor and he could give her something to calm her although mum is a strong person and she will be alright. I think she is still in shock and reality hasn't sunk in and it will be that way until after the funeral."

"Yes I can see that happening."

"Mum knows how to hold her head high in public and on the 30th she will be dressed to perfection and she will do everything in order that needs to be done. After it's over the grieving really begins."

"She's right dad. Mum will be fine in public. She won't want to let Steven down. We will need to look after her once it is over."

The next day Victoria decided to go and see Steven. She had struggled with not knowing what to do and in the end she realised that if she didn't go she would regret it. She went downstairs to find Emily and Jack and as she walked through reception flowers had began to arrive. Emily came through to see the flowers and Jack was reading the cards.

"These are so beautiful. A lot of people really liked him. Jack would you keep the cards after the funeral so that I can write and thank people.

"Yes that would be a lovely thought."

Steven's mum came down and admired the flowers. She was very pale and still had a look of disbelief on her face. After a few minutes she went through to the living room and Victoria followed her. This really was too much for her. Victoria found her in tears sitting on the sofa. She sat down and put her arm around her.

"Mum I'm so sorry that you and dad have to go through this. The shock has made you ill with grief."

"Steven was my son. I loved him and I always will. To know that he was driving and had been drinking, well, he should have known better. If he was here now I could hear myself telling him off for doing such a dangerous thing but he's not here now and I can't bear it."

"I know this is so hard for you and I know how much you loved him. The love a mother feels for her child is like no other love so I can only imagine how painful this is for you. I loved him as a husband and Chloe's father but I know that my love for him was different to yours."

"Victoria I know that Steven could have been a better husband to you and I'm sorry that he wasn't. Sometimes I wished he could have been more like his father or Jack."

"Mum he didn't want to be like anyone yet he wasn't happy being himself either. He chose his lifestyle but that didn't make him happy. I thought if I loved him and believed in him that things would change for us but now that will never happen."

"I know you were a good wife to him and that's what makes his behaviour so hard to understand. I don't know how I'll ever get over this. Somehow we won't be the same ever again."

"Mum you need to give yourself time to grieve, we all do. The next few days will be difficult but we will get through them. We need each other now and we'll support one another."

"Victoria you are a lovely person and you are right about the days ahead. We will be there for each other."

Jack and Emily came in. "How are you two?"

"We are fine. Mum and I have been sharing our thoughts about Steven and how much we loved him."

"Victoria if you would like to go to the chapel of rest, Emily and I will take you. Mum I think dad wants to take you."

"I'm still not sure Jack."

"Mum today will be the only opportunity you will have so think carefully before you decide against it."

The chapel of rest was a secluded building, tastefully decorated and around the alter candles were burning and the atmosphere was peaceful. Victoria was surprised at how personal and intimate it was and she was pleased with the surroundings. She lingered at the back while Jack and Emily went up to the front to were the oak coffin stood.

"Jack you two go ahead. I'd like to be alone for a few minutes."

"Are you sure?"

"Yes. I'll meet you in the car park."

Jack and Emily left and Victoria walked slowly towards the front of the chapel. As she got closer to the coffin she could feel her heart-beat quicken. This was her first experience of the death of a loved one and she felt apprehensive. She stood a few feet away from the coffin and then she moved closer to place the single red rose that she had brought. Steven looked different, his body cold and so still. Victoria never realised that death brought such stillness to the body. She gazed at the man she had loved and what remained was the empty shell of the human being she had committed her life to.

Standing at his coffin she felt a sense of hopelessness. She had lost her husband and Chloe had lost her father and it had been so unnecessary.

If only he hadn't been drinking that night. She wondered how many times other families had said the same thing.

"Victoria are you alright?"

"Yes Emily. I have seen enough." She turned to leave knowing she would never see his face again. "Good-bye Steven, rest easy."

"Come on and we will take you home."

"No I can't get into the car yet. I need some air."

"There's a seat in the garden we can sit on."

Jack was waiting outside and he noticed how pale Victoria looked. "Are you alright?"

"Oh Jack I don't know if I'll ever be alright."

Jack and Emily sat down beside her and she cried. They both held her but no one spoke. Victoria needed to cry so they comforted her.

"I know my life is going to change now that Steven is dead but I don't just feel the loss of him, I feel abandoned. I know he didn't always treat me right but at least I had a future for Chloe and I. Now I don't know what direction my life will take."

"Victoria remember back in Ireland when we walked along the beach talking about God?"

"Yes Emily and I felt so much at peace then but I didn't know this was in front of me."

"Victoria, God can give you peace in any situation because he never changes.

I know the next few days are going to be difficult for you but when they are over I want you to consider coming back to Ireland. You will have time to rest and think about the future."

Jack nodded in agreement. "Victoria I think you are so close to surrendering your life to God and when you do he will give you all the direction you need."

"I have thought about having a relationship with God the way you and Emily have but then when Steven died I felt so confused. I'll think about going back with you if only for a few weeks."

"Good, I'm sure it will help you."

Victoria stood up. "I think we should get back now. Jack, your parents want to come here but I'm worried about mum. Seeing Steven like this could make her worse."

"My dad will look after her and we will look after you. You need to rest when we get back because you know what's ahead tomorrow."

"Yes, I think it will be quite a long day."

21

IT WAS LATE in the afternoon when the car stopped outside the chapel of rest.

George hadn't been looking forward to this and he still had doubts about being here. He really should have been behind the bar at the casino but he had reluctantly agreed to come here.

"George I need you to come in with me in case his family are there."

As he was about to get out of the car he saw two people coming out the door of the chapel. The woman was very upset and the man with her was trying to support her.

"Hold on a minute Sophie. Those two must be Steven's parents."

They waited in the car and the driver moved off.

"Sophie are you sure about this?"

"Yes George. I have to see him one last time. I'm still having trouble believing he is dead and it's not as though I'll get an invite to the funeral."

"No that certainly isn't going to happen."

They went inside and Sophie stopped when she saw the coffin.

"Are you alright? Sophie you don't have to do this."

"I'm fine and I do have to do this. Now you wait here for a minute."

George sat at the back and Sophie went and stood by the coffin. She saw that someone had placed a rose but she wasn't to be put off so she put her rose beside it. She looked at the man she had loved and who had also broken her heart. She loved him still and she was sorry they couldn't be together.

She knew that he had hurt her that last night she had saw him but she never realised that when he walked out on her that it would be the last time she would ever see him again.

"I love you Steven. Good-bye my love."

George stood beside her. "Come on Sophie, there's nothing else you can do."

"It really hurts me to think that he died alone. I wish he had stayed with me that night."

"I know Sophie but it was his choice to leave and you can't blame yourself for that. Steven always did what he wanted and he never thought there would be consequences."

"George he looks so still and cold. I wasn't sure what to expect but I don't like it."

"Sophie he's dead, the man you loved is gone and that's just his body there. It's like we are looking at the shell of the person we once knew."

"I know you're right. The man I loved is gone but I'll always remember him and the happier times we shared."

"Let's go Sophie. We both could use a drink."

"I agree, I think I've seen enough."

As they were leaving another car arrived and two people got out carrying flowers for the funeral. Sophie was about to get into George's car when she heard her name being called. George looked surprised. "Does someone know you?"

Sophie turned and saw Emily. "Yes George someone knows me. You wait in the car and I'll just be a few minutes."

Emily walked towards her. "Hello Sophie, I wondered if you would come to see him."

"What do you expect Emily? I was a part of his life and I loved him. I came quietly today because I wouldn't want to offend his wife or family by showing up at the funeral."

"I can understand that Sophie."

"How's his wife?"

"As you can imagine she is shocked and upset. His parents are devastated and his daughter is trying to understand why she won't be seeing her daddy anymore."

"It must be very difficult for them."

"It is but I'm sure it's just as hard for you. I know you loved him Sophie."

"I did and I suppose I still do. I won't try to hide my feelings from you Emily. I know the relationship between Steven and I was wrong but it happened and I'm glad it did. For a short time I'd found someone who loved me and made me feel special. I'll always have those memories."

"I know he loved you but you have to get on with your life now. Did you see him the night of the accident?"

"Yes I did. He wasn't in a good mood that night and he had been drinking. We had an argument and he left in a terrible temper and that was the last time I saw him. I know from the news reports that he drove in the opposite direction from the hotel, maybe he thought a drive would calm him. I don't think he realised how much alcohol he had drunk but then Steven thought he could do anything and he still would have driven the car. The police have been to see me as I was the last person to see Steven. I could tell they looked on me as the other woman in his life who had no right to be there. I've been to the scene of the accident and left flowers, I don't really know where I go from here."

"Sophie I'm sorry. I know you are hurting as much as anyone else in the family. There will be a service here early tomorrow morning and then Steven's body is being taken to London for burial."

"I appreciate you telling me but I won't be coming. I wouldn't want to upset anyone. I came today and said good bye to him, I preferred it to be private but then you can understand why."

"Sophie I wish I could help you."

"You can't Emily but thank you for the offer."

"Sophie I have prayed for you and if only you could see that God has the answer to every need in your life."

"I know what you mean Emily. Let's be honest, I've had a few relationships in my life that have been a waste of time and all of them ended painfully."

"Sophie you seem to look for someone to be all that you need in your life and that's a high expectation. I know that only a relationship with God can meet all your needs and give you the love you have longed for."

"I know I make the same mistakes over and over again and I'm sure what you are saying is true. I just don't know if I want to take the risk of trusting God for my life, that's a big involvement."

"Sophie you have trusted just about everyone else but God. You have just lost someone you loved and you have been hurt. I don't think you have anything to lose by trusting God to work things out for your life. Trusting him would give you a clearer perspective on the future."

"I suppose since you put it that way I've nothing else to lose. I have to go now but I'll be thinking about what you said. I will also be thinking about all of you at the funeral tomorrow. I know it will be a difficult day for you and his wife and family. Maybe we will meet again one day. Good bye Emily."

"I'll keep praying for you and if you ever need to get in contact with me you have my address. Good bye Sophie."

"Bye Emily." They reached out and hugged each other.

"Sophie maybe one day we will meet under different circumstances."

Sophie smiled as she turned and walked towards the car.

Emily watched her and she sensed the pain inside her. "Oh God she needs your love more than anything else in this world."

"I will have mercy on whom I'll have mercy and compassion on whom I'll have compassion."

Sophie got into George's car and she was crying.

"What's the matter and who was that woman you were talking to?" Sophie reached into her bag for tissues. "One question at a time George.

That woman is Emily Dillon-Spence and she is Steven's sister-in-law. We knew each other years ago before she ever married Jack.

She is a special person George. She knew about Steven and I but she never judged me although she didn't like what was happening. She has a way in making people feel they are worth something, maybe it's because she is a Christian and she sees things in a different way to me."

"Is her husband also a Christian?"

"Yes and they seem to have a wonderful marriage. I suppose they have problems like any couple but they manage to overcome theirs."

George started the car and they drove to the casino. "I used to be a Christian but it was years ago. I was also married at the time and I thought my life was just fine."

Sophie was surprised. "So what happened?"

"My wife died from cancer and I lost my faith after that. I suppose I was angry at God because I'd lost the one human being I loved with all my heart."

"Would you ever go back to that lifestyle or are you still angry with God?"

"I don't know. I think I still have some anger that hasn't been resolved between him and me. Anyway I need a drink, all this talk is heavy stuff today."

Sophie laughed. "Too much for one day."

Driving back to the hotel Jack was curious about the woman Emily had been talking to. "Was that woman someone from the town or a staff member?"

"She lives in town and she knew Steven. That woman was Sophie."

"She was the one that Steven was involved with."

"Yes. She and I grew up in the children's home together."

"She must be very upset about the accident."

"She is and the police have questioned her which upset her even more. Sophie was the last one to see Steven before he died. He left her that night and he had been drinking. He drove off and that was the last time she saw him."

"Does Victoria know any of this?"

"No and she doesn't need to right now. Sophie is grieving too for the man she loved but not everyone will have any sympathy with her."

"She was the other woman in his life Emily."

"Yes and she loved him. I know Sophie well and she would have done anything for Steven. When she gives it's all or nothing."

Jack sighed. "Isn't life strange? Steven didn't treat women with respect yet there are two women grieving for him. I don't think he realised how much he was loved."

"I agree with you. Steven used to try and intimidate me and he got so annoyed when it didn't work. I always got the impression that there was a side to him that no one got close to. Women might have loved him but he held back on them. He only gave the little he wanted to give; maybe it was his way in keeping control of his life."

"Emily even if all that is true I still find it hard to accept that his life ended the way it did."

The next morning the cars arrived at the hotel for Victoria and the rest of the family. Some of the hotel staff and people from the town gathered in the chapel of rest for the short service.

Victoria had chosen lilies to be placed on the coffin and a smaller wreath of roses from Chloe.

The service was kept simple and the local minister addressed the gathering of people and he talked about how Steven had been an asset to the community and how his family had brought employ-ment to the town. He praised what good points Steven had and expressed sympathy to the family circle and promised the support of the people in the days ahead.

The journey to London seemed to take forever and Victoria was feeling the strain before they arrived at the church. This was the part she had been dreading although Steven's parents had arranged everything so she just had to get through it.

The cars stopped outside the church and the family went in first where seats had been reserved for them. The Dillon-Spence family circle were already seated and friends and business acquaint-ances were there filling the church to capacity. Victoria and Chloe sat at the front with Steven's parents and Jack and Emily. The minister stood at the front and music played softly in the background. Victoria could feel her heart beating faster and her head ached, she hoped this part of the proceedings wouldn't take to long or she might faint.

The music stopped and the minister asked everyone to stand and as they did the coffin was carried to the front of the church. The first hymn began and Victoria tried to focus on the words in the order of service. She was seated opposite Steven's coffin and for a minute she wondered what he would have thought of all this fuss. A trace of a smile crossed her face because she knew how much he hated pomp and ceremony. His parents had arranged this part of the funeral and Victoria realised it was their way of helping to come to terms with his death so she had to respect their wishes. She drifted through the service and was relieved when the minister got to the last prayer. All she needed now was to get out into the fresh air and breathe deeply.

Everyone had been invited back to the Royal Court Hotel in Kensington where refreshments had been prepared. Victoria mingled with the people, smiling and saying the right words as sympathy was poured out to her. This part seemed unreal to her and she struggled through it. Finally she had had enough and went outside to the gardens to escape, she felt annoyed inside because all of this was false to her. Everyone had been sympathising over the death of a wonderful young man, who was successful in business, a credit to his family and a loving husband and father. They were concerned how Victoria would manage without him. They really thought that Steven was so perfect because he was the son of the Dillon-Spence family. She knew the truth but for the sake of his parents she had to pretend that the sympathetic words of kindness were true.

She went to the back of the hotel and sat down on the garden seat. Tears poured down her face and then she sobbing. Her head still hurt and she felt so tired and alone with the truth as she knew it.

"Victoria would you like me to sit with you or would you rather be alone?"

She looked up and Emily was beside her. "Please sit down. I just had to get away from all the people and the talking. I'm feeling so tired today."

"You have coped very well these last few days but I'm sure you want some peace and quietness now the funeral is over."

"Yes I do. Steven once told me that he could depend on me to behave in an appropriate manner whatever the occasion. I'm still living up to his expectations. When I was inside I felt like I was pretending to be someone that I'm not. People think Steven was so perfect and I've been agreeing with their sentiments but I know that none of it is true."

"Victoria it's the Dillon-Spence family name, that's enough to make anyone appear to be a saint."

Victoria smiled. "Yes I suppose it is. There are so many people inside that I've never met before and Steven didn't know them either but they are talking like he was their best friend. Today has been like a performance to me and while I know I'm grieving for Steven, it's not in the way those people think."

"Victoria I know the truth about Steven so you don't have to pretend with me. I think today was about giving his parents the opportunity to do something for Steven just one last time."

"I know and that is why I went along with the arrangements but I'll be glad when it is over."

The immediate family stayed overnight at the hotel and the next day began with Jack and his father in a meeting concerning the future of the Edgewater Hotel.

Jack went to his father's office to find him staring blankly into his coffee.

"How are you dad?"

"I feel inside that we still have a business to run and decisions need to be made concerning new management for the Edgewater but there's also a big gaping hole in me. I think it's going to take some time for me to get round this one Jack. Steven was my son and he's gone and I can't quite take it in. I'm trying to be whatever I'm supposed to be for your mother's sake but then I'm not sure what I'm supposed to be. No one can ever prepare you for something like this so we stumble through and hope we eventually get it right."

"Dad I've been praying for you and mom and I don't have any magic words that are going to take away your pain but I believe God will give you the strength you need to get through this."

"Jack I don't know about that. I believe in God but for me he is someone who is out of my reach. I suppose I've never really taken the time to find out."

"Maybe you will now. Dad I'll be praying you and mum through this and I'll do whatever I can to help with the business."

"I know you will Jack. I can depend on you."

"Dad the immediate needs are the management of the Edgewater Hotel and then we will see what Victoria wants to do regarding her living arrangements. I don't think she will want to stay there for an indefinite time."

"I know she wants to get back today so I've arranged a car for her and Chloe."

"Yes, she mentioned to Emily about getting back today. I think she needs to be in familiar surroundings in order to accept that Steven is gone."

"Yes I agree although she needs to be assured that she is still family and she and Chloe will always be looked after."

"I think she knows that dad. She loves you and mom a lot."

22 SARAH WOKE UP to find that her husband had already left their apartment to start work. She lay very still trying to imagine that the emotions she was feeling were not real. She felt tired from the sleeping pills the doctor had left for her and she desperately needed a cup of tea. She telephoned for room service and asked for a light breakfast. She hadn't been eating much these last few days and she felt weak and sick inside. Tea and toast was her remedy for everything and she had to eat something.

Sitting at her dressing table Sarah brushed her hair and tried to make an effort to look presentable but everything seemed so difficult this morning.

She picked up a photograph of Steven and Victoria and she thought how handsome her son looked and then she burst into tears. Memories of Steven when he was a baby flashed through her mind, she could see him learning to walk, playing with his first bike and his little cars. She remembered when he had took measles and he was so sick that she had sat beside his cot all night just watching him breathe. "Oh my son. My son." Sobs shook her body as all the pent up emotion and grief poured out and she cried until she felt exhausted.

Room service sent up her breakfast and the waitress was sensitive enough just to leave the tray and go. Sarah didn't want to talk; she felt too tired to talk to anyone. She had her tea and a slice of toast and tried to compose herself. Memories of Steven as a young man trying hard to impress his father flashed through her mind. Sarah had doubts about Steven going into the family business. As a child he had wanted to be a doctor, something that was dismissed as childhood imagination. When he grew up he had mentioned to her that if he hadn't gone into the family business he would have liked to have gone to university to study medicine. Sarah wondered if he had gone into the business to impress her and his father and maybe his life would have been different if he had done what he really wanted to do instead of what had been expected of him. Inside her heart she felt as though there was a raw open wound and the pain was unbearable. She would have given anything to have her son back and she realised now just how final death is and she felt utterly hopeless.

Sarah went into her bedroom and it seemed that all around her there were pictures of her family and now one of her children had gone. It was too much and as she broke into sobs again she fell on her knees, "Oh God help me, please help me. I love my son." Sarah had been a religious person in that she went to church but she realised now it was more of a social exercise. Someone like her had a reputation to live up to and the family name was known in high places, being a church going family was the thing to do. Being in church had been more about who had a new hat or who had worn the same outfit twice! Sarah didn't always understand what the minister said and although she had always believed in God she didn't connect with him the way Jack and Emily did.

As Sarah cried on her knees to a God she hardly knew something inside hungered to be satisfied and only he could help her.

She heard someone at the door and she ignored it at first but then she heard Emily's voice and she went to let her in.

"I'm sorry Emily I really don't want to see anyone now." Sarah was painfully aware of her eyes, red and swollen.

"I won't stay long. Why don't we have some tea?"

"The tea I ordered earlier will be cold now."

"It's alright I've already arranged it." The door knocked and

Emily went to answer it. She took the tray off the waitress. "Thank you that will be all."

"Thank you Emily. I just don't want to see anyone. I know I look awful."

Emily smiled as she poured two cups of tea. "Listen to you. You don't look awful and you have every right to be upset. These last few days have changed your life mum and it's understandable you don't want to see people."

"Thank you for being so sensitive but why are you disturbing me?"

"I care enough to disturb you even at risk of you throwing me out!"

Sarah laughed. "I'm not that bad."

"I know that you're not but I care enough to risk it."

Sarah sipped her tea. "Thank you. I don't really know what I'm supposed to do today. Everything that used to be important to me isn't anymore and I've found myself questioning my whole life and I'm not sure yet what the answers are."

"Mum grief affects people differently and it is something you have to work through in your own time."

"You know Emily the hardest thing is knowing that my son died before me. No parent imagines that they will see their child buried before them, it's not right. I feel as though a part of me has died too and that something deep inside of me has been amputated." Fresh tears ran down her face and Emily went over to her and got down on her knees in front of her. In her own heart Emily ached for the pain she knew this woman was suffering.

"Mum I can't take away your sorrow, I wish I could. I can't say that I understand your feelings because I've never felt what you are feeling. I can only be here for you and pray with you. Sometimes we need God to take us through our pain and he does if we allow him too."

"I don't know Emily. God has never been very real to me. I know I have lost my son and my life can never be the same again. I believe what you are saying about God is true but he seems so far away from me."

"Pray with her Emily."

There was no mistaking the still small voice in her heart but Emily was hesitating. She had never had a conversation like this with her mother-in-law before but she knew that God wanted her to pray.

"Mum you need to know that God is very near and he can give you the strength to get through this. He can begin to heal the pain in your life if you will allow him."

"I don't know Emily, I feel a little sceptical. To me God is someone I associate with religion and going to church and for me to be a good person. I think I am a good person and I'm involved in numerous charities and fund raising for good causes. However I have still lost my son so where did I go wrong?"

"You didn't go wrong mum. Do you blame God for Steven's death?"

"I'd like to blame someone and it would be easy to blame God but I know I can't. We know that Steven was drinking that night and probably driving too fast, it was his choice Emily. I can't blame God for something I know that Steven did because he wanted to. He was a law unto himself. However he was my son and I love him no matter what his choices were."

"Mum that is exactly how God loves you. His love is unconditional."

"But how do I know that he is with me and he will see me through this?"

"I don't know if you have ever accepted Jesus as Lord of your life."

"I know enough that he died on a cross for the sins of this world."

Emily smiled. "Let's forget about the rest of the world and just think about you. If you had been the only person in this world Jesus would still have died. God loves you that much that his Son gave up everything for you and he doesn't end there. He had a plan for your life and he can give you the strength you need to get through this time. He knows all about sorrow and he can heal the pain you are experiencing now."

"But he won't give me back my son."

"No but he will teach you to accept what has happened and move on in your life."

Sarah began to cry again. "This makes his love for me very personal and I've never saw it like that before. I've always felt disconnected from him because for me going to church was a social thing to do. I mix a lot with people who do the same and I see now that it is wrong for me to continue as I am but how do I change?"

"You don't have to be concerned with how to change, you learn to listen to him and he will direct you. When you are in a relationship with God he will let you know what he wants you to do. The bible is full of promises to anyone who believes in him. It is not a history book; it is what you need to live the way in which he wants you to. In the weeks ahead he can give you what you need, one day at a time you can talk to him whenever you like. Would you like me to pray with you?"

"Yes. I want to know Jesus as Lord. I believe he can fill this void in my life and give me purpose. I realise there has always been a void and I simply tried to fill it up with other things. I want my life to be different now."

Emily smiled and held her hands. "Mum, God says in Isaiah 43:1

"But now thus says the Lord who created you, O Jacob, and He that formed you, O Israel: Fear not, for I have redeemed you; I have called you by your name; You are Mine."

"Mum he already knows all about you."

"Once I make a decision for him then what happens?"

"You begin to learn to trust him for your life. There's a story in the bible of a potter shaping a piece of clay. This is how God wants to be in your life. He wants to be the potter that moulds you as seems best to him and mum God only gives the best of anything. Your part is to be willing and say yes to him."

"I've decided. I need him in my life."

"Then let's pray."

Jack and his father had spent the morning discussing the future of the Edgewater Hotel. They had gone through files of people they had previously interviewed who had management experience and now they faced the task of contacting them and going through a new selection procedure.

Jack had studied several people but kept going back to one particular file.

"Dad I think this guy might be what we are looking for."

"Let me see his profile." He glanced through the folder and Jack could see that intense frown his father wore when he was serious about something.

"I seem to remember this man being here so he must have made an impression on me. Daniel Seymour married with two children and has been in the hotel business since leaving university with a degree in business studies. He is thirty six so he would have quite a lot of experience and when we last saw him he was assistant manager at another hotel."

"I could give a call and see if he would be interested in coming to see us."

"Yes Jack, you do that. I like his profile and if he is interested it would save us a lot of time conducting more interviews provided he and his family would be willing to live in at the hotel then he could be the man for the job."

"I don't think the move would be a problem. When we interviewed him before we were clear that job involved moving to live in at the Edgewater and he was agreeable."

"If I remember he liked the idea of moving out of London and Bournemouth isn't a million miles away."

"If he is the one for the job we will need to be sensitive in the way we handle the timing of moving in a new management. As yet Victoria doesn't know what she is going to do with her life. She is still in shock and although I don't feel that she will want to continue living at the Edgewater we would need to consult with her about moving in someone new."

"Yes I appreciate how hard it would be for her so soon after Steven's death to move in a new manager but I think she's wise when it comes to business matters and she will know that we need someone down there. I suppose I'm hoping she can separate the business side from her personal feelings and that way she won't be offended."

"Well I think she realises we are not putting her out of her home but we do need a management structure for the hotel."

"Yes, she may even be relieved when there is someone else to take over the responsibilities because she is in no state to do the things she used to do with Steven. Anyway I think we have worked hard enough this morning so how about a sandwich and coffee?"

His father didn't answer and when Jack looked up from his paperwork he saw him gazing at a family portrait on the wall.

"Dad are you alright?"

He turned towards Jack and there were tears in his eyes. "I don't know if I'll ever be alright again. I've lost my youngest son and how am I supposed to get over that? I know that Steven was foolish at times but I loved him just like I love you Jack. I wish he had taken more care about his responsibilities in life. Victoria was a good wife and he had a comfortable living in a family business and I just don't understand why it never seemed to be enough for him."

"Dad I know how much you loved him but Steven liked to play by his own rules. He was an adult with a mind of his own and he made his choices."

His father sighed. "Yes and that's what got him into trouble and probably cost him his life." He slammed his fist on the table.

"Jack why did he have to waste everything that was good in his life? I'm torn apart with grief inside and at the same time I'm angry because it shouldn't have turned out this way."

"Dad the hardest thing is accepting that Steven is gone and there is nothing you can do about that. I can understand your anger because Steven was young, foolish at times and that makes his death so unnecessary. It should never have happened but it did and we have to live with it. In time you will begin to deal with your anger dad and Emily and I will be praying for you and mom."

"Son I never was into all this church stuff and I'm not sure I believe in God. For me going to church is something you do for marriage, christenings and funerals. I suppose I believe that there has to be something after this life but I'm not sure what."

"Dad, God is real and he can give you the strength to get through this time and maybe one day your way of thinking about him will change. You just need to be open to him but for the present he knows what you are thinking and feeling right now and he cares about that."

"I'm glad because right now my thinking is all over the place but I'll remember what you have said."

Just then the door opened and Victoria came in followed by a waiter with a lunch trolley. "Hi you two. I thought you would be working hard all morning and you would forget to eat."

Jack laughed. "I had just said to dad we needed to stop for a sandwich."

Victoria poured out the coffee. "I hope you don't mind if I join you. I will be leaving shortly and I wanted to spend some time with you before I go."

"It's good of you to join us Victoria. You know we are concerned about you right now."

Victoria saw the strain on her father-in-laws face. "Don't worry about me. Steven was my husband but he was your son and I know this is hurting you dad."

He smiled at her and nodded his head. Victoria knew that he would keep busy with work and do whatever to keep his mind occupied but inside the grief would still be wounding him.

"Dad I expect you two have been discussing the future of the Edgewater Hotel and who will manage it."

"Yes Victoria there are some things we had to discuss and we want to consult with you on everything. While the hotel needs a new management structure we are aware of the need to be sensitive to your needs."

"Dad I can tell you now what I've been thinking. I didn't sleep well last night and I began to think about issues that are important to all of us. I know that I have the love and support of this family for myself and my daughter and I really appreciate that. Although I have lost my husband I still feel secure within the family. You both know that I'm returning home today and I need to begin accepting what has happened. Steven's personal belongings has to be sorted out and other things in the apartment and I know I need to do this in order to help me accept the reality of the last few days. I've also thought about the hotel. I realise that you need to get a new manager in there soon and I don't want you to hold back on this on my account. When I go home I'll be preparing for someone else to come and take over the responsibilities of running the hotel. I haven't decided where Chloe and I will live and I feel it is to soon to be making major decisions but I think it would be a good idea if we went back to Ireland and spent some time with you Jack and Emily.

This would give me breathing space and allow the Dillon-Spence Group to move in a new management for the Edgewater."

Jack smiled and he admired the strength of this woman. "Victoria we would love to have you come to Ireland with us and I believe it will be good for you and Chloe."

"I must say I'm proud of you Victoria and I love you as my daughter. I was almost dreading having to discuss future plans with you in case it upset you to much but you have thought this through in such a sensitive manner. Now there are a few things I do want you to be aware of and I suppose now is as good a time to discuss them. You know how much we love you and Chloe and that there is a trust fund set up for Chloe's future. There is also a large insurance policy which the company had on Steven's life and that will be paid directly to you. We can advise you on ways you might want to invest some of it in the future. There is also a monthly allowance paid to you and Chloe. When she is eighteen she will receive the first part of her trust fund, then again at twenty one and twenty five. With regards to the expenses for Steven's funeral they are already covered and you don't have to concern yourself with that."

"Thank you dad for the way in which you are caring for us. I really love you all for everything you have done and the way our future needs have been provided for us."

"Victoria if you decide to come back from Ireland then we will help find a suitable home for you."

"Thanks dad. I know I can rely on you all."

"Hello, I couldn't find any of you so I thought you would be in here. Is there any coffee in that pot?"

"Yes darling. Sit down and I'll pour you a cup and there are sandwiches on that tray."

"Emily I've decided to go back to Ireland for awhile and that will give dad and Jack time to implement new management structures at the Edgewater."

"I'm glad Victoria. A rest is what you need right now and you will have plenty of time to think about the future, there is no hurry."

"Victoria I know you said you wanted to get back today but would you not consider staying one more night. It is New Year's Eve and I don't like to think of you being alone tonight."

"I know dad but I'd prefer to spend it quietly and then maybe tomorrow I'll begin to sort things out in the apartment. It will be good therapy for me."

"Jack and Emily are you staying over?"

"Yes we will both be here tonight and then Emily will return the day after tomorrow but I'll be staying on to help you with business."

"Son I appreciate that. Emily I know you miss the children and I'm grateful that you have stayed this long."

"I do miss them but they are fine. I telephone everyday and speak to them. I think Anna is spoiling them because we are away and they will be enjoying that."

"I'm glad they are not fretting. Emily I'm worried about Sarah. Maybe you could talk with her. I don't want her locking herself away and grieving alone. She doesn't often speak about how she really feels; I suppose she had been used to putting on a brave face and getting on with things."

"Don't worry dad, I've already talked with her this morning. She will be fine and like all of us she needs time to accept what has happened.

Victoria left the Royal Court later that day. The journey back to the Edgewater gave her time to relax and Chloe slept most of the way.

She was lost in her thoughts as the car sped down motorways and it seemed in no time she was back home.

The staff welcomed her and offered sympathy and Victoria was grateful for the care they had shown her.

Victoria got Chloe settled into bed and then sat down with a coffee. There was a lot of post waiting for her, mainly letters of sympathy and cards. She decided anything else could wait until the next day as she needed time on her own to begin to accept what had happened. She wondered what she would do with her life now that she wouldn't be sharing the business responsibilities at the Edgewater. If she wanted to continue to work within the family business then a position would be created for her but she didn't have to. Financially she and Chloe were very comfortable and she was relieved that she didn't have to worry about money. Now she was more concerned with trying to get some perspective in her own life because for the first time she had the freedom to choose. The last few days had been strange for her because she was surrounded by so many people yet most of the time she felt lost. She would be standing in a room full of people and feel completely alone inside.

Just before midnight she decided to go to bed. Quietly she went in to her daughter's room and she was fast asleep. Victoria kissed her cheek. "You look so beautiful Chloe. Happy New Year darling." She whispered. Slipping out the door she promised herself that the year would be a fresh start for her and Chloe. Her little girl was so precious to her and she would do her best to be the loving mother her child needed.

Victoria got into bed and she realised just how big the bed was without Steven although there had been nights when he stayed out late and she had gone to bed alone. The telephone rang and Victoria wondered who would be ringing so late.

"Hi, it's Emily. How are you?"

"I'm fine and I'm in bed with a hot drink."

"Victoria I want to wish you a happy new year and I mean that with all my heart. You have come through so much and I pray that next year will be good for you."

"Thank you Emily. I believe next year will be different and there will be new things for me to discover. I wish you a happy new year and give my love to everyone there."

"Yes I will. I'm looking forward to going back to Northern Ireland. We can go for walks along the beach again."

Victoria smiled. "Yes I did enjoy that even if it was freezing."

Emily laughed at the thought. "Victoria will you be alright until I see you again?"

"Of course I will. I have a lot to do before I go away. Preparing for the trip will be good for me so don't worry."

"Well good night and God bless."

"You too. Bye."

Victoria turned off the lamp and the darkness brought much needed rest and she gladly surrendered to sleep.

23 VICTORIA WOKE UP on New Year's Day with hope in her heart that this year would be a time of change and as it stretched ahead she had plans to make for the future.

The nanny had already dressed Chloe and she was having breakfast so Victoria decided on a long soak in the bath before she began the day. After tea and toast she began to clear out stuff that had cluttered up the place for too long. This year was a new beginning but Victoria couldn't move on until she had shed things that belonged to the old life.

Steven's closet was full of suits, ties, casual wear and formal clothes and of there were shoes to match everything. Victoria decided to bag up the clothes and give them to charity and she worked all morning packing it all up. She felt good about herself, this was a new start and she was grabbing life with both hands.

The telephone rang and she was tempted not to answer it but everyone would think there was something wrong with her.

"Hello."

"Madam this is Justine at reception. The police are here and they would like to speak with you."

"Alright. Would you have someone bring them up to my apartment please?"

In the few minutes that it took the police to arrive Victoria had combed her hair and put on lipstick. She opened the door. "Hello please come in."

"Hello I'm detective Tony Scott. I'll only take a few minutes of your time. I understand how difficult this is. The death of your husband must have been devastating for you."

"I'm fine. Can I get you a coffee?"

"No don't bother. I'll get straight to the point." He placed a large brown envelope on the table. "These are your husband's personal effects that we removed from the scene of the accident. They are your property now."

Victoria stared at the envelope as the reality of Steven's death began to hit her again.

"Madam are you alright? Can I get you a glass of water?"

"No I'll be fine. I'm still trying to get used to the fact that he is never coming home again. Thank you for bringing this for me, I appreciate it."

"I'll go now if you are sure you will be alright."

"Yes really I will and thank you again."

Victoria showed him out and as she shut the door an overwhelming sense of loss went through her. "God what has happened to the girl who was feeling good about herself?"

She picked up the envelope and held it not knowing what she would find inside and she felt almost afraid to look. "Now I'm being silly."

She opened the envelope and let the contents spill out onto the table. There was his watch which had been a present from her on his birthday. She had it engraved on the back and he seemed to like the personal touch. There was his wedding ring, cuff links and his wallet which contained some money and his bank cards and a photograph of her and Chloe. Victoria picked up each item remembering the times she had bought them for him and then she put them back into the envelope. She went to Steven's desk and put it in the drawer; she could sort that out later too.

It seemed all she had left of her marriage were clothes in bags and a desk of personal stuff and a brown envelope. She sighed and decided it was time for a coffee.

In the afternoon Victoria began clearing out the big oak desk. There were lots of business papers and junk mail that Steven hadn't bothered to put in a bin. Any documents concerning the hotel she put to one side and Jack could have those. She found his desk dairy and opened it and saw that he had pencilled in appointments for the next month. How strange that he was no longer here to keep them. At the back of his dairy was a leather pocket and she noticed a photograph in it along with a business card. She pulled it out expecting it to be of either her or Chloe but it wasn't. The picture was of an attractive smiling blonde haired woman and Victoria new instinctively that it was Sophie. She stared at the picture and she realised that she had saw her before in the hotel bar and she wondered how long Steven had been involved with her. She picked up the business card and saw it had the name and number of an estate agent on it. Since it was with Sophie's photograph she guessed there had to be a connection between the two. She wondered how Sophie was coping with the loss of Steven and if she had her own special mementoes of their relationship. She felt angry that Steven had caused so much pain in everyone's life, it wasn't just about her and another woman but his family were devastated he was dead. Picking up a photograph of her and Steven together she threw it to the floor. "How dare you Steven." She shouted.

"You thought you could hurt everyone's life and then you died and the rest of us are left to pick up the pieces of our lives. I'm left alone without a husband and our Chloe is going to grow up without her daddy. Whoever Sophie is she is probably as heartbroken as I am and it's not all her fault. You did your share of the chase until you got her where you wanted her. I should know, you once did it with me all those years ago when you told me you loved me. We could have had so much happiness and you had to go and spoil it all. I wish I'd never loved you."

Victoria began to cry and she knelt on the floor beside the photograph and sobbed until she was exhausted. She went to bed feeling the pain of raw emotions inside her and a lot of questions still left unanswered. Victoria took the sleeping pills the doctor had left for her and soon sleep took over her tired mind as she drifted into darkness.

The next morning Victoria woke up early and got up and made tea. She had a headache and her body felt sore and tired. A warm shower revived her and she dressed and styled her hair.

"Mummy I'm hungry."

"Hello my darling." She picked Chloe up and sat her on her knee. "Did you have a good sleep?"

"Yes but when I woke up I remembered that daddy isn't here."

Victoria kissed her. "I know darling and we miss him but mummy will always be here for you."

"I loved daddy but he went away. I know he is in heaven but I'd like him to come down so I could give him one more hug. I feel sad without him."

"I know darling but daddy had an accident and that's why he is in heaven. He can't come back down Chloe but we have lots of good memories of daddy. Remember the times he took you to the park? We also had lovely holidays together when daddy played in the swimming pool with you."

"Yes I remember and we had lots of fun."

"When you feel sad then you should think of all the happy times with daddy and that will help you."

"I will. Can I have a picture of daddy in my room and it will be my special picture?

Victoria hugged her. "Of course you can."

"I love you mummy but I'm still hungry."

Victoria laughed. "Then we have to do something about that."

"Chloe I wondered where you had got to. Good morning Victoria."

"Good morning Tracey. Madam here is complaining she is hungry."

Tracey picked Chloe up in her arms. "Well we can't have that so I think we should go into the kitchen and make something lovely for you."

Chloe laughed and hugged Tracey. "Yes, yes."

"Victoria can I get you anything?"

"When Chloe has her breakfast I would like some tea and toast please."

"Fine, I won't be long."

The telephone rang and Victoria answered it in her room. "Hello."

"Hello its Emily. How are you?"

"Oh Emily I'm not sure how to answer that. I feel in such turmoil and everything is going around in circles."

"What has happened?"

"Oh it's just Chloe is missing her daddy and I feel hurt for her and angry at Steven. My emotions are all over the place Emily."

"Victoria I will be so glad when you can join us in Ireland."

"So will I but there are things I must do here first and then I can begin to put it all behind me. How are you?"

"I'm fine and so are the children. Jack is staying in London and I miss him but he needs to help his father right now. I hope he will get home for a few days even if it means he has to go back again."

"I know everything has been such an upheaval for everyone."

"Never mind everyone I'm more concerned about you."

"I'm just angry inside and I know at some point I will have to deal with that but not now. I loved Steven and so does Chloe yet I feel he has spoilt everything. I know he is dead but I resent him for the pain he caused to other people's lives."

"Victoria it's only natural that you are feeling the way you do. It is going to take a lot of time for you to come to terms with all that's happened. Please understand that I'm here for you and I will do anything I can to help you through this."

"I know Emily and I love you for the support you are giving me but there is so much pain inside me. I feel so raw inside, like there is a big open wound in my heart and I don't know if it will ever heal."

"Victoria I believe your pain will heal but you need more than me to help you. I want you to close your eyes and try and relax. I'm going to pray with you because I know the Lord can help you right now."

Emily prayed and as she did Victoria felt her mind and her body become calm and deep inside her something responded to Emily's prayer."

"Emily, thank you I appreciate that and I feel much better but I think I need to know God more. Remember when we walked along the beach on Christmas day and I said I wanted to talk to him like you do?"

"Yes Victoria I remember and that's exactly what you need to do. Begin to talk to him like you talk to me. He loves to be up close and personal with us and all you have to do is open your heart to him. Say yes to him Victoria and your life will never be the same."

"I'd like to do that. Emily I'll speak to you later. Bye."

Victoria sat down on her bed trying to remain calm and keep any turmoil at bay. "God I don't really know what to say to you. I feel so small and you are a big God and maybe I shouldn't even be talking to you. I've never known you but I know I need you in my life. I can't begin to go forward on my own.

I know you love me and my daughter but your love hasn't been real to me before. The proof of your love was when you sent your Son to die for me and that was a high price for him to pay. I want to call you Lord of my life so I give you my heart and all of me. I ask your forgiveness, there is so much emotion inside me now yet I believe you want to heal me. Lord my life, my future and every desire I have I surrender to you."

Inside Victoria she could feel her heart begin to melt and become soft and the gentleness eased the pain. She cried as she recognised that the Lord was pouring his love into her and his inner healing had begun in her life. She got down on her knees and in her heart she knew she was bowing before him. As she surrendered to the love that was drawing her she knew that every hurt and emotional wound, the betrayal and rejection by her husband, all of this her Lord was washing away as she cried. In her heart she heard a still small voice. *"I've prepared a way for you and I am making all things new."*

"Oh God I heard you." Her heart experienced joy for the first time. "I need you so much and thank you Lord. You are giving me a fresh start and I feel so safe because I can trust you."

Victoria decided in beginning her new life she had first to put the old one behind her. She took the business card and rang the estate agents number.

"Hello Norwood Estates, can I help you?"

"Hello I'd like to speak to Ben Addis please."

"And your name is?"

"Mrs Victoria Dillon-Spence."

She waited a minute before being put through and she got annoyed at the silly Christmas music that played while she was on hold.

"Hello this is Ben Addis. How may I help you?"

"I wondered if I could meet with you today. It is quite important but not something I wish to discuss on the telephone."

He hesitated. "I'll need to check what other appointments I have."

"Mr Addis I've just buried my husband and I'm now in the process of sorting out his business. I need to meet with as soon as possible."

"I'm sorry. I know that your husband died and I didn't mean to be insensitive. Please come in this morning and we can talk then."

"Thank you I'll be there within the hour. Bye."

Victoria put down the telephone and she felt a new strength inside and a determination to get to the bottom of whatever went on in Steven's life.

Ben Addis picked up the file on his desk. The name inside was Mr Steven Dillon-Spence and he knew just how confidential the details were. There were business deals that did not go through the outer office but remained in a confidential file locked away in Ben's office. Now he had to decide how much to tell Victoria. He would wait until he met her and then decide what she needed to know.

The internal telephone rang and he picked it up. "Mrs Dillon-Spence is here to see you."

"Thank you Cathy, please bring her through."

Victoria walked into his office and his first impression of her was overwhelming. She was very beautiful, dressed in a camel wool suite that was tailored to perfection, her hair styled and make up subtle. Ben stood up and shook her hand. "I'm pleased to meet you although I'm sorry that the circumstances are difficult. Losing your husband so suddenly must have been a dreadful shock for you."

"Yes it was. Now that the initial shock has become a reality for me I must sort out my husband's business. Mr Addis I'll come straight to the point. I found your card in my husband's desk. I've never heard him mention you before yet I knew a lot about the business. I'd like to know how you knew Steven."

Ben was surprised at her directness and he wasn't sure how to deal with it.

"Mrs Dillon-Spence I'm sure that being a woman in business yourself you will understand that it is the nature of our business to treat each client with respect and assure them of confidentiality."

Victoria stared at him. "Mr Addis I'm not a fool so don't treat me as one. Your client that you treat with such high regard is dead therefore you need not concern yourself with being sued for breach of contract. However, I'm your client's widow and there are certain financial matters I need to sort out before I can move on with my life. Now I will ask you again. How do you know Steven?"

Ben picked up the file. "I hope you realise what you are asking of me. The contents of this file may not be whatever it is you are expecting to find.

I'm going to give it to you and leave you alone for a few minutes then I'll come back with coffee for us."

Victoria took the file. "Thank you. I appreciate you may be trying to protect me but there is no reason to protect Steven. I need to do this or I wouldn't be here."

"I understand. I'll leave you to read it."

Victoria opened the file and the first page were Steven's personal details and information about the business. She skipped over to the next page and read details of an apartment with an address not far from the hotel. Curiosity began to rise in her. Why would Steven want a luxury apartment on a residential side of town when he managed a five star hotel? She read that the apartment had been bought by Steven but the property deeds were signed over to Ms Sophie Howard. Victoria was shocked. Not only did Steven have a relationship with this woman but he had bought her an apartment. It seemed that her husband had led a totally different life outside of their marriage and the hotel. Victoria wrote down the address of the apartment and put it in her bag. She wasn't sure what to do about it but at least she knew the truth.

Ben came back with coffee and he knew by the look on her face that she had read the file thoroughly.

"I'm sorry you had to find out this way. I don't know much about Ms Howard except that she was a close friend of your husband's."

"I think we both know how close their friendship was. According to your file the apartment was signed over to her. Is there anything I can do about that?"

"I don't think so. When the deal was arranged your husband bought it for her regardless of their friendship. It was a gift to her."

"Yes and he probably claimed it back in expenses with his income tax. To be honest I don't know that I would want to do anything about it. I'm more annoyed because of the deceptive life my husband has led."

"I understand and I'm sorry. You can't undo Steven's past but you can look forward to the future. You have a life of your own, learn to live it."

Victoria smiled. "Yes I think you are right. Thank you for your time and for being honest with me. Truth has been in short supply in my life." She stood up and shook hands with him. "Good bye Mr Addis."

"I wish you happiness Mrs Dillon-Spence. Good bye.

When she left Ben sat down at is desk with the image of Victoria on his mind. He found it hard to believe that Steven was willing to risk so much when he had a beautiful wife at home. He sighed as he turned on his computer. "Back to work, there are some people I'll never understand."

Victoria drove through town to where the apartment was. She parked in a side road and sat for a few minutes looking over the area. It was beautiful, private and obviously expensive. She had to fight back tears as she thought of the double life Steven had going for himself. His lifestyle must have cost a lot of money and now she realised why he felt under so much pressure when his father began questioning the accounts at the hotel. It all made sense now but she still felt angry at the deception and the lies he must have told her and his father in order to cover his other life.

Victoria sat in the car trying not to allow the turmoil to take over her mind again. "God what will I do? I can't just let this go."

"The truth will set you free."

Victoria puzzled over the words in her heart. How could finding out about Steven's life set her free? Suddenly she realised that her mind had been in a fog she had been trying to get through and as she learned the truth the fog began to clear. "Lord what do I do with the truth? How do I get free from the hurt Steven caused me?"

"Victoria this is the way. Walk in it."

"I think I see what you mean. The truth is something I need to face up to and you will help me to deal with it. Each hurdle I get over sets me free from it and the pain associated with it. As I face up to the things that were wrong in my marriage to Steven then I can accept that it is over and I can move on with my life with no more secrets. This must be what you meant when you said you would make all things new for me."

She felt an inner peace inside and she knew what she had to do next. Getting out of the car she walked towards the apartment ready to face another truth.

Victoria rang the doorbell twice and waited. Her heart was beating a little faster but she wasn't going to walk away from this. The door opened.

"Hello."

Victoria looked at the woman, tired, pale and still in her dressing gown.

"Hello my name is Victoria Dillon-Spence and I'd like to talk to you."

"Oh I see. Come in."

Victoria followed her through to the lounge and she was impressed at how neat it was.

"I'm sorry I'm not dressed yet. It's a struggle to get through my day. Sit down. I think it's obvious why you're here so that cuts out the formalities."

Victoria sat on the sofa. "Sophie I know you had a relationship with Steven and I'm not here to argue about that. Steven is dead and that is something we have to accept. I'm not sure why I'm here. I suppose I had to meet you just to know that what I'd suspected was true and I wasn't going mad. I'm hurt that Steven betrayed me at a time when I thought we should have been working on our marriage. It sounds foolish now."

"No it isn't foolish. Steven loved you and his daughter. He would never have left you regardless of problems in the marriage."

"Well I'll never know that now that he is dead."

"Believe me Victoria, he loved you and Chloe. You were high on his list of priorities even if you didn't feel that way. I got to be at the bottom. I know you're thinking that I deserve whatever because I got involved with him but it does take two and I didn't get into it by myself."

"Sophie you still chose to be with him."

"Yes and I take responsibility for that choice but it was difficult to say no to Steven."

Victoria felt the shadow of a smile on her face. She knew exactly what Sophie meant. "Tell me about the Steven you know. It appears he had another life."

Sophie relaxed a little; after all she had a lot in common with Victoria.

"Steven saw me as a distraction from his other life, his marriage and the business and his family. His father had high expectations that Steven found difficult to live up to. He had to have an escape route from all of that and I was his means of escape. He told me from the beginning that our relationship was on his terms, he never promised me a future with him and he liked to be in control. He made it clear that he loved you and he would never leave you. I'll be honest with you, I loved him but I knew my place in his life. He saw me whenever he could but it was in his time and I accepted that as the other woman in his life there were certain rules I had to live by. Sometimes I felt like second best but there's a price to pay for everything. Loving Steven meant I had to do things his way or not at all."

"Sophie I don't know what I'm supposed to feel. Part of me wants to be angry with you yet there is no point to that now. It's obvious you are grieving and at some point you are going to have to move on with your life."

"I'm not ready to make plans yet. I've still got my job although I've taken some time off. There's one other thing that is bothering me and since we are being honest I'll tell you. I received a letter from a lawyer today telling me that now Steven is gone the apartment is mine."

"Yes I know that."

"Well until today I didn't know. Steven never told me that this place would be mine in the event of our relationship breaking up, obviously he didn't realise he was going to die. You are Steven's widow and maybe you would want to sell this place, I don't blame you but if you let me know to begin looking for somewhere else."

"Sophie the apartment is yours and it was a gift from Steven. I don't have any claim to it and I wouldn't want to. This place has nothing to do with Steven and me."

"Thank you."

"Before I go I have one more question. On the night that Steven died I'm sure you are aware I was in Ireland. Did you see him that night?"

"Yes I did and I think it was the worst night I have ever spent with him."

Victoria was puzzled. "Surely with me out of the way he would have been spending time with you."

"I thought that too but Steven seemed to be under a lot of pressure. He didn't always discuss his problems with me. Remember I was a distraction from anything that troubled him. He was in a terrible mood that night and he had been drinking. We had an arguement; I won't go into the details as it still hurts me. Anyway, he didn't stay long and when he left I thought that by the next day he would have calmed down. I waited for him to telephone but he didn't. I tried his mobile but there was no answer. I found out about the accident when it came on the local news. I'll never forget the shock I felt. Being the other woman I didn't expect an invitation to the funeral but I did go to the chapel of rest to say good-bye to him. I wish we hadn't argued that night. Now you know the truth Victoria, I've nothing more to tell you."

"I think I should go now. Thank you for being honest with me. I intend to make a new life for myself and my daughter. I suggest you do the same. Good bye Sophie."

She left Victoria to the door. "I'm sorry for everything you have been through. I never intended to hurt you or your marriage."

"I can believe that. Steven was a very charming man and he didn't like a woman to say no to him, infact it was difficult to refuse him."

"Good bye Victoria."

Victoria smiled as she walked away. She had faced up to another truth about Steven and now she had to let it rest.

She felt good about herself as she got into her car, it was a feeling of achievement and she liked it. As she was about to drive off she was aware of an uneasiness in her heart. She waited a few minutes, something wasn't right and her peace was disturbed.

"Lord what it is? I thought I handled that situation the way you would have wanted me to. I wasn't nasty to Sophie and I don't want her apartment. Lord why do I feel I've offended you?"

"You talk of facing the truth and of putting the past to rest but there's one thing I require of you. You need to forgive."

Victoria felt like a bucket of cold water had been thrown over her. Surely God didn't mean she had to forgive Steven for the way he betrayed her and the lies he told her. How could she forgive Sophie? She could understand how Steven made her feel second best but she knew what she was getting into with him and if Steven wasn't dead they would still be seeing each other. "Lord I can't do what you are asking of me. It doesn't seem right that I'm the one who has to forgive when I didn't do anything wrong."

"My son was betrayed and lied about but before he died he forgave those who had treated him badly. He died that you might go free."

"Oh God I see that but how do I forgive?"

"Victoria the truth sets you free. Unforgiveness leads to resentment and it will harm your life and it will hinder your relationship with me.

Unforgiveness won't harm Steven or Sophie but it will hurt you. You are my child, I love you and I don't want you to be hurt."

Victoria felt surrounded by his love, pure love from the inside out. "Lord I hurt when I think of the double life Steven had but I want to be able to forgive. Teach me."

"Forgiveness isn't a feeling it is an act of will. Feelings come and go but releasing your will to me is a decision you make, it is your choice. I love you no matter what you decide but I want to bless you. My desire is that you have my best in your life and unforgiveness will only hinder you."

"Lord I want what you have for me. I can't pretend with you because you know my heart and I can't change the way I feel right now. I want to have my will in line with yours and I'm choosing to forgive Steven for any wrong he did during our marriage. I can't change the past but with your help I can have a better future. Lord I forgive Sophie for her involvement with Steven, only you know why she did it. Hear my heart and as I forgive help me to let go of the past."

Victoria shed more tears as her anger and resentment began to melt away as she obeyed her Lord but one thing puzzled her. "God how am I supposed to deal with the emotions that well up inside me? How often do I forgive?"

"Victoria keep on forgiving and keep moving on with me."

Suddenly she felt her heart at peace and joy welled up within her. "Thank you Lord. I've so glad you are in my life. I love you."

"I have loved you with an everlasting love. I rejoice over you with singing and you will know the fullness of my joy"

24

EMILY STARED OUT of the window as she drank her coffee. It had begun to snow that morning and it was bitter cold outside. The trees in the gardens looked forlorn without their leaves and the lawns were covered in a wet white blanket of snow. In a way it looked like a beautiful picture of winter but Emily saw it as cold and without life.

"Lord I'm sorry for being so negative this morning. January is usually a time for new beginnings but Steven's death has overshadowed everything. I suppose I realise that there's never a good time for death to happen and it comes when we least expect it to. Everything seems so bleak and yet you are still God and you never change."

Emily opened her desk drawer and took out her bible. She opened at the psalms and one line caught her attention. "Oh give thanks to the Lord for his love endures forever."

"Lord I want to thank you for your love. No matter what happens in my life or how I'm feeling your love remains constant and endures forever. I'm glad it doesn't depend on anything I need to do or say. You love me unconditionally and that love strengthens me."

"Emily look beyond the circumstances and you will see that my love has brought you this far and will take you further. I see the sorrow that

death has brought to your lives but I am your healer. I will strengthen you in the days ahead and enable you to be my source of love in the lives of other people. Look out of the window again. What you see isn't a bleak cold picture of winter. No, what you see is my hand at work. I change the seasons, I water the earth, and I know what the ground needs in order to prepare for spring. Look with my eyes and see what your God has done."

Emily went to the window and looking out saw what her Creator wanted her to see. "Lord forgive me. Your words are life and they change my whole perspective. Thank you for the miracle of winter and in it's time will give birth to spring."

She went back to her desk and began work with joy in her heart that helped her to get through the mountain of paper work and post that had been waiting for her.

Amy came in with coffee. "I thought you might need this. There is a lot of post this morning. I sorted through advertising mail but there is still a lot of personal mail."

"I know Amy and thanks for the coffee. I'm still receiving letters and cards from people who recently found out about Steven's death. There are some that Jack will want to reply to personally so I'll put those to one side. We are going to put a notice of thanks in the newspapers and the hotel trade magazines. The rest can wait until Jack gets home."

"I'll put them in a folder. When will he get home again?"

"I'm not sure Amy. He is helping his father with employing a new management for The Edgewater Hotel. I think he will get home for a few days and then he will commute between here and London until everything is in place. He is also a great support for his dad and mom but I do miss him here."

Amy picked up the diary. "You have a few appointments today."

"Tell me it's not going to be a long day."

"First, you have Mrs Evans the housekeeper. She said to me about needing more staff on the housekeeping side although I thought this was a quieter time of year to be needing extra staff."

"Usually that's true but we had some people leave at Christmas. Mrs Evans likes to spring clean the place from top to bottom well before spring arrives.

What else is there?"

"The chef wants to go over new menus with you."

"Surely the catering manager can do that."

"Apparently not as these ideas need your stamp of approval."

"Please tell me there are no other appointments."

"No but we are behind in correspondence so there's plenty of paperwork."

"Right I suppose we could do that after lunch. You go through the letters that need to be answered and write a list for me. Any routine mail you can deal with and sign on my behalf. I need to check over some accounts later so I'll maybe do them tonight when it's quieter."

"I looked over the appointments book in reception and we are already taking bookings for conferences and weddings for spring/ summer."

"I know I had a look myself and we are in for a busy season. I want to make an appointment with the conference manager so you check when she will be free. I'm thinking of having some redecoration done to the conference rooms and a different look maybe for the dining rooms."

"A make over for the dining room. What about a theme and a total new colour scheme."

"Yes that sounds good although Jack expects me to work within a budget so don't get carried away Amy."

She sighed. "I don't like that word budget; I prefer to let my imagination flow."

Emily laughed. "Unfortunately it doesn't flow into the bank account. I've also been looking at our promotional material that we send out to people and I think we could do with upgrading our package. I'm not sure what I want yet so I'm open to ideas, within the budget Amy."

Amy smiled. "You do realise that Mrs Hollings doesn't like disruptions in her planning. If the present package works she won't see why you want to spend money changing it."

"Yes well that's the reason I'm the boss and she isn't. We have to move with the times."

The day went quickly and Emily just had time for a quick lunch. Amy left at 6pm and Emily was still in the office at 7:30pm when the telephone rang.

"Hello."

"Hello darling."

"Hello Jack, it's so good to hear voice."

"I telephoned the private line in our apartment but Anna told me you were still working."

"It has been a busy day and I miss you so much. It's like I've double the work to do."

Jack laughed. "So now you realise that I do work when I'm there."

"You do a little." She teased him.

"I suppose you are doing accounts."

"Yes my least favourite task. Jack when are you coming home?"

"In a few days, I promise. I've helped my dad sort out just about everything to do with the Edgewater and we are interviewing for new staff. Once we get through the final selections I'll be able to come home for a break. We still have one guy who is a definite possibility so I'm hoping it all moves quickly and smoothly."

"We are busy over here. Already we have bookings for spring and summer."

"Sounds good. We should have a busy season in front of us."

"How's your parents Jack?"

"It's hard to say. My father is working harder than ever and it seems to be his way of coping with the grief inside. He has taken on the task of sorting out the Edgewater and although I'm helping him, it is very much his project.

My mum is a lot better from you talked with her and although she is still grieving, she is reading her bible and she seems to be looking for a new purpose in life."

"I'm glad. I believe your mum has sincerely opened her heart to God and in time she may be able to help your dad."

"That would be something. My dad doesn't mention Steven often, he just wants to work and I'm concerned that he is pushing himself to hard."

"Jack we have to trust God for your parents. He knows their pain and that they need his healing so try not to worry about them. How are you Jack? You seem to be the strong one yet Steven was your brother."

"I'm not sure how I'm feeling. I suppose I've put any grief on hold because my parents need me. Sometimes I have to remind myself that this is real. Emily I'm looking forward to seeing you again. I miss you and the children and I love you so much."

"I love you Jack and I hope to see you soon."

"Yes you will. Bye darling."

Emily left the office and she felt alone. She missed Jack more than she realised and talking to him didn't help. She wanted him here, holding her and she wanted to reassure him. "Oh Lord bring him home soon." She whispered.

The children were ready for bed when she let herself into the apartment.

"Hello I'm home."

"We're in here mum."

Emily followed the direction of the voice to Rosa's bedroom. Nathan was sitting on the bed and Rosa had a story book opened.

"Hi you two. I missed you today." She sat on the bed and hugged both of them.

"Where's daddy? Why isn't he home?"

Nathan was too young to understand that Jack was still away.

"Darling, daddy is staying with granddad and nanny but I talked to him on the telephone and he will be back soon."

Nathan wrapped his chubby little arms around her neck and kissed her.

"Thank you darling, mummy needed that."

"What did daddy say to you today?"

"He said he misses you and Rosa and he loves us very much."

"Mummy are you sad? I think you miss daddy."

"I do miss him Rosa but I'm trying not to be sad because he will be back in a few days."

"Then we will be together again." Rosa hugged her.

"Together!" Nathan shouted.

Later when the children were asleep Emily went to her bedroom and lay on the bed. She opened her bible at Isaiah 51 and read verses 11 -12.

"So the ransomed of the Lord shall return, and come to Zion with singing, With everlasting joy on their heads, They shall obtain joy and gladness;

Sorrow and sighing shall flee away. I, even I, am He who comforts you…."

Closing her eyes she worshipped God and in her heart she knew how close he was to her. "Lord I love you and thank you that you are the one I run to, the one that comforts, there is none like you. Showers of loving tenderness flow over me when I worship you, thank you for your comfort and your peace."

The stillness in his presence was healing to Emily's heart and she got into bed and lay with her eyes closed but her mind still on worship.

"Stay in my rest and let me bathe your life with my love, peace and strength. My love for you is so vast and I set you free to serve me with your life. Rest as I breathe fresh life to you."

Emily drifted into a peaceful sleep and in the morning she awoke refreshed and ready to face the day. She stayed with the children while they had breakfast and she had toast and tea. "Mummy has to go to work now. Rosa you get dressed for school and have a good day. Nathan I'll come up and see you at lunch time. Be a good boy for Anna and I'll see you later."

The post had arrived at reception and Emily went through it. "I'll take these and leave the rest for Amy."

She walked into her office as the telephone was ringing. "Hello."

"Hello Emily, its mum."

"Hi, this is an early morning surprise. How are you?"

Sarah laughed. "I'm fine. I just wanted to talk to you and say thank you for the way you have helped me. From we prayed I'm discovering a new life with God and I'm searching for a new direction. I feel like there really is a purpose to my life and its nothing like the deceptive social whirl I've been living in for years. I look back and so much of my life was just for show and it wasn't real."

"Mum I'm so happy for you. You sound so positive and at peace with yourself."

"I am Emily. I'm still grieving for my son but I know that God is with me in this. I spend a lot of time reading my bible and I've bought some books. I don't go out as much and apparently some of my friends are worried about me. Little do they realise I'm getting to know God more and I'm content with the things he is teaching me."

"I'm so glad for you mum. I can only imagine how you must feel about Steven but you are working through your feelings and God will continue to help you."

"I believe that too. I'll go now and you have a good day."

"You too mum, bye."

The day was busy and Emily got through a lot of paperwork. At lunch time she went to the apartment to see Nathan and she had a sandwich while she was there. The afternoon was spent talking with staff members about changes for the spring/summer season and by 6pm Emily decided she had done enough. She needed to be with the children and she was looking forward to a family night. Bath time, stories and lots of hugs and kisses was the thing that Emily loved with them and she never took it for granted.

When she was little and growing up in the children's home she used to imagine what it would be like to be part of a family were she would be loved. She used to dream of having parents who would make her feel safe and they would do lots of things together and have fun days out. She had missed out on that in her own life but she made sure Rosa and Nathan had plenty of love and happiness in their lives.

Emily sat down to relax after the children went to bed and Anna brought her a coffee. The telephone rang and Emily hoped there were no problems downstairs. "Hello."

"Hi, it's Victoria."

Emily breathed a sigh of relief. "Hi, just give a minute. I'm going through to the bedroom to lie on the bed. It's been a busy day."

Emily picked up the telephone beside the bed. "Hi, I'm back. Now tell me how you are."

"I'm fine and Chloe is good too. What about you and Jack?"

"Jack is still in London with his parents and I miss him but he hopes to get back for the weekend. The children are fine although they miss their dad."

"I know that feeling. Chloe is finding it hard to understand why her daddy can't come down from heaven just one more time."

"Oh Victoria that must be very difficult for you."

"It has been but I find if I give her the time to talk about what she is feeling then she is alright. Lots of hugs also help."

"And how are you coping Victoria?"

"I believe that God is making me into a new person. I made my decision to surrender my life to him and I've been putting things in order that I was trying to avoid. I'm learning to face up to the truth of how things really are."

"That must be painful for you too."

"Yes it has been but God is teaching me how to face the pain and not hide away from it. Emily I've cleared out so much of Steven's belongings and then the police called with his personal items that they removed the night of the accident. I was going through his desk when I found an estate agents card and a photograph of Sophie. I traced her to an apartment that Steven had bought for her. She was surprised to see me but I did talk to her. I had to face the situation Emily with no more sweeping things away or putting them on hold.

Emily, God has told me that the truth will set me free and that means facing situations and learning to forgive. I'm doing things now that I never thought I could do and it's all because of my relationship with the Lord."

"Victoria I'm so happy for you. I know that he can give his joy in all circumstances, even the painful ones. You have accomplished so much from we last spoke and it is wonderful the way you are coping."

"Emily learning to trust God has been my breakthrough. I've been praying about the future and I've decided that Chloe and I need a fresh start. I know that there will be a new management put here soon and I really don't want to be here any longer than necessary. We will be coming to live in Northern Ireland and begin a new life there."

"Oh Victoria I'm so happy I could cry. Praise God this is great news. My spirit is full of joy for you and I believe God has such a wonderful new life for you and Chloe. It's amazing just listening to you. It's not just the words but I hear your heart and it is beautiful to hear you talk about the Lord and your relationship with him."

"Emily I have found it amazing that I'm in the midst of difficult circumstances and yet my heart is at peace. Only God could do that."

"Just tell me when you are coming over."

"I've still a few things to sort out here and I want to meet with mum and dad before I leave. I'll probably fly from London to Belfast. I'll be talking to dad tomorrow to find out more about the new management here and I'll ring you again when I'm sure of the date."

"I look forward to seeing you so much and the children will love having Chloe here."

"Yes she needs company now so they will be good for her. When I arrive then I'll begin to think about what I want to do in the future. I look forward to walking along the beach again and it will mean so much more now that I'll be talking to the Lord. I'll speak to you soon Emily, Bye."

"Bye Victoria." Emily sat back on her bed and with a grateful heart praised God for what he was doing in Victoria's life. She felt amazed at the turn around in the way she talked and the way in which she had coped since Steven's death.

A knock at the door disturbed her. "Anna must have gone out without her key."

She went down the hall barefoot and she was aware that her eyes were puffy from the tears she had just cried for Victoria but they were tears of joy.

She smiled at that thought as she pulled open the door and then she gasped for breath. "Jack, oh Jack you're home." She threw herself into his arms and cried some more. "I have missed you so much."

"Darling I've missed you." He kissed her. "I'm so glad to be here."

"I must look awful and now I'm crying again."

Jack put his bags in the hall and picked her up in his arms. "You look beautiful. Now I've had a long day and I want a shower and an early night with my wife."

"That sounds like a great idea."

25

BY THE END of January with Christmas and New Year behind them the hotel began to prepare for spring.

Emily and Jack were planning out the months ahead and Amy was taking notes. They were relaxed in the sitting room, having coffee and chatting about how they would like next season to be.

"Anyone like another coffee?"

"I would Amy. Thanks."

"Emily do you want a top up?"

"No I think I'm fine." Emily was making a list of jobs to be done and where they would begin.

"I think I have some order to this now. There are things that we need to get started on and we know how anxious Mrs Evans gets about the housekeeping."

"We'll go over them and Amy you write them down in order of priority, and feel free to give us your input."

Emily laughed. "You are so important to us Amy."

Amy smiled. She was used to Jack teasing her.

"There is no one who can make my coffee like you Amy."

"I know Jack. You could never do without me. Now can we get some work done?"

"Emily she is becoming very bossy."

"That's because you need to be told what to do. Now shut up or she will throw you out."

The telephone rang and Amy answered it. "Jack it's for you and it's your father."

"Amy put it through to my office and I'll take it there. I suggest you two carry on the meeting without me."

"I'm sure we'll manage Jack. I know what you are like when you and your dad start talking on the telephone."

He left and Amy picked up her notebook. "Mrs Evans asked me to remind you about the housekeeping. You are right about her getting anxious."

"Yes I spoke briefly to her yesterday and she gave me a list of suggestions. I think we could start with housekeeping and let her get started with the spring cleaning. That will keep her busy and happy."

Amy smiled as she ticked off her list. "Did you talk to Jack about your other ideas?"

"Yes. I'm still thinking about redecorating the dining rooms where we host wedding receptions. We could freshen them up with a change of curtains and tableware. Mrs Evans has suggested new curtains and matching bed linen but we need to work out a proper budget for that."

"The reception is fine. It was only decorated last autumn although I suppose we could have the sofas and carpets steam cleaned."

"Yes that would be a good idea. Brighten it up a bit without to much expense."

"We need to remember that we need additional staff for house-keeping or you will have Mrs Evans complaining."

Emily laughed. "Mrs Evans is an excellent housekeeper and very well organised but she doesn't let me away with anything."

"I'm glad I don't work in housekeeping. I'm much better in the office."

"Watch it Amy, I could have you transferred."

"No. Jack can't do without me. By the way before I forget to tell you. I had a call yesterday from the tourist board. They want you to confirm any changes to last year's brochure."

"I need to speak to Jack about that. I think we could improve on promoting the hotel more and mention a few more details about the place."

"Yes I agree. We are situated in a good place for tourists. If they want to go further up the coast they head towards Ballycastle and there's Whitepark Bay and Ballintoy. If they want a good place to shop they can drive to Coleraine and there is lots of choice in the town. We are in a good place here and we could highlight the areas we are close to."

"Amy you are a gem. Any other ideas?"

"Yes. I was looking through our bridal promotional pack and I think we could update that. The hotel is great for photography, the gardens are beautiful and then there is the bridal suite. I feel we should improve on the material we send out to people. Create a better image."

Emily laughed. "You are in top form today."

"And don't forget you also wanted something done about the conference rooms. We were busy last year with conferences and staff residentials so I think we should get in contact with employers who have used us in the past and maybe offer an incentive for them to come back again."

"Yes we could maybe get in some more bookings. I'd really like to boost our promotional material this year. We have now established a good reputation within the industry and having laid the foundation we need to build on it. Amy if you type up your notes I'll go over them with Jack and see what he thinks."

Amy went through to her office as Jack was coming out of his. "We got through a lot Jack. I'll type this up for you and you can discuss it with Emily."

Jack smiled. "I'm sure you two have a lot of ideas that will cost a lot of money."

"That's the one thing we are good at Jack, spending money."

The next few weeks brought changes to the hotel and the staff worked hard at giving the place a new look. Emily was pleased at the preparation being made for the next season and she felt proud of the way their work had been blessed and they had staff that were reliable, efficient and enjoyed working for them.

She had her morning coffee in the sitting room and as she relaxed on the sofa she realised how tired she felt. She had noticed it over the weeks but a lot had happened in their lives and she had felt stressed at times. She had also been working longer hours when Jack was away in London so maybe all she needed was an early night. A good rest should help her now that Jack was home. The telephone rang and disturbed her thoughts. "Hello."

"Hi, it's Victoria."

Emily immediately perked up. "How are you?"

"I'm fine and I'm making progress. I was thinking of coming over next week. I should have everything sorted out by then and I wondered if you could meet me at the airport?"

"I'll do better than that. I'll come over there to you and we can travel back together."

"Emily I'd love you to but I know you are busy and I didn't like to ask."

"Victoria you know I'd do anything to help you through this time. Now I'm coming over and that's settled. Have you organised your personal belongings to be sent?"

"Yes I have. I've arranged with a company that will be collecting my boxes and transporting them for me. I didn't realise how much Chloe and I had until I started packing up but it's finished now and when we leave I'll have two cases and hand luggage."

"How are you feeling about everything? You have had your life turned upside down."

"Yes it's feels that way. It has been difficult at times and yet it has also been rewarding. Planning the move to live in another country has kept me busy and it has given me a focus in my life. It's been difficult because I know that leaving here is my way of saying good bye to the life I shared with Steven. I suppose it is bittersweet but I'm trying to remain positive."

"I can understand that. You are leaving the place that has been your home for so long but you have lots to look forward when you get here."

"I have been thinking of some ideas but I'll talk to you about them once I get over there."

"What day are you planning on leaving?"

"My boxes are being picked up on Monday morning so I want away from here by mid week."

"Fine. I'll arrive on Monday evening and we can plan to leave by Wednesday."

"Sounds great. Let me know what flight you will be on and I'll have a car waiting for you. When I told Chloe we were moving to leave in Northern Ireland she was so excited at being with Rosa and Nathan again. I think this move will be good for her because she associates this hotel with Steven. She always called it her daddy's hotel and that's how she still thinks of it."

"I agree with you. Coming over here will be the fresh start you both need"

"I'm grateful that no matter how hard it has been I've found an inner strength in God and I can still praise him, even in the worst moments."

"I'm happy for you Victoria. You have made wonderful discoveries with God and there's more to come. I'll ring you with my arrival time and I'll see you Monday evening."

"Yes I look forward to it. Bye."

Emily sat back on the sofa feeling really happy for Victoria and excited that she was coming to live here. She relaxed, putting her head on a cushion for a few minutes rest.

"Emily are you alright darling?"

Startled she sat up straight and yawned. "Oh Jack I didn't mean to fall asleep. I don't usually do that."

"Are you feeling alright? Do you feel ill?"

Emily laughed. "Jack don't fuss, I only fell asleep. I'm just tired from all the hard work I do."

Jack was still concerned. "You are going upstairs right now to have a proper rest."

"I can't I have things planned for today."

"Emily they can wait. You need to rest and no arguments."

"Alright I'll go and have a sleep. I was talking to Victoria and she is coming over next week, I said I'd go over there and travel back with her."

"It depends on how you are feeling. I could go over and check up on the hotel while I'm there."

"That might be a good idea. How are things at The Edgewater? I don't like to talk business with Victoria."

"We have a couple moved in last week and at present they are living in the guest suite until Victoria moves out. They have two children and have been in the business for years. I think they will do a good job there. The hotel needs a boost, it has a five star rating but Steven didn't work to keep it there.

We need to promote it and work hard at living up to what it's supposed to be. Anyway, you go upstairs and have a rest. I'll ring Victoria about next week. I want to check everything is going according to plan over there."

The next week Victoria, Chloe and lots of boxes arrived at the hotel. Jack had travelled with her and he was pleased at the way the Edgewater was running. Business seemed to be increasing and Jack felt a new management with fresh ideas was just what it needed.

Victoria and Chloe stayed in the guest suite and Rosa and Nathan loved having Chloe living there. They had the security of being together as a family and that was good for all of them.

Walking through reception Emily saw Victoria go towards the main entrance.

"Good morning. Going anywhere nice?"

"Yes I need some fresh air."

Emily laughed. "Enjoy the beach Victoria."

Victoria made her way from the road and down the steps that led onto the rocks. The view looking out to sea was beautiful as she walked along the shore. There was no one else about and even though it was cold she felt warm inside. "God you are awesome and this place is the evidence of your wonderful creation. You have given me a new start and a family that loves me and my daughter. Thank you for my life, I never imagined it could be like this."

"I'll always be with you, loving you and supplying your every need. Trust me."

"I do Lord. I trust you for my life, my future and my daughter. You are everything to me. Most of all I've never known such love and acceptance like I've found in you." She sat down on the rocks and took a small bible from her jacket. Looking over the pages she stopped at Hosea and read down the second chapter.

"And it shall be in that day, says the Lord that you will call me, My Husband..."

"I will betroth you to Me forever; Yes, I will betroth you to Me in righteousness and justice, In lovingkindness and mercy; I will betroth you to me in faithfulness, And you shall know the Lord."

Victoria wept as her heart spilled over with love for her Lord. "Lord I look back on my life and I don't know how I lived it without you. I never want to let go of you."

"You won't have to. I have come to give you life abundant."

Victoria walked for awhile and stopped at a rock pool where she picked up a few shells and put them into her pocket. She had an idea for a new painting and the shells would be a reminder of this day when she walked along the beach with the Lord for company.

Approaching the road she realised she had walked further than she had intended. "Why did I do this? I'm tired now and I have to walk back again."

As she turned in the direction of the hotel she felt an urge to keep walking in the direction she had been going. "Lord I'm not sure what this is about but I believe you want me to keep going."

Victoria turned down the path and the lane led towards the beach. "Oh this is lovely." She walked a bit further and then she saw it. She stopped and stared in amazement. "Lord is this the reason you wanted me to come down here?" Just down the lane was a cottage and she felt compelled to go closer and see it. At first she thought there were two cottages but upon closer inspection she realised that it was one cottage and it was quite big. What thrilled her the most was that there was a for sale sign outside it. She took a mental note of the estate agent and began walking back towards the hotel. She felt excited inside and she knew she wanted that cottage. Images of what she could do to it flashed through her mind and she knew it would also be a proper family home for her and Chloe.

When Victoria got back to the hotel she went to see Emily.

"Hi did you enjoy your walk?"

"Oh yes and the Lord told me wonderful things as we walked along the beach. I read from the book of Hosea and his promises are awesome."

"Yes I love it when I read his word and I know he is talking to me through it. You look excited so tell me why."

"Pour me a coffee and I'll tell you. I was making my way back to the hotel when I felt the Lord wanted me to go further along the road. I was feeling tired by this time but I knew not to resist him. Anyway I came to a lane and when I walked down it I came to a lovely big cottage with a for sale sign. I remember the estate agents name but I need to look up his number."

"Don't you want to stay at the hotel?"

"For a time, yes but eventually I'd like my own home. When I married Steven I knew I would be living in at the hotel but at times I resented it when the business began to take over Steven's life. I know that he allowed it to happen but I wasn't always happy living on the premises,"

"I understand that. Jack and I love our lives here and we try to see the advantages in living and working in the same place but we do have to set boundary lines or the business would take over our home life. Now tell me about this cottage."

"It looks quite big but I didn't see much because it has lace curtains on the windows. I knocked on the door but it seems to be empty."

"The best thing to do is telephone the agent and make an appointment to view it. May I come with you?"

"Oh yes I'd like that. I'm so excited yet I've never lived on my own before and I don't know how I'd feel about it."

"We will go and see the place first and take things one step at a time. You don't have to rush into anything."

"You're right. I'm learning to make decisions for myself now although I pray about everything and that makes a big difference. It still feels strange though not having Steven telling me what to do."

"Do you miss him?"

"I miss the man I married. Steven was kinder and loving. I'm not sure when he began to change, it was a gradual thing. He began to take on new projects for the hotel and then he developed other interests outside of work and associated with people I never got to know. I don't miss the person he became but the man I fell in love with I was missing long before the accident."

"That must have been difficult for you, watching the changes in Steven's character. I'm glad though that you are making a new life for yourself and Chloe. I believe you have lots of good things to look forward to."

"Yes I think so too. Learning to do things for myself is turning into quite an adventure."

They both laughed. "Victoria I'm going to enjoy the coming months."

Victoria picked up a slice of chocolate cream cake. "And I'm going to enjoy this now."

26

"GOOD MORNING SLEEPY head. I've brought you tea and toast."

Emily sat up and yawned. "Thank you Jack. I don't know what is wrong with me lately but I seem to be tired all the time."

"I've noticed. Maybe you should have today off. Rest for awhile this morning and then have a relaxing bath."

"That sounds so appealing. I think I will Jack."

He kissed her. "Well I'm off to work but I'll come up and see you later."

"Oh I've just remembered that I'm going out with Victoria later. We are going to view the cottage I was telling you about."

"Don't be over doing things Emily."

"I won't. We are just going to have a look at it and then back here."

"Good. No shopping trips. I know you and Victoria and it isn't always a good idea you two going out together."

She laughed. "I promise to be good and come straight home." She teased.

"I should think so. Bye for now."

As Jack left the children came in and climbed into bed beside Emily.

"Mummy why are you not going to work with daddy? Are you sick?"

"No Rosa I'm just tired and daddy thought I needed to rest today."

"Are you staying in bed?"

"Yes Nathan for a little while."

"Mummy we like it when we get into your bed." Nathan hugged her.

"I know you do and I love having a cuddle with you both in my bed."

"Mum I really like having Chloe with us. I feel like I have my friend living in the same place as me and its great."

"I'm glad because she needs a friend right now."

"I know. She told me her daddy is in heaven but she misses him down here."

Emily smiled at her childlike innocence. "I'm sure she does miss him but she has you as her friend and that will help her. Everything is new to her now she is living here and it will take a little time for her to get used to it."

"I know mum but I prayed for her and she knows that Jesus loves her."

"That's really good Rosa. She needs lots of love now."

"Mummy I know that Jesus loves me and you do too."

Emily laughed and kissed Nathan's head. This was one of the times when her heart was so full of love for her children she thought it would burst.

"Rosa and Nathan I have your breakfast ready." Anna came in. "Come on you two, I think your mum needs to rest now. You can see her later."

"Thank you Anna." The children jumped off the bed and raced out the door.

"If you need anything, just call me."

"I will. I'll rest this morning but I have to go out for a short time later."

"I'll leave you in peace."

Emily slept for two hours and then she had a warm bath. She dressed in a comfortable trouser suit and she felt better as she styled her hair and put on her make-up, thankful it covered the dark circles under her eyes.

Anna had fresh coffee ready for her and she brought it through to the lounge with a sandwich. "I thought you might like something before you go out."

"Thank you Anna that was very thoughtful of you. Was there any post sent up for me."

"Yes there was one letter for you." She picked it up of the table and gave it to Emily.

Sipping her coffee Emily looked at the envelope and noticed it was hand written so the letter was personal. The post mark was Bournemouth and she was puzzled about the sender. She opened the envelope and took out two sheets of paper; there was no address on the letter.

Dear Emily

I wasn't sure if I should write to you after everything that has happened. I know that Victoria has left for Ireland so I hope I don't place you in an awkward situation, that is not my intention.

I wanted to thank you for being the person I needed you to be. We have known each other for years and no matter what situation I got myself into I could always depend on you. You never judged me and you said the things I needed to hear even when I didn't like it. Emily I have never told you how much I looked up to you and in a way I still do.

My other reason for writing is to tell you about George. Now before you go thinking that I've found a replacement for Steven, it's not like that. George is someone I work with and we have been friends for a long time. He was with me the last time you saw me outside the chapel of rest. I told him you were an old friend and that you are a Christian. He then told me that he used to be a Christian but then his wife died and he got angry with God about it. I think he is still hurting inside. Anyway, George and I both realise that we have made a lot of mistakes in our lives and we haven't yet worked out what to do about that. We have gone to a church together although neither of us has made any commitment to God yet. I think I'm getting my life on the right track and I hope George is too.

Emily thank you for being who you are. I'm grateful that you have been a part of my life. I haven't given you my address because you don't need to reply; besides I wouldn't want to compromise you with your family.

Love and God Bless

Sophie

Emily was pleased and surprised by the letter. At least Sophie was trying to get her life sorted. She was delighted that she and George had gone to church. Maybe they would give God the opportunity to bless both their lives.

Emily placed the letter back in the envelope and was still thinking about it when the door opened and Jack came in.

"Are you here to check up on me?"

"Yes I thought I'd catch you out doing paperwork."

"No way darling. I slept this morning and I enjoyed the rest. Jack I got a letter from Sophie. It's there if you want to read it."

Jack frowned as he took the letter out.

"It's alright Jack, there's no need to look anxious."

He smiled at the way his wife knew him so well as he began to read the letter. Afterwards he put it back in the envelope and handed it to Emily. "I never got to know Sophie but I hope her life is beginning to change for the better. Maybe this man George will be good to her and together they will find some purpose to their lives."

"Jack I'm feeling a little guilty. I wondered if I should tell Victoria that I knew the woman that Steven was involved with."

Jack sat down beside her. "Slow down Emily. Victoria is still grieving and I know that she's here to begin a new life and it's great she has a relationship with God but she is still vulnerable. If you tell her about Sophie she may feel hurt or betrayed. You have to be careful."

"I know that Jack but I feel I'm deceiving her and that she will feel betrayed anyway."

"Emily pray about this because you need God's wisdom and his perfect timing."

"I will Jack and I won't say anything unless I believe God wants me to."

At 2:30pm Victoria and Emily sat outside the cottage in the car. The estate agent had agreed to meet them there and they watched as a silver car drove up behind theirs.

"Let's go and meet the man Victoria."

"Hello I'm Mr Harvey pleased to see you."

They shook hands and then he opened up the cottage for them.

"I'll leave you ladies to look around. Call me if there's anything you want to know."

"Thank you."

They went inside and Victoria gasped at the size of the living area.

"Emily it's bigger than I imagined. The details say it has two reception rooms, kitchen, three bedrooms, bathroom and the attic has been converted."

"So that would give you four bedrooms."

"No it wouldn't. The attic would be my studio. Emily I'm going to paint again and this place would be perfect."

Emily saw the smile on her face and she looked radiant. "That's great news. I was hoping you would begin again."

"You know I feel like a light has been switched on inside me. I have an image in my mind of an artist studio with my pictures in it. I want to buy this cottage. The location is perfect; I have the mountains at the back and the ocean in front of the cottage."

"Victoria it needs some work done to it. I think it has been empty for a long time and there is some renovation work to be done."

"Oh I know that. I'd also want it all decorated as well but I can see the potential this place has and I like it."

Victoria I'm sure it will be beautiful by the time you have finished with it."

"It will be alright if we stay at the hotel while the work is being done?"

"Of course you can. You are family and the hotel is your home for as long as you want it to be. It will take a few months to get this place the way you want it but it will give you something to aim for. I'm glad you are beginning to realise that there is a purpose to your life."

They went outside and found the agent. "Do you like the cottage then? It has a lot of potential."

"Yes I do like it and I'd like to buy it."

"That's good news. I can have the paperwork ready by tomorrow as there are no other offers in. You do realise that there needs to be some work done to the cottage. It has stood empty for quite awhile."

Victoria smiled. "That's because it was meant for me. I will be staying at the Cedar Lodge Hotel so if you can arrange to bring the paperwork to me then we can go over it."

"I'll telephone you tomorrow and we can meet later in the week."

"I look forward to it."

Victoria was like an excited child all afternoon. "Emily there are so many changes going on in my life I can hardly believe it. The cottage will be perfect for Chloe and I and it will be beautiful when it is completed."

"Think of the fun you will have choosing colours for it and furniture for all the rooms."

Victoria laughed. "I will love every minute of it."

"I'm glad you decided to paint again. I know you have always said that it was just a hobby but I know your work and it's good. I hope you begin to take yourself more seriously. You could have a whole new career if you wanted to."

"Yes I have thought about that. I've also been praying about another idea. It would take a while to plan it out so it's for the future."

"Tell me?"

I know you are involved in the children's home and you and Jack have several projects up and running. I'd like to do something worthwhile with my life and also to enrich other people's lives. I believe I'm to paint, it's a gift that God has given me and I aim to use it. My idea is to encourage children and teenagers in art. I would like to develop a programme that will give children the opportunity to develop their artistic talent. So many times it is left unused or not given the attention it deserves. I'm sure there are children who are creative and I want to take what they have and build on it. I know from experience the satisfaction I get from sketching or painting, and I feel good about what I do. If I can teach the children to develop their talent then I believe it will also help to boost their confidence and raise their self-esteem."

"Victoria that is a great idea. The children need people to take an interest in them and encourage them and you would be good at it. I know you have said this idea is for the future but can I share it with the matron the next time I talk with her. I'd like to see what response it would have."

"Yes and then it would help me in developing the programme."

The next few weeks were busy for everyone and it was a time of accepting Steven's death and how it had changed each one of there lives. They had to accept that they would never be the same people they were before the accident. While they had to move on with their lives they also had to adjust to the void that was left. Time would help them come to terms with the loss but only God could fill the emptiness that now existed within the family as a whole.

Jack was becoming more anxious about Emily as she was always tired and several times she came into work and by the afternoon she had to go and have a rest. Jack had tried to get her to see a doctor but she kept insisting she wasn't sick. He wasn't entirely convinced.

Sitting at his desk trying to do some work he was finding it hard to focus. He realised he was feeling a little insecure and he knew that wasn't the way God wanted him to be. "Lord what is with me? I need your assurance."

Suddenly he realised that having recently lost his brother he knew he couldn't deal with anything being wrong with Emily. "Lord I'm sorry, I shouldn't be getting on like this."

"Be still and know that I'm God. Jack don't be afraid for Emily, trust me."

"You know all about her and she's your child so I'm choosing to trust you for her."

Amy came in with his coffee. "What's up with you? You look depressed."

"I'll be fine. I've been a little worried about Emily but I've prayed and God knows what she needs better than me. Have you seen her this morning?"

"No I thought she might be having a rest."

"She seems to be doing a lot of that lately."

"Why don't you suggest that she sees the doctor?"

"If I suggest going to the doctor once more I dread to think what she will do to me."

Amy laughed. "She can be a little bit stubborn."

"That's the understatement of the year. She is a lot stubborn."

"Are you talking about me?" Emily walked into the office.

"Would you like a coffee?"

"Yes please Amy and close the door after you so that I can torture my husband."

Amy smiled at Jack. "That would be my pleasure."

"Honey are you feeling better?"

"Of course I am." She walked towards him and the room began to spin. Jack jumped up and grabbed hold of her before she fell. "Steady darling. I'll get you to the sofa'

She set down and Jack rang through to Amy. "I need a jug of cold water and ice. Emily isn't feeling well.

Amy was back in two minutes with the water and some lemon slices she knew that Emily liked. Emily sipped the water. "I feel better now; I must have stood up to quickly."

"Emily no more excuses. You are going back to bed and I'm telephoning for the doctor."

Emily felt too tired to argue. "Ok Jack you win."

The doctor arrived in the afternoon to find Emily lying on top of the bed.

"Hello doctor, I feel such a fraud bringing you out here."

"I'll be the judge of that Emily. There has to be something wrong for you to be this way. I'll do a few tests and see if we can figure out what the problem is." Doctor Green was with her for what seemed a long time and Emily watched him scribble in his notepad as he checked her blood pressure and did a few other tests. He didn't speak much but there was a frown on his head as he concentrated on what he was doing. "Now I think I know what is causing you to be so tired, you are pregnant Emily."

She felt shocked. "I can't be. I shouldn't be." She got flustered. "Now how did that happen?"

The doctor laughed. "I think we know how it happened."

"Yes of course I do. I'm just surprised."

"I'll send off this blood test just as a routine check and if you are tired you must rest more."

"If you see Jack on your way out don't say anything."

"I won't. I'll leave you to surprise him."

After the doctor had gone Emily rested. "Lord this baby is a surprise. I think I'm shocked and pleased at the same time."

"Don't be anxious about this little one. It is my gift to you and Jack."

"Thank you Lord I'm overwhelmed by you."

As she lay with her eyes closed the bedroom door opened and Jack came in looking anxious. "How are you darling? What did the doctor say?"

"He took a blood test and said I needed to rest more."

"Is that it? Surely he could see there is a problem. I'm not happy Emily."

"Jack there is nothing to worry about. I'm normal."

"Emily you nearly passed out this morning, now that isn't normal."

"Jack that sometimes happens to pregnant women."

"Maybe so but you're not...."

Emily laughed.

"Darling are you pregnant?"

"About two months and I never even thought about it. What a surprise."

"I think shock is a better way to describe it." He looked serious.

"Jack are you alright? I know we hadn't planned this baby but I'm getting to like the idea."

He kissed her. "I'm happy too. This little one is a gift from God and a blessing in our family now. It will give us something to focus on and my parents will be delighted."

"Yes, God's timing is perfect. I'd like to keep it to ourselves for a while at least until we get used to the idea."

"Yes, that's fine with me."

He kissed her. "I love you Emily and this is going to be a special time for us."

"I love you and this little one is a lovely gift from God."

27 VICTORIA BOUGHT THE cottage and had plans drawn up for major renovation work. She involved herself as much as possible with the work as it gave her the drive she needed to get on with life after Steven. Most of the time she didn't think about him but there were times when she wished their marriage had been more loving. She had more unpleasant memories than good ones and she felt sad about that.

"Hi Victoria what are you doing this morning?"

"I've been looking over some brochures for fitted kitchens but the builder doesn't need a final decision just yet."

Emily sat down on the sofa. "Are you alright? You seem to be a bit down this morning."

"Oh I'll be fine. I still get days when I miss Steven and I'm sorry our marriage was such a sham. It isn't just me that he hurt; there was the other woman in his life. Sophie has been left to pick up the pieces of her life too."

"Victoria you are supposed to be looking forward to the future not dwelling on the past."

"I know and most of the time I'm fine. I get a bit curious about Sophie and why she would want to get involved with Steven. We know that she wasn't a one night stand so they had an on going relationship."

Emily began to feel uncomfortable. She could see that Victoria was still hurting and looking for answers to satisfy the feelings she had about Sophie.

Emily whispered a silent prayer. "What will I do Lord?"

"The truth will set you free."

Emily immediately saw the sense in being honest. It would help Victoria and put a stop to any curiosity she felt about her. Being honest would also help her because she felt she had been deceiving Victoria and because they had grown so close she didn't want any secrets between them.

"Victoria what do you think you would gain by knowing more about Sophie?"

"I'm not sure. At present I struggle with my imagination. I didn't know Sophie so I think she must have had something that I didn't or Steven wouldn't have got involved with her. I really tried to be a good wife to Steven but when I found out about Sophie I felt so inadequate. It was the most awful feeling and I'm not sure that I'm over it. I mean, here I am beginning a new life here, buying a cottage and planning to paint again but am I only fooling myself? Can I really do the things that are in my heart to do?"

"Of course you can. You have a wonderful future ahead of you."

"Yes but how do I deal with the past?"

Emily took a deep breath. "Victoria you know how much Jack and I love you and Chloe. We would do anything to help you and protect you from being hurt any more than what you have been."

"Yes I know that but what has that got to do with Steven and the other woman he was involved with?"

"I know who the other woman is. I know Sophie."

Silence seemed to hang in the air as Victoria tried to take in what Emily was saying. "Do you mean you actually knew her?"

"Yes. When you hired the private detective months ago and he wasn't able to find information about Sophie's past I realised then that I knew her. Sophie grew up in the same children's home as I. She was a very shy insecure girl and she didn't mix easily with the other children. After we left we both got jobs in a hotel. Sophie never stayed long in one place and eventually she left and moved on to a different place. We lost contact with her continual moving around and I heard nothing more until she got involved with Steven."

"Emily why didn't you tell me?"

"I had no evidence at first. I suspected it was the same girl but because I wasn't sure I couldn't risk telling you in case I was wrong."

"When did you become sure?"

"Just before Christmas when I came over to stay with you and Chloe. I'd gone for a walk in the hotel gardens and she was there. She had been waiting for Steven but he had stood her up so she left."

"Did you see her again?"

"Yes the day before the funeral. I'd gone to the chapel of rest to deliver some flowers and she come to say good-bye to Steven. Victoria believe me you have no reason to feel inadequate. Sophie may have been the other woman in Steven's life but she was as much a victim in all this as you are. She made the mistake of falling for someone who took advantage of every situation."

"What else do you know about her?"

"I know that Sophie was always looking for someone to love her and take care of her. Every relationship she got involved in she built her life around that person. If the relationship went sour then she fell apart for a time. I used to try to advise her against building her life around one person and that she needed to find peace within herself. She had such high expectations when she got into a relationship."

"I get the impression that she lived in a fairytale and that she was waiting on prince charming to come into her life and take care of her."

"Yes she was like that and we both know that it doesn't happen like that. Sophie didn't always face reality and men did take advantage of her. Steven used her and she was so desperate to be loved she believed anything he would have told her."

"When did you last speak to her?"

"Before the funeral, however I have received a letter from her. She hasn't given me a return address because she doesn't want me to contact her. She is sorry for everything that happened and she is trying to learn from her mistakes and put the past behind her."

"Maybe this time she will get it right."

"Victoria you are taking this very calm but I don't think you are telling me how you are really feeling."

"I suppose I'm wondering how you could keep something like this from me. It feels like a betrayal yet I know you would never hurt me. It feels strange knowing that you knew Sophie and she was involved with Steven."

"I'm sorry if you feel hurt by this but there wasn't a right time to tell you before. I struggled knowing something that you didn't and now I'm glad I've told you. I didn't want to deceive you but when Steven died I could hardly tell you then because you were in no fit state to hear news like that."

"I know you're right and I'm not hurt at what you have told me. I know the truth now and I can face up to that."

"Victoria I don't expect to hear from Sophie again so can we agree to put this behind us now."

"Yes it belongs in the past and we will leave it there."

Emily went upstairs for a rest and she felt so tired. Sharing her heart with Victoria had cleared up the situation but now she was emotionally drained. She slept for a while and then Jack brought her tea and she told him about her conversation with Victoria.

"I'm glad you have told her the truth because I know it bothered you. Now that it's sorted out I'm still concerned about you."

"Jack I'll be fine. I was tired the first few months I was pregnant before. I'll make sure I rest every afternoon until I'm feeling better."

"I'll hold you to that. We have been invited to a gala night at the Royal Court.

Our parents are being presented with an award for their service to the industry and we all have to wear formal dress."

"It sounds exciting. I'm glad something nice is being done for them. They have worked very hard to achieve their success in business.

They deserve an award. We could have the children present flowers to them that night or some special token they can keep."

"Yes that would be very thoughtful. I spoke to my dad earlier and mum is busy having the main ballroom decorated and she is adding to the guest list by the day."

Emily laughed. "I can imagine her organising everyone but it will do her good to stay busy. Have you told them we will be there?"

"No I wanted to talk to you and Victoria first."

"I'm sure she will love to go. She needs to get back into social events again."

"I was thinking we could tell my parents about the baby when we go over there."

"Yes it will be a lovely surprise for them and hopefully add to the celebrations."

"I believe this family is going to experience lots of newness in our lives. It's just something that is in my spirit and I feel excited by it."

"Jack this new baby is a good example and only the Lord knows what else is in store."

28

THE ROYAL COURT Hotel was a buzz of excitement. The main ballroom had been decorated and the sheer luxury of the room was breathtaking. The décor in colours of gold, red and ivory with chandeliers lighting the large room in an aura of glowing colour as the crystal drops reflected like a rainbow hue.

The furniture of walnut tables and chairs upholstered in red velvet seat covering complimented the red carpeting. The tableware of finest china and solid silver cutlery, crystal goblets, water jugs and a variety of glasses and crystal champagne flutes. The tables were adorned with beautiful flower arrangements and candelabras with red and ivory candles were appropriately placed down the centre of them.

The hotel was one of the most prestigious in Kensington and stepping through its doors was stepping into excellence of the highest degree. The furnishings throughout the hotel were chosen carefully and the rooms were decorated with a no expense spared attitude. The guests received the utmost service from the staff that had been trained to perform their duties by seeing that every guest was an individual who was treated as though they were the only person in the hotel. It was important that a guest would leave the hotel satisfied by their stay and having the desire to return again.

All of the Dillon-Spence family had arrived at the hotel for the gala dinner being given to honour Jack Senior and his wife Sarah for their years of service to the hotel industry. There were lots of friends and business acquaintances invited to this special occasion and the hotel staff were just as excited by the atmosphere in the hotel.

Sarah was in their penthouse getting ready for the evening ahead. She had chosen a long emerald green satin gown decorated with sequins, she had her hair styled back from her face and her make up immaculate. She wore a white diamond necklace with a green emerald and matching earrings and on her head a white diamond tiara.

Jack senior dressed in a dinner suit and bow tie looked elegant and Sarah smiled as she watched him in the mirror and she remembered so well the reasons she had fell in love with this handsome man all those years ago. She sat down at her dressing table for one last look before they went downstairs. He came and stood behind her smiling. "Sarah you are beautiful but then you always have been."

"Thank you darling and you are still that good looking man who swept me off my feet a long time ago. Jack I know tonight is a happy occasion but in some ways it is bittersweet. Steven isn't here to share it with us and I miss him so much."

"I know sweetheart and I miss him too. At least we think about him and because he is our son I suppose he will always be there inside our minds."

Sarah stood up and turned and faced him. "I love you Jack even more now because we have come through so much and worked so hard. We stuck together and we became stronger."

"Yes that's all true. You are my soul mate Sarah and I will love you forever."

She kissed him. "I think we should be joining the family now."

As they were about to leave the door knocked and in came Jack and Emily.

"We were about to go downstairs. Is everything alright?"

"Everything is running on time mum. Tonight is going to be perfect for you and dad."

"You two look stunning. Mum you are so beautiful, I've never seen anyone wear emerald green like you do. You really sparkle."

Sarah laughed. "I think the diamonds have something to do with that. Very appropriate."

Emily kissed her father-in law on the cheek. "You are so hand-some and I'm really proud of you both."

"Thank you my dear. You flatter me and I like it!"

"I think we need to be going downstairs now. I wouldn't want our guests to be kept waiting to long."

"In a few minutes mum. Emily and I have something we want to share with you."

"There's nothing wrong?" Sarah looked anxious.

"No mum not at all."

Jack was smiling all over his face and Emily grinned at him. "Go on, tell them."

"Mum, dad we would like you to be the first to know that Emily is pregnant and you will soon have another grandchild."

"Congratulations." Everyone hugged each other.

"What a lovely surprise to begin our evening. We are so happy for you both; this is great news for our family."

They went downstairs and all the guests had arrived and had been directed to the ballroom were staff in charge of the seating arrangements saw to it that everyone sat were they should be. The Dillon-Spence family entered the room together and everyone stood and clapped as they walked to the top table and were seated. The dinner began and as the staff served the meal there was a hub of chatter as people talked and ate their way through each course.

After the meal the floor was cleared for the dancing and the band got under way. It was a time of social enjoyment and the first that the family had come together from Steven's death. Jack and Sarah led the first dance and soon other couples joined them. Family friends made sure Victoria didn't feel left out and she had no shortage of dancing partners.

The children were excited at being allowed to stay up late and Rosa and Chloe loved being dressed up in formal dress. Nathan wore a little suit and bow tie but he stayed close to Anna, he wasn't sure he liked all this fuss.

At an appropriate time the children presented their grand-parents with gifts, a gold pocket watch, engraved for Jack senior and a gold locket, engraved for their grandmother and a basket of flowers. Photographs were taken of the moment and then the children were taken by their nanny upstairs to get ready for bed.

The director and all the board members were present and Mr John Taylor presented Jack and Sarah with a trophy of crystal and gold for their years of service to the industry.

The evening was a great success and the family felt such a release from the stress and pressure of the last few months.

Later when everyone had left or gone to there rooms in the hotel Jack sat in their living room sipping a brandy. Sarah sat down facing him. "Our family and friends gave us a wonderful evening Jack, everything about it will always be so memorable."

"Yes I'm very proud tonight. The Dillon-Spence name has again been honoured and it has been worth all the years of hard work."

"And knowing you there will be more years to come. I can't see you retiring and going off somewhere quietly."

Jack laughed. "You know me so well Sarah. Retirement is something I don't even think about. Besides we aren't that age for a few years yet."

Sarah kissed his cheek. "I'll leave you in peace with your thoughts. Good night."

"Good night darling."

Sarah got into bed and picked up her bible and read through John chapter fourteen. "Lord I'm grateful for the peace you have given to me and that you comfort me in every situation. Thank you for a lovely evening with my family. You know my heart and I don't need to pretend with you and I don't have to wear a smile to try and deceive you. I miss my son Lord and I will always love Steven but I believe you will give me what I need each day to get through. I thank you for the news of our new baby, you are the giver of new life and you are restoring unto us a precious gift."

"I've given you my peace and my love. I know your sorrow but you can trust me to give you the strength you need for each day. Lean harder, I can take the strain that you don't need to carry. I'm here for you for today and all of your tomorrows. This new life is my gift, enjoy what I'm doing Sarah."

Sarah closed her eyes to savour the peace in her spirit as she realised that her relationship with God was one she could embrace with all of her heart. She was never afraid to be vulnerable in her prayers to him and in his presence she found fullness of joy.

The next morning Jack and Emily were having breakfast with the children when the morning papers arrived. Jack looked over them while Emily had a second cup of tea in peace as Anna had taken the children off to get dressed.

"Emily you should see the papers. There is a small column about last night and pictures of my parents and the family group. There is one of us together which is quite good."

"Let's have a look? I didn't expect to be in the papers."

Jack opened another paper and there were more pictures and a write up. "I think the Dillon-Spence name must be famous."

"Alright Jack; don't let a few pictures go to your head. It's news today and history tomorrow."

The door knocked and Emily answered it. "Renee come in." They hugged each other.

"Good morning you two I thought I'd come by for a quick chat before we all go our separate ways."

Jack stood up and Renee hugged him. "How are things going for you Renee?"

"Jack my life couldn't be better. The hotel is beautiful from the Dillon-Spence Group took it over and completely renovated and decorated it. The hotel is busy and already showing a bigger profit"

"I'm glad Renee. You seem to be a lot happier from the last time we talked."

"I am and I have so much to be thankful for."

"Jack will we let her in on the secret?"

Jack smiled. "I knew you couldn't keep it quiet."

"What secret? Don't keep me in suspense."

"Go on Emily. Tell her."

"Renee we are having another baby."

Renee hugged her and Jack. "That is wonderful news."

"We have only told Jack's parents but I knew you would be happy for us."

"I'm happy and surprised."

"Same here Renee. I thought Emily was over tired because she works so hard and neither of us thought she might be pregnant."

Renee laughed. "Jack you make sure she doesn't put in long hours now. I know her of old."

"I'll take care of her."

"I have to leave now but I'll keep in touch with you. I love you both."

There were good bye hugs and Renee left to return to South Devon.

The family returned to Northern Ireland and it felt good to be home. Work was going well on Victoria's cottage and she was beginning to get her life back on track. Accepting Steven's death still proved difficult at times but mostly she hurt for Chloe who had lost a daddy and still missed him. She knew the sorrow his parents were going through and that hurt her too because there was nothing she could do to take away their pain.

When the cottage was completed Victoria was looking forward to moving in and planning her career as an artist. She knew there would always be opportunities to work within the family business but she wanted to launch out on her own.

Emily began working fewer hours as her pregnancy progressed. She loved every moment of this special time and as she got bigger in size she blossomed even more. Standing in front of the mirror she placed her hand on her tummy as the baby kicked. "Jack come and feel this. I'm sure this baby is a boy and a possible footballer."

Jack laughed as he felt the little one move around. "Emily this is such a miracle and you look beautiful darling."

"I don't know about that. It's hard to feel beautiful when I'm growing bigger by the day."

"Being pregnant suits you. There is a lovely glow in your eyes and your face is radiant."

"I'll take all that as a compliment and believe you mean it. I wouldn't want God to strike you with a bolt of lightning."

"Very funny Emily. I'm glad I know my heavenly father better than that."

"I'm going out this morning. I had a telephone call from Iris Boyd and I said I'd call up to the children's home today."

"Any problems?"

"There could be. Iris wants me to talk to one of the girls, I'm not sure why but I'll find out soon enough."

Emily drove to Cedar Children's Home and parked her car. Getting out she saw the younger children play in the garden. She stopped to watch them and in her heart she prayed for them that whether they were placed in families or spent their time in here in the home that they would know that they were loved. She prayed they would know the love of God in their lives and that love would be demonstrated through those who came into contact with them.

"Hello Emily. I'm glad you could come."

Emily turned around. "Iris, I've just been watching the little ones having fun."

"Yes I saw you and I'm sure you have already prayed for each one of them."

Emily laughed. "You know me so well Iris. Shall we go inside?"

"Yes I need your advice. We can talk over our coffee and I think a slice of chocolate cake. I know you can't resist Emily and you make me feel good about myself."

"Lead the way Iris, I'm all yours."

In the lounge Amanda sat staring out of the window. She had been biting her nails and her fingers had bled. Her complexion was pale and there were dark circles under her eyes, her shoulder length hair uncombed, she looked so lost.

"Hello Amanda, I'm Emily."

The girl looked up but she didn't speak and her expression remained blank.

"Can I join you?"

Amanda lowered her head. "That's up to you, there are plenty of seats."

Emily sat down beside her and she could almost feel the emotions and pain that were going on inside Amanda.

"Amanda, I know you are new here. How are you settling in?"

The girl looked up with a cold stare. "What do you want to know for? Are you some kind of social worker or just some do gooder come to visit?"

"I'm neither. I do some work here and I also work at a hotel down the road. Some of the older children come and work there too."

"Well I'm only fourteen so I won't be working at your hotel unless they do child labour here."

Emily smiled. "No Amanda they won't be sending you out to work yet. I understand you have been moved to several different places to live."

"I've been in and out of foster care lots of times and I've been passed from one home to another. I'll be glad when I'm old enough to get out of here and get a job and a place of my own."

Emily looked at her and saw herself all those years ago when she was in care and her heart ached for her. "Lord help me to love her with your love."

"Amanda I know it is difficult for you now and with all the moving around you have never had a chance to settle in one place for long but you will have the opportunity to do that here."

"What's the point? Tell me what I have to look forward to?"

"That depends a lot on you."

"How do you work that out? I hadn't planned for my life to turn out the way it has. I don't enjoy not having a proper home. I once had two parents; I know you might find that hard to believe. I used to think I was a normal kid but my mum left, went off with someone else. She told me she would come back for me but she never did. I was six years old and I used to watch out of the window hoping she would turn the corner and I'd be ready to go with her. Guess what? It never happened. I still had a dad but when mum left he began to drink. He became this horrible person who wasn't like my dad at all. When I first went into care I realised then that my mum loved someone else more than me and my dad loved to drink more than he loved me. No one in his family wanted me; he was a drunk who had managed to turn everyone against him. When the social worker came and took me away I heard someone say it was for the best. Best for who? Now tell me Emily, what do you mean when you say that it depends on me?"

Emily was torn at the rejection that had furiously vented itself on her.

"Amanda I'm so sorry that the people who should have loved you most were the ones that let you down. That must be very painful for you. I understand your anger and disappointment."

Amanda looked defiantly at her with eyes that blinked back tears. "Sure you understand. You would be surprised at how many people tell me that they understand but it doesn't change anything. Since I can remember, it all stays the same."

"Amanda it doesn't have to stay the same. You can make a difference to your own life."

"But how…?"

"I know there is nothing that you can do about the things that have happened in the past, you can't change what has happened but you can aim to have a better future. You can learn to accept responsibility for your life and you can stop blaming everyone for your unhappiness."

Amanda sat up straight and pushed her hair behind her ear. "You mean I'm to do things like schoolwork and accept I'm going to be in this place until it's time for me to leave and get a job. I don't know, I feel so lonely at times. I don't seem to be able to get to know people although I can get into a fight with no problem."

"Amanda what is it going to benefit you by making life hard for yourself? If you take your anger out on other people then they won't want to be with you. Now that seems a lonelier option."

Amanda began to cry. "Maybe I don't want to live. Sometimes I wish that I'd never been born."

Emily reached out and took hold of Amanda's hands. "Listen to me. Amanda it is no mistake that you were born."

"It had to be. Nobody has ever loved me enough to keep me in their life. I feel like some package that always gets delivered to the wrong address and then it's return to sender as in social services. I used to dream of being hugged and of having a mum to read me a bedtime story. I seem to have started out alright but then it went wrong. I know I will never trust anyone because they only let you down. I wish I'd never been born."

Emily stood up and put her arm around her. "Believe me. You are not a mistake, you are beautiful and your life is precious."

"How can you say that? I'm not nice looking and I'm angry all the time."

"You are angry because you have been hurt and let down by people you needed to depend on. It's alright to feel angry; it's what you do with that anger that's important. Don't allow it to eat into your life anymore than it has."

Amanda stamped her foot. "I keep telling you that I don't have a future. Why are you here anyway? You wouldn't know how it feels, just look at you. The clothes you wear, the make up and your hair. You are pregnant so I suppose you have a husband who loves you. How would you know anything about my life and how it feels?"

"You are right Amanda. I do have everything that you have said but it wasn't always like that. I grew up in a children's home and then when I left I got pregnant to a man who didn't want to know me."

Amanda was surprised. "How did you survive?"

"I always believed in God and even as a child in the home I knew he loved me. The matron of the home loved all of us and when it was time for me to leave she helped to get me a place to stay and a job. I met a man and fell in love for the first time and because I'd been so lonely I thought this person would look after me. He did love me but he didn't want children so he left me."

"You must have been very frightened."

Emily smiled. "Yes I was but I remembered that God loved me no matter what and I decided to commit my life to him."

"Oh I've heard all that God stuff before but I've never believed it."

Emily laughed. "I don't know what you have been told but the truth is, God loved you so much that he sent his Son Jesus to die for you. He loves you now Amanda and he has a future for you but it's your choice."

"Sorry but I don't get it. How would someone dying for me give me a future and before you tell me it's got something to do with sins I've got so many of those I wouldn't even tell you about them." Emily could see that Amanda was already taking a step forward in being vulnerable. "Amanda everyone commits sins but you need to see things the way God does. What I mean is, God loves you and it was because of the sin in the world that he sent Jesus to pay the price for sin so we don't have to. When he died it was for your sins and mine and the shedding of his blood covers our sin. You don't need to try to make yourself better; God loves you as you are."

"Aren't you supposed to ask for forgiveness?"

"Yes. If you are willing to accept Jesus into your life and you are sorry for things that you know were wrong and then you are forgiven. Having a relationship with him makes all the difference to your life. You can trust him and he won't let you down and even when we get things wrong all we do is tell him we're sorry and move on."

Amanda went quiet as she puzzled over what Emily had told her. She wasn't so sure about trusting anyone not even God.

"Tell me what you are thinking?"

"You make it sound like my life could be different and I want to believe you yet it sounds too good to be true."

"Amanda it's true. Remember when I first started to talk with you. You said that you were a mistake."

"Yes that's true."

"No it's not. God doesn't see you as a mistake. There's a verse in the bible in the book of Jeremiah, chapter one. It says, "Before I formed you in the womb, I knew you…" Amanda God knew you before you were formed in your mother's womb and he still knows you now."

"I didn't think the bible said that."

"I'll give you one more. Psalm one hundred and thirty nine, "For you formed my inward parts; You covered me in my mother's womb. I praise you for I am fearfully and wonderfully made;" "Amanda he is talking about you. The bible is not just a history book; it's much more than that. We can learn all about what God thinks about us and how he wants us to live in order to have a great future, one he wants to bless us with. It's all true and you can depend on it."

"So it really means that God cares about me? I know some foster parents cared about me but I always felt like a charity case and I know I didn't always make life easy for them. I like talking to you. Will you come back and see me?"

"Of course I will. If you need to talk to me at any time then Iris can reach me."

"I'm still not sure about the trusting God bit. It's a lot to take in."

"He understands that. Amanda you can make life better for yourself while you are here. Iris isn't just the matron because it's her job, she really cares and she can help you a lot."

"But you'll still come back?"

"Yes I've said so. I'll help you in any way I can. I know from experience how difficult life can be but you don't have to go through it alone. Now why don't you begin by looking after yourself? You have lovely hair so take care of it."

"I will and I'll go to school."

"That is a good starting point. Now I have to go but I'll come back again soon."

"Emily do you have a bible I can read. I'd like to know more before I make any decisions."

"I'll get you one before I leave. I'll be thinking about you." Emily hugged her and Amanda put her arms around her. Emily could sense the urgently within her to be loved. "Bye Amanda, remember what we talked about today."

"I will. Bye."

Emily went to see Iris in her office. She sat down and felt drained emotionally.

"Well Emily, tell me what you think about Amanda."

"She is a frightened, insecure young girl who is afraid to trust anyone yet she is so lonely and longs to be loved."

"I agree with you although she has caused quite a lot of arguments with the other children from she has arrived here."

"Yes, she admitted she sometimes makes life difficult but I think I made a breakthrough with her. I tried to get her to see that her life is worth living and while she can't change the past she can make the future something to look forward to. She asked if she could have a bible to read. I think she is searching for answers to questions that are inside her and at present she is afraid to trust even God."

"I'll go and see her later and bring her a bible. Hopefully she will begin to see me as her friend and not just the matron of the home."

"I think we will see some change. She has said she will begin to look after herself more and do her school work."

"Good, I'll be encouraging her and if she improves then I'll begin giving her some responsibility and try to build her confidence."

"Yes that would be a good goal to aim for. I'm going to have to leave you to it. I must get back before Jack sends out a search party. Call me if Amanda needs me. I want to support her anyway I can."

"Thank you Emily. I'll keep you informed of any changes and hopefully they will be good ones."

As Emily drove home she prayed for Amanda. "God I can only tell her about you but she needs to experience you in her life. She needs to know your heart of love that heals the pain that has been inflicted on her through neglect and rejection."

"Don't be anxious for Amanda. I care for her just like I care for you. It will be my love that will draw her."

Emily smiled. "Lord the lovely thing about your grace is that through every event in my life you had the way prepared and your grace covered me."

"Build relationship with Amanda. My grace also covers her and my love is moulding her for the future."

"Thank you Lord that you are my best friend. Use me and let your love flow through me to her, showing her acceptance and favour."

Emily arrived back at the hotel and went into the office where Jack was working. She hugged him and kissed his cheek.

"Hello darling. Why am I getting hugs and kisses?"

"Jack I love you and I love what God has blessed us with. I've just spent a long time with a young girl who believes she is a mistake. I think I've helped to change her mind but it made me realise that we have what we have because of his grace and if he can use me to help to heal one wounded life then my life will be worthwhile."

Jack stopped work and stood up from his desk. He saw the look of tenderness in Emily's eyes and he knew her heart would ache for that girl. He kissed her and then she put her head on his shoulder. "Emily, God has used you today just like he's used you before and there will be more people in the future that he will want you to reach out to. Keep loving them with his love and be assured that your life has been worthwhile."

29 VICTORIA WAS DELIGHTED with the work that had been done to the cottage.

The decorators were in and they were almost finished. She had spent a lot of time out shopping and she drove to Coleraine several times a week. She had ordered large items to be delivered and smaller items filled the car. The hotel porter was helping her unload everything when Emily came outside.

"Hi is there anything I can do?"

"No not in your condition although you could have coffee with me when I eventually get inside."

"I'll see you in my sitting room. I fancy a chocolate cream cake."

Victoria frowned. "I suppose I'll have to have one with you. We can't have you eating alone."

"Right I'll see you soon." Emily disappeared with a smile on her face. Being pregnant was affecting other people when it came to her food notions and they just had to support her!

Victoria arrived like an excited child. "Emily I've had such a good day. There is nothing like retail therapy to keep me happy."

"You look radiant Victoria. I'm glad you bought the cottage because it has been good for you to get involved in something new. How soon will everything be completed."

"I hope to move in about two weeks and I have my art studio finished. I bought some materials today and I've been doing some sketches."

"You are a changed woman Victoria. Coming to Northern Ireland has been a great move for you. I'm glad you have some focus in your life now."

"So am I. Sometimes I think back to the life I had with Steven and it seems such a long time ago. It is as if it happened to someone else and not me. Do you think I'm in denial?"

"No I think you are learning to think for yourself. You used to be so afraid of making decisions in case they were wrong or you upset Steven. Now you are learning about you and you have a new life here. Today you bought painting materials and that's something you wouldn't have done when you were with Steven."

"I know I was always afraid back then. Now I feel I'm becoming the person that has always existed inside me but Steven wouldn't have approved. I feel like so much of me has been hid away and now I've bursting to be free."

Emily passed her the plate of chocolate cakes. "Celebrate with a cake."

Victoria laughed. "Emily you are not always good for me."

"I know but its fun. We can diet when the baby is born. Victoria I love the real you and I think you should always be true to yourself and never allow anyone to take over your life the way Steven did."

"I won't. Now I have a relationship with the Lord my life is changed completely and I have a lot to make up for."

They finished their coffee and Victoria sighed. "I really enjoyed that but now I'm going to go down to the cottage and I might go for a walk. I'll see you later."

Victoria parked her car outside the cottage and had a look inside. The decorators were still working so she left them to get on with the job. She walked down the road that turned onto the path that led to the beach. Stepping over some rocks she jumped down onto the sand. The waves were rippling in land and soon the tide would be in. It was a beautiful afternoon and the sky was clear blue as shafts of sunlight beamed onto the waves making them glisten like diamonds. She walked along the beach and her heart melted with love for her Lord. "My life is so wonderful because of you and my heart is full of joy that I never thought was possible. Lord it is because of your great love for me that I have come this far and I know we have only just begun. I believe you have so much for Chloe and I to look forward to. You are an awesome God and I worship you with my life."

She walked along the water's edge holding her shoes in her hand. The cold water covered her feet and she felt revived. The sea air cleared her head and she felt newness inside. "Lord I feel like I'm falling in love all over again but it's with you. My heart is bursting for more of you and your love is such an intense revelation to my spirit. I feel a reckless abandon of my heart to you as I bathe in your embrace. You are everything I need in abundance and there is none like you."

"I delight in your praise. I have brought you to the place of reckless abandonment of your heart, your life and everything I created you to be. I am a husband to you and I have betrothed you unto me forever. I can do so much in the life of one who is surrendered to me. I'm the potter and you are the clay in my hands and I'm shaping your life for my purpose. I have prepared the way, walk in it and rest in my love."

Victoria sat down on the rocks and watched as the waves lapped around her. She sensed the stillness of his presence in her heart and she felt totally surround by his peace. She bowed her head in grateful acknowledgement of her Lord and his love that covered her life.

Emily and Jack went to the hospital the next morning for a routine appointment. "Jack I feel so much bigger with this baby."

Jack smiled. "Emily I don't think it is the baby but the amount of chocolate cream cakes you have been eating."

"That could be true. Victoria and Amy are beginning to avoid me. They have begun to put on weight since I became pregnant."

Jack laughed. "You are a bad influence on people. I thought you told me you were going to eat only healthy foods."

"I do most of the time but when I take a craving for cakes then I just have to have one."

"Yes and so does everyone else!"

The consultant brought them into his office and the nurse did the routine tests. "Emily we will do a scan now and see how the baby is doing."

Jack helped her onto the bed with a smile on his face.

"I don't know what you're smiling about. Be thankful you are a man."

The doctor laughed. "I've heard that statement quite a few times. Now just relax Emily and we will take a look at the monitor."

The doctor studied the screen. "The baby certainly is active this morning."

"I know I can feel him practising his football moves."

"It could be a girl darling."

"Well then she's the sporty type."

The doctor continued to watch the picture on the monitor but Emily sensed he was quiet. "Is anything wrong doctor?"

Jack held her hand and she felt tense.

"Nothing to worry about Emily. I just want to make sure." He continued to scan. "There it is, I thought as much."

Jack stood up and looked closer at the screen. "Is the baby alright?"

The doctor smiled. "The babies are fine. You are having twins."

Emily gasped in surprise and looked at Jack. "It wasn't just cakes!"

Jack laughed and kissed her.

"I had to be sure Emily. One baby is lying almost behind the other so we wouldn't have known before today."

"I had a feeling something was different right from the beginning. I felt like there was more than one tiny baby there."

The doctor laughed. "Women sometimes get a feeling when the pregnancy is different. There's a lot to be said for women's instinct."

Jack and Emily left the hospital with more scan pictures and they were surprised but happy at the news. "Jack how are we going to manage with two babies to care for? They are hard work and so demanding."

"We have Anna to help."

"Jack she already helps with the two children we have and she cooks."

"She doesn't have to cook; we live in a hotel and can have food sent up anytime."

"I know but she likes to cook. We will have to tell her we are having twins and if necessary we will get someone in to help her."

"We need to tell her gently in case she resigns."

Emily laughed at him. "Jack finding out I was pregnant was a surprise but now we know it's twins I feel overwhelmed."

"Emily God is simply giving us a double blessing."

"Yes I suppose although I'd have been just as happy with one. Jack just think how big I'll get with twins, and I was worried about eating too many cakes."

"Emily you will be big and beautiful so let's enjoy this pregnancy, at least it is different."

Jack couldn't wait to tell the family about the twins. Emily was quieter but it was more shock than surprise. Anna was delighted and assured them she would help in any way and she wouldn't resign. Jack telephoned his parents and they were delighted. It was good for them to receive such happy news. They would come over to Ireland when the babies were born and Sarah was planning on a big shopping trip to Mothercare.

Emily lay on her bed for an afternoon rest and she patted her tummy. "God I haven't taken the time to say thank you for these two little ones. I was surprised at the news but the lovely thing is, you knew right before conception that there would be two babies. It's lovely that we are in your care and as our babies are developing I want to embrace this special time in my life with you and thank you for your blessings."

"I will bless the fruit of your womb and I will cover you as the eagle covers her young. I know your heart and your willingness to serve me and I rejoice over you with singing."

"Lord you really know how to make me feel special." She closed her eyes and drifted into sleep.

The weeks went by and Emily blossomed in health and as she got bigger she revelled in the joy of knowing two little miracles were growing inside her. Jack insisted she work as little as possible and she rested more. Her rest times were becoming a special time between her and God and she knew she was experiencing his blessing on her life. She and Jack seemed to have a closer bond in their relationship as they enjoyed this pregnancy, even when Jack had to rub her back in the middle of the night.

Victoria and Chloe had moved into their cottage and were enjoying settling into their new home. Now that Chloe had started school Victoria spent most of her time in her studio. Her desire was to paint enough pictures and have the opportunity to show them. She talked with Emily about beginning a project with the children at the home as she knew so much artistic talent could be buried under a mountain of difficult circumstances. Victoria wanted to design a project that would be creative and stimulating for the children. She and Emily were planning a meeting with Iris and then if she liked the idea it would be listed on the agenda for the committee members that met each month.

It would take time but Victoria had prayed and planted the seed and she believed in its season there would be a harvest.

Emily worked for a few hours each day and it was usually paperwork. Amy had taken on extra work and she would bring anything important to the apartment. Anna would have tea ready for them and Amy got to stay for a chat.

"I've brought some post for you to go through. There's some promotional material and I can deal with booking requests."

"Thank you Amy. You're a star. What's this one on top, it's unopened."

"That's because it says, personal and your name is on it."

"Oh right. What would I do without you? I'll read it later."

Emily had a sandwich at lunch time and her cravings for chocolate cakes seemed to have gone away. She patted her tummy and thought there would be no more room for cakes now. The twins were getting bigger by the day and Emily felt enormous.

"Anna I'm going to rest for awhile. I'm tired today."

Anna smiled. "You need to rest, now off you go."

Emily was about to lay down when she remember the letter. She had put it in the pocket of her trousers, folded over. She took it out and looked at the envelope but didn't recognise the writing so she tore it open.

Dear Emily

I hope you are well. I saw your picture in the newspaper with your husband and you look beautiful. It's taken a lot of courage for me to write to you but I couldn't put it off any longer so I'll get straight to the point.

The last time I saw you was the day you were taken from me and placed in care. I'm your birth mother Emily and I've never stopped thinking about you. There are lots of things I'd like to say to you but they will keep for now.

I want you to know that I love you and I really would like to meet with you. Maybe a telephone call to begin with might be an idea.

If you don't want any contact with me then I will understand but I hope you will think about it. I'm sorry if this letter has opened old wounds as it is not my intention to hurt you. I can't go on with the rest of my life without at least having tried to contact you.

I hope to hear from you.

God Bless

Mum (Maria Gibson-Wallis)

Emily was stunned. She looked at the letter again and she felt numb. She still had the silver locket and the letter that had been given to her on her birthday when she was in care. She never expected to hear from her birth mother again and now this letter. She wasn't sure how she was supposed to react. This woman had given her away and although Emily understood the reasons why, it had all happened a long time ago. She wondered if she should just ignore the letter after all this woman was a stranger to her. If she decided to make contact then she had to think about how this would affect her family. There were a few people who knew she had grown up in care but there were lots who didn't. This letter would merge the past with the present and this woman would become part of Emily's future. She had to think of her children and how would she introduce a new grandmother to them? Yet another part of her wanted to get in contact with the sender. Renee would remember her birth mother but it had been such a long time she would be just as surprised.

"Oh Lord why am I thinking of her as this woman, she is my birth mother and after all these years she hasn't forgotten about me. What am I to do?"

When Jack came in he found Emily upset and he thought that something was wrong with the babies. "Honey what is it? You have been crying."

"Jack I received a letter today. It's from my birth mother. After all these years she has found me."

Jack sat down beside her and put his arms around her. "This isn't a surprise Emily it is a shock, no wonder you are upset. How did she find you?"

"There's the letter and it has a London postmark on it. She mentions seeing the photographs in the newspaper."

"That would have been the night of the dinner at the Royal Court. There were lots of photographs taken that night. I'm puzzled how she was so sure that it was you in them."

"I don't understand Jack."

"This woman hasn't seen you in over thirty years yet she recognises you from a photograph. Finding our address wouldn't have been hard because of the business but I feel she had to have more to go on than a picture in a newspaper."

"She could have hired a private detective to double check the photograph was mine. That way someone else does the work for her."

"She signs her name Gibson-Wallis. I wonder why?"

Emily sighed. "I don't know. Right now I have more questions than answers. My immediate concern is, do I ignore the letter or do I make contact with her."

"Honey you need to think of the consequences of what could happen if you contact her or if you will regret it if you don't? I'll support you no matter what you decide but it's your choice."

"I know that. Before you came in I'd considered ignoring the letter, after all, she put me into care all those years ago and while I understand her reasons for having to do it, I don't know if I could face her now. It might be too late. I've had two children and now I'm pregnant with the twins and there is no way I could give my babies away." She began to cry.

Jack held her. "Emily you also need to remember that because you are pregnant you are very sensitive at the moment. Your birth mother made a decision over thirty years ago when she had no family support or money. You have to allow for how difficult the circumstances were for her. She probably made her decisions out of fear or her family made those decisions for her and she had no option but to go along with them."

"Jack I can understand and I've forgiven her for the past. My struggle is in knowing that if I make contact with her I'm unlocking the past that few people know about. This will have an effect on our family and how will your parents feel about it?"

"Emily I appreciate your concern about our family but we can cross those bridges if and when we have to. At present this letter is about you and you need to be thinking about how you are going to react."

"Jack I honestly don't know. I'll leave it for a day or two and I'll need to pray about it. It just feels like such a shock at the moment."

"That's a good idea and when you are ready we will talk about it again."

Emily felt restless in the days ahead and being pregnant with the twins didn't help. She felt enormous and clumsy and patience was not her strong point. Working in the office sorting the post she was in sombre mood.

"Emily you don't need to be here. Why don't you go upstairs for a rest?"

"I'm fine Jack." She burst into tears.

"Emily you are not fine. You are feeling tired and under pressure. Take some time out."

"I think you are right Jack. I'll go for a walk in the garden and clear my head."

"Good idea and when you get back go upstairs and I'll come and see you."

"Yes I'll do that." She picked up her jacket and as she put it on she knocked over some letters onto the floor. "Oh sorry."

Amy bent down to pick them up. "It's alright Emily, you go on."

Emily laughed. "You mean, get out of my office before I destroy it. I feel like an elephant these days."

"Well you don't look like one although maybe the elephant behaviour could be a problem." Amy teased.

"Ha ha, I'm out of here."

Emily didn't walk very far, just to the flower garden in the hotel grounds and she down on a bench. She felt empty and frustrated inside. Looking over the gardens the flowers had begun to bloom and soon the area would be an array of colour. Emily relaxed as the cool air helped clear her mind but she was aware of emptiness inside her. "Lord I'm tired yet looking at the beauty of the flowers reminds me of the colours that you have created. I always find it awesome when I see the result of your creativeness." She looked up towards the hills behind the hotel and the amazing shades of green and while she was in awe of God there was still something in her spirit that remained empty. "Lord it says in your word, I lift up my eyes to the hills, where does my help come from. My help comes from the Lord, maker of heaven and earth.

I need your help. I feel so restless and it's has nothing to do with being pregnant. It's the letter Lord and I don't know what to do about it. So many memories have been reawakened and I feel a longing to meet the woman who gave birth to me but she is still the same woman who gave me away. I need to hear you Lord because I just can't do this myself."

Emily the answer is in front of you. You don't have to look any deeper."

She sighed. "Now you really have me puzzled." Emily got up and walked along the pathway where she stopped at the bridge that overlooked the stream running through the gardens. Along the side of the bank she saw clusters of forget-me-nots in colours of blues and lilacs. "Lord they are so small and yet so lovely although they could get swept away being at the edge of the stream."

"At least they have taken the risk."

Emily stood still; there was no mistaking his voice. "I think I see what my problem is Lord. The issue is not about whether I reply to the letter or not, it's about taking a risk. Am I willing to take the risk of being vulnerable with the one person whom I've always wanted to meet? Am I willing to experience the effect it will have on my family and on me as a person?" Emily looked down at the flowers again growing at the edge of the water; although they were at risk of being swept away they still continue to bloom. "Lord I've made my decision and I'll go and talk to Jack."

"Be strong and of good courage. I'll always be with you."

Emily returned to the apartment and Jack was there looking for a folder. "Hi honey, did you see the papers I was reading last night? I thought I left them on the desk?"

"They are in the bedroom Jack. You had them there this morning. I know you are in a hurry but can I talk to you for a few minutes."

He stopped and stood in front of her. "You have reached a decision?"

"I have. I'm going to reply to the letter. I realise that fear has been holding me back. I wasn't sure if I could take the risk of being vulnerable with the one person whom I wanted love and acceptance from. Jack I've prayed about it and I'm willing to take the risk."

"Emily I'm glad. You sound a lot more positive about it so what was the deciding factor?"

"I was standing on the bridge where the stream goes through the gardens when I saw some forget-me-nots growing along the edge of the bank. It was then the Lord allowed me to see the risk they took blooming at the edge of the stream yet they could easily be swept away."

"Maybe the forget-me-nots are symbolic reminders that your birth mother hasn't forgotten you and she obviously doesn't want you to forget her."

"Yes I believe that."

He kissed her. "I'm glad you have reached your decision and you know that I will support you in every way. Just think, I might just get to meet my mother-in-law."

Emily laughed. "I never thought of it that way. Thank you Jack for your support, I need you so much."

After Jack had left Emily sat down at her writing desk and took out her personal stationary.

Dear Mum

I hope you don't mind me calling you that although I suppose it sounds strange to the both of us. It has taken me a few days to think about the implications of replying to your letter but everything in life carries an element of risk. I realise that you took the risk of writing to me not knowing if I would reply, now I'm willing to take that same risk. I'm feeling quite vulnerable as I write this but I would like to talk with you and hopefully we could meet each other.

I understand why you made the decision to let me go when I was a baby. I believe you loved me but the circumstances you were in must have been very difficult for you. I feel everything was stacked against you and you didn't have any control over the events that happened. It must have been an awful time for you. I'm sorry you had to go through that and there seems to have been a lack of support for you at a time when you needed it most.

I still have the silver locket and the letter I was given on my sixteenth birthday; I also have your photograph.

I'd like you to telephone me if you still want to. There is so much for us to talk about. I'm married, as you know, and I have a daughter, a son and I'm pregnant with twins. My husband is a wonderful man who would like to meet his mother-in-law! I hope that thought hasn't frightened you off. We are both Christians and our relationship with God is such an important part of our lives. It is good to be able to pray about everything and know that no matter how difficult the circumstances that there will be a way through them.

I look forward to hearing from you.

Love

Emily

After the letter was posted Emily worried that she hadn't made it long enough or maybe it was too informal. Already she was wondering when her mother would get in contact with her and she was curious about what she looked like. The photograph that Emily had was taken when her mother was sixteen and she had held her in her arms. One photograph of a young girl was all she had to connect her with the past.

"Lord I have so many questions I want to ask her."

"*Patience Emily. Be still and know that I am God. I know the end from the beginning and I am making all things new.*"

"My security is in you Lord because you do see the bigger picture, from start to finish. I surrender myself to you and I trust you with the response to the letter."

Emily felt at peace because she had taken a step forward by writing to her mother. It was like a huge step for her because she knew that her past would soon merge with the present. Although she had never met her mother she felt she loved her and to love was a risk at any time.

"Lord you took the biggest risk of all when you loved me enough to die for me. I'm glad you did because you have taught me how to love and I believe I will have the opportunity to show that love to my mother."

30 JACK AND EMILY stood in the arrivals waiting area of Belfast International Airport. Emily was feeling a little apprehensive and her body felt heavy in the last weeks of her pregnancy. The twins were due within two weeks but Emily didn't think she would have to wait that long.

Jack squeezed her hand. "Are you alright Emily? I think we should sit down."

"I'm fine. I just hope my waters don't decide to break in the middle of the airport." She giggled at the thought.

Jack frowned. "That's not funny. I think the sitting down idea is a good one."

He guided her to a seat. "Would you like a coffee?"

"No Jack. One coffee and the twins become hyperactive and play football on my bladder. You know something Jack? I don't think I could do this again, ever!"

He laughed. "It won't be long now and within two weeks it will all be over."

"I can hardly wait."

Jack walked over to the monitor to check the incoming flight times. The flight from London came up on the screen and he went back over to Emily. "Honey the flight has just arrived."

"Oh Jack this is it. I suddenly feel so nervous. Maybe she has changed her mind and she won't be on the flight. Or she will take one look at me and get back on it again."

"Emily stop it. She is probably just as nervous as you are but it will be fine. You both have waited a long time for this meeting."

"Jack why don't you go over to the reception desk where we arranged to meet. I don't think I could stand, my legs are sore."

"You wait here and I'll go and ask for her."

]Emily tried to calm the butterflies in her tummy and at the same time the babies tried to turn around. "You two behave, I'm supposed to be calm." She whispered. "Lord I've waited so long for this moment and I thank you for the way in which you have brought it about. Today I'm going to meet my mum and I feel like a child again."

She saw a woman approach the desk where Jack was standing. She had dark hair like Emily and she was slim, unlike Emily! "That's my mum." She whispered and then she felt the tears and a feeling of overwhelming love rose up inside her. She stood up and began to walk forward as Jack turned and saw the woman. She looked like Emily and he smiled. "Welcome Maria, I'm Jack, Emily's husband."

"Where is she?"

"Mum I'm right here."

Maria turned around and the look of love in Emily's eyes brought tears to her own. "Oh Emily, my beautiful daughter." Tears flowed freely as they hugged each other and all the years of praying and hoping for this wonderful moment was the miracle they had hoped it would be.

Maria stood back and wiped the tears from Emily's cheeks. "You are as beautiful as I imagined you to be. I have longed so much to hug you and I have done it so many times in my dreams but today it is real."

"Mum this is the best day of my life. From I was a little girl I have wanted to see you just so as I can call you mum."

Jack put his arms around both of them. "We have a car waiting outside and you two can get better acquainted."

"I must see to my luggage."

"Maria that has been taken care of and it is in the car. Let's go girls."

They laughed as they walked through the airport to the waiting car linking each others arms.

The drive back to the hotel was relaxing and Maria was amazed at the beauty of the scenery as they drove to the coast. Emily was surprised at how natural their conversation flowed, just as if they had known each other all their lives.

When they arrived at the hotel Maria was taken to the guest suite and after she had freshened up she met Emily in the sitting room for tea. Jack stayed for a few minutes and then excused himself; he knew they need time alone together.

"Emily, scones with fresh cream and jam, how lovely."

"I know. I blame all my extra weight on being pregnant but I'm really just deceiving myself."

"Enjoy it while you can. I'm so happy I'm here while you are still pregnant. There is so much I have missed out on."

"Well you will be meeting the children later but I thought we could have some time on our own. I had so many questions I wanted to ask you but now that you are here they don't seem to be as important now."

"Maybe it would help if I begin by telling you about myself and then if you still have questions I can answer them then."

Emily smiled and at that moment her mother reached out and held her hand. "I know how vulnerable you feel but we need this time to be honest. We can't change the past but we can enjoy the present and with all my heart I want to be a part of your life and your future."

"I feel the same. I want you to know that I love you and you will always be in my life from this day on."

Maria curled up on the sofa with her tea. "Emily I know that you received the letter I'd left for you when you were sixteen. After you were born my family didn't give me any choice about keeping you. My parents were ashamed of me and your biological father disappeared overnight. I wanted to keep you but I had no job, no money and no support. The social worker assigned to be was in favour of the adoption, everyone thought it was for the best but no one asked me what I thought. I asked my family if we could keep you but because they were so angry with me they threatened to throw me out. No one was concerned about how I felt or the pain I was going through knowing that I had to give you over to the social worker. In my memory I always see myself holding you for the last time, kissing your baby soft skin and telling you over and over again how much I loved you. The day they took you away none of my family came near the home to visit me until it was over and then they brought my clothes and we went home. We left town soon after and I wasn't allowed to talk about you. They treated me like it had never happened but how could I forget you? Every birthday and Christmas I used to imagine what you looked like. I didn't know that you were in a children's home. I was led to believe that you were going to be adopted so I always thought of you as being part of a family and being happy.

Eventually I met the man I married, James Wallis. My parents approved because he had a good job, he was an accountant and he sang in the church choir. I think I loved him when we married, I'm not sure but I grew to love him over the years. I hadn't fallen in love with him; I had never experienced those feelings with anyone. Those real feelings of intense love had died in me the day I lost you and my heart remained closed for a long time after that. James was a good husband and provider and I never had to go out to work after we married. Sometimes I would have liked a job outside the home but James didn't like the idea. We had two children, David and Ellen and of course they have grown up now. David is married but no family yet and Ellen is a career girl, she became a nurse and now she is a midwife. She would come in useful for you. James, my husband died two years ago from a heart complaint. I miss him sometimes but I always kept a part of me separate from him and the children. Through the years I have always thought of you but I assumed that you had been adopted and I was afraid that if I tried to find you I would upset your life. James knew about you but he thought trying to trace you would only lead to more unhappiness.

In a way he was quite protective towards me but at the same time we had a comfortable life and I don't know how he would have coped with any change in our circumstances. David and Ellen never knew about you until their father died. It was then I knew I had to try and find you and I hoped that it wouldn't upset your life if I succeeded. I knew I was taking a risk but when James died it happened suddenly and I realised that you don't always get a second chance to do the things you want to do. I had this urgency to find you so I hired a private detective and set my plan into action. I told my children about you and they were surprised to learn that they had a sister somewhere although David couldn't imagine his mum being pregnant and not being married. I had to remind him that it happened a long time before he was born. Ellen is more outgoing and after she got over the surprise she thought it a great idea to find you. They both want to meet you but only when you are ready."

"You and James were involved in a church so were you both Christians?"

"James was a very committed person but in many ways I was the opposite. I went to church because my parents made me go but because I had lost you I didn't really believe in anything or anyone. Looking back I suppose I was suffering from depression but that wasn't a subject people openly talked about then. When I began going out with James I knew he was a good catch for a husband and he was kind, however, I wanted to be honest with him. At first he was shocked when I told him; he found it hard to believe that a quiet girl like me could be in that situation. He thought my parents had my best interests at heart when they said I couldn't keep you. I knew that I could love James but I'd never be in love. After we married I made excuses not to go to church and after a few arguments we agreed I would go to any special meetings there was, like Easter and Christmas. It stayed that way for years until one day I was tidying some boxes in the attic. We kept all sorts of things up there and I found an old purse of mine. I opened it thinking there might be money in it but instead I found something more precious. It was the little name band that was round your wrist after you were born. Suddenly I felt as though my heart was breaking and I sat down on the floor and cried. I felt so alone and unhappy and my life with James was a different one to the one I craved. It was pretence in many ways and yet he seemed content with what we had. I got on my knees with the baby band in my hand and I prayed and as I opened my heart to God for the first time in years the pain of longing eased. I knew then that one day I would find you and I believed I had entered into a different kind of relationship with God. I didn't begin to go to church then but I started to read my bible and when I talked to God he became real to me."

"What about my dad? No one could ever tell me anything about him."

"That's because there isn't much to tell. He came and worked on the farm and his name was Rodney. He had such a funny sense of humour and he was like a breath of fresh air to me. My parents were very religious and very serious about life but Rodney was carefree and loved to laugh. I fell for him that summer and he used to tease me and I'd blush. He was a few years older than me and when I became pregnant he intended to stand by me. He went to talk to my father and the next morning I was told that Rodney had left and he wouldn't be back. I think my father thought that he wasn't good enough for me and he gave Rodney the impression that my family would look after me and the baby. In a way they tricked him into leaving and I know that my father could be very persuasive."

"Are your parents still alive?"

"My mother isn't but my father is although he is ill and in residential care."

"You wrote in your letter that you saw my photograph in the newspaper but how could you be so sure that it was me?"

"The private detective I hired was able to trace your whereabouts up until you got married. The Dillon-Spence name is known in London and I felt quite proud that you had done so well in your life. The detective had contacts within the newspaper that gave us the information we needed to confirm that the photograph was you and Jack. We knew about the Royal Court Hotel in Kensington, I mean, most people do; then we discovered that there was a hotel in Ireland and that you and Jack were the management."

Emily looked puzzled. "If you traced me until I'd married and you were aware who the Dillon-Spence family were then why wait until now to write to me? Jack and I have been married for a long time."

"I agree there was a gap from the time I found out about you until making contact recently. My husband was still alive then and I didn't tell him or our children what I was doing; besides he might have tried to talk me out of it.

I also was a little afraid that you might not want to have anything to do with me so I had to prepare myself for that possibility. I'm so glad that hasn't happened."

"Mum your life is amazing. You coped with so much yet you kept your feelings to yourself and believed you would still find me. As a child growing up in care I was always aware of God in my life, I knew him from story books and learning to pray and I loved it when the local minister used to come and visit us and have a special children's meeting. I spent a lot of my life praying for a family and I was in foster care several times but as I got older I had to accept that no one wanted to adopt an older child. I suppose inside me I always believed that one day I would be part of a family but the way in which it came about was something only God could have done for me."

"What happened to you when you left the home?"

"I got a job and I began to lead my independent life but somewhere along that path I lost sight of God. It was as if he wasn't a priority in my life, maybe because I was grown up and I'd still never lived within a family I might have felt disappointed that he hadn't answered my prayers. Rosa, my daughter, isn't Jack's child although he has adopted her and he is a wonderful father to both our children. The man who I had Rosa to was the first man I'd fallen in love with and for the first time in my life it felt good to be loved by another person. When I got pregnant he didn't want to know and I had to make a choice, it was either him or the baby but I couldn't have both. I made my choice and for several years I was a single parent but the hotel I worked in was managed by a wonderful woman called Renee. She had no family of her own and she became very protective of me and she cared for me while I was pregnant. I had living accommodation at the hotel so I was able to keep working. Renee was with me when Rosa was born and we have remained close friends ever since."

"How did you meet Jack if you were in South Devon?"

"Renee knew his family and he came to see her about business but it so happened it was my birthday and Rosa was three years old at the time. Renee had planned a surprise tea with Rosa and Jack was there when we arrived. I was introduced to him and we became friends. I was very cautious at first but by this time in my life I had become committed in my relationship with God and prayed about everything. When I found out that Jack was also a Christian I was happy about seeing him. We fell in love but I knew that this time the relationship would be different to the one I'd known in the past. I think I was a shock for his mother." Emily laughed at the thought.

"Why?"

"Sarah had always imagined that Jack being her oldest son and very attractive would fall in love with someone with a little more breeding than me. She had dreams of a big society wedding and family names covering the pictures in the papers. Instead she discovered that I was a single parent with no parents of my own and I had grown up in a children's home."

Maria laughed. "I can imagine you were a surprise."

"Things improved after Jack and I married because then I wasn't a single parent but Jack's wife. Sarah is now a Christian and she and I are very close but back then I never thought I could ever have a good relationship with her.

I'm grateful to God for the husband I have and the family I married into. It's like he knows the desires of our heart and if we trust him he does work out situations and circumstances. All those years ago I prayed and he heard and now I'm in my sitting room having coffee with my mother."

"Yes I agree with you that we both have received answers to prayer."

"I'm glad you are staying for a few weeks and I'm sure Victoria will just love to take you shopping. She calls it retail therapy, I call it spending money."

"Who's Victoria?"

"She is Jack's sister-in-law and she left England to come and live over here. Jack's younger brother Steven died a few days after Christmas so the family have gone through a difficult time. Victoria has bought a cottage not far from the hotel and she hopes to pursue her own dreams now. She has a little girl, Chloe, who has just begun school so they have settled and are making a new life."

"My goodness there is so much for me to catch up on and new people to meet. I feel like God has just given me a wonderful gift of a daughter, son-in-law and grandchildren, infact a new family. It's so exciting being here with you."

"I feel the same because I've yet to meet your children. It's like God is weaving together the whole picture for us just like he saw it long ago."

Maria enjoyed spending time getting to know her grandchildren and they thought it was great having a secret granny that could now spoil them with treats.

Victoria met Maria at dinner that night in the apartment and she was happy for Emily. She knew how much she longed to meet her birth mother and finally it had happened.

Emily finished her meal and sipped chilled water. "I enjoyed that so much. I didn't realise how hungry I was."

"You need a little extra in your condition although you haven't long to go."

"No, less than two weeks and I'll be glad when it's over. I'm very tired these days and it frustrates me that I can't do as much as I used to. I feel I'm near the end of a long road."

Maria smiled proudly at her daughter. "There has been a lot of excitement in your life these last few weeks and you could be overtired now. You do need to rest as much as you can before the babies come."

"I keep telling her that Maria but she can be a little strong willed."

"I'll have a rest day tomorrow and keep everyone happy."

"Maria since Emily won't be in our way tomorrow, why don't I take you shopping. I know some great stores and shopping is such good therapy, if you happen to need any. We could have lunch and get better acquainted."

Emily and Maria looked at each other and burst out laughing.

"What's so funny?" Victoria turned to Emily.

"I was just telling my mother today that you would love to take her shopping and you probably have had more therapy than anyone I know."

"Victoria I would love to go with you. I want to see so much while I'm here."

"I shop in Coleraine a lot and then we could go for a drive round the coast. You will have a wonderful day Maria and I assure you that despite what Emily has said about me, retail therapy simply means that you forget about everything else and come home with lots of bags and a smile on your face."

"I suppose I can't ask for more than that."

Jack was amused as he observed the three women. "Maria I'm sure you and Victoria will get on very well together while my wife has a rest day tomorrow. I think it's just great that we are all together and so many new things are going on in all our lives. God is a good God."

Maria reached over and squeezed his hand. "He is Jack. I'm so happy to be here."

The next day Jack arranged a car to drive Victoria and Maria shopping. They arranged with the driver when to pick them up and Maria wanted a leisurely drive round the coast. Emily was in reception to see them off although she felt a little sorry for the driver. How was he going to cope with two excited ladies all day long?

"Have a lovely day and I'll see you for dinner tonight."

"We will. It's shop until we drop."

"Victoria I hope I can keep up with you."

"Believe me Maria, you won't have problem because you will be enjoying yourself so much."

When they reached Coleraine, Victoria began her guided tour of all the shops she knew in Bridge Street and Church Street and lunch at the restaurant in Queen Street. Maria wanted to buy presents for everyone in her new family especially the grand-children and Chloe. She smiled to herself.

"What are you grinning about?"

"Victoria I just never thought I'd be shopping in Northern Ireland for my new family. The only time I've heard of this country has been on the television news and it hasn't always been good."

Victoria laughed. "This country is a great place and I'm so pleased I got to take you on your first shopping trip."

It was late in the day when the two women returned to the hotel. Emily was relaxing in the sitting room when her peace was suddenly disrupted.

In they came followed by a porter with lots of bags. He put them down and looked at Emily. "Will I have tea sent through madam?"

"Yes please and some cakes." She grinned at Victoria who was all smiles and her mother, smiling but looking a little tired. "I can tell you two have had a good day."

"Emily it was wonderful. Victoria does know how to shop, however my feet are complaining so I'll have to take my shoes off."

Emily stood up and rubbed her back. "I've been a little uncomfortable today. I couldn't lie down because my back has been sore."

"Have you told Jack?"

"No Victoria. He is busy and I don't want to interrupt him because I've a sore back. I think the twins are just putting pressure on me and that's the cause. It can't be very comfortable for them now because there isn't a lot of room for them to move about. Now tell me about your day. Mum I'm sure Victoria had you in every shop in Coleraine."

"Well I don't think we walked passed many but it was a wonderful day. I understand now about retail therapy and I can't wait to tell Ellen this is what you do."

"Ellen? Oh Emily I've just realised you have a sister Ellen."

Emily shook her head and laughed. "Victoria what are we going to do with you?"

She sat down and suddenly felt a sharp pain in her back. She frowned as little beads of sweat broke out on her forehead.

"Emily what is it."

"Mum I think I've just had a contraction. Victoria ring through to the office and get Jack. I don't feel so well."

Maria was by her side and took her hand. "Emily you'll be fine. I haven't waited all these years for something to go wrong now."

Emily instantly felt secure. "Mum I'm so glad you're here this time. It really makes all the difference."

Jack arrived a few minutes later. "Emily I'll call the doctor."

"Jack it might be to soon. Maybe I should go and rest on the bed for awhile."

"No Emily. This is twins and we were told to ring the doctor when you had the first contraction."

Before Emily could answer she felt the pain as her body contracted. "I think you might be right Jack."

"I'll go and check on Chloe and then I'll come back later. What about Rosa and Nathan?"

"They will be with Anna now."

"I'll take them with me and give Anna a break. Don't worry about anything Emily."

Jack telephoned the doctor who told him to bring Emily into hospital.

"I want mum to come too."

Jack smiled. "Of course, a girl needs her mum at a time like this."

Maria laughed. "Thank you Jack."

The next few hours seem to pass although Emily felt time had stood still as each contraction became stronger than the last. The doctor had given her an injection and she felt like she was floating above it all. She was glad Jack was there beside her and encouraging her but she wanted the pain to end. She remembered that her mum was in the waiting room, determined not to leave until the babies were born. "Jack." She whispered. "It's good that my mum is here."

"I know honey, it means a lot."

Midnight came and went and Emily was exhausted and prayed silently for her babies to be delivered safely. Another contraction and Emily felt an inner strength. "I need to push."

"Yes Emily it's time." The doctor knew how tired she was and he had felt concerned although he hadn't said so. The nurse stood beside her. "Emily at the next contraction, you push."

Jack held her. "Honey this is it."

Within minutes the first baby was born and Emily breathed a sigh of relief.

"Well done Emily. You have a little girl." The baby cried and the nurse wrapped her in a blanket and passed her to Jack. "Emily she is beautiful."

He placed the baby against her shoulder. "Hello my darling."

She took another contraction.

"Emily it's time to push again. You're doing well." The doctor was relieved it was nearly over.

The nurse took the baby from Jack and he held Emily as she delivered her second child. The baby was born and Emily heard that first cry.

"Congratulations you have a son. One of each is as good as it gets."

The baby was taken by the nurse and wrapped up in a blue blanket and brought over to Emily. "Meet your mommy little one."

Jack held their little girl and in that moment he thanked God for his wife and family. "This is truly one of life's special moments."

"Jack they are so beautiful and they are ours. I'm so happy and so tired." She gave their son to Jack and she held their daughter "She has lovely eyes and a tiny button nose."

The doctor knew how tiresome the labour had been for Emily but seeing her smile now had been worth it. "The babies are a good weight and very healthy. Have you though of names yet?"

"Our daughter will be called Hannah Maria and our son, Peter James."

The nurse wrote their names on little bracelets and placed them round their wrist. "Welcome to the world little ones."

"I'll go and see your mum. She's been out there a long time."

"Jack we will be moving Emily to her room shortly and then her mother can see her and the babies."

Emily was resting with her head on the pillows and beside her bed two contented babies asleep in their cots. She was aware of movement in the room and opened her eyes. "Mum I'm glad it's you."

Maria kissed her daughter. "Well done darling." She looked at each baby and stroked their heads. The little boy was asleep with his thumb in his mouth. "Peter James you are lovely." He stirred and woke up and Maria felt tears in her eyes.

"You can hold him Mum."

Maria picked him up and held him close to her. "Emily you have been blessed with these babies." She kissed his head.

"Pass him over to me mum." Emily held him close and smiled at the tiny miracle in her arms.

Maria picked up the little girl and then she saw her name. "Hannah Maria. You called her after me. That is so wonderful. Thank you."

"Jack and I thought you would like that and besides I think she looks like her granny."

Maria laughed. "She is beautiful just like you were the first time I held you. Emily and Jack, the Lord has given me back so much, I feel blessed in abundance."

Within a few days Emily came home with the babies and the hotel staff were excited and had a welcome home banner across the front entrance. Presents were soon pouring in and there was a steady stream of visitors and cards arriving. Jack's parents came over from London and stayed for a few days and they were delighted to meet Maria. The first two weeks were exciting but tiring and when Jack's parents and Maria returned to London she realised she needed to rest. There hadn't been much time for her to be alone with God except when she was feeding the babies late at night in the nursery. It was a special time for her to bond with them and to praise God for them but now that visitors and family had come and gone she wanted to get the babies into a routine and have some time to herself.

Jack had the nursery decorated and sometimes they both sat in here at night and just watching the babies sleep. Emily loved the smell of their soft skin and they were so perfect she felt her heart would overflow with love for them.

Sitting in the rocking chair Emily watched over her little ones, she was at peace inside and she knew the grace of God over her life as her spirit praised him.

"Lord thank you for the miracle of life and the double blessing you have given us. I look at the twins and I think of you, I love you for the life you have given me. I remember when Rosa was born and I felt alone because I had no husband. Lord I soon learned that you were a husband to me and you have supplied every need through the years. I love you and yet I know that your love for me is awesome and you can't love me anymore than you do. I feel so secure in you and I pray that all of my children grow up to know you and grasp hold of the plans you have for them."

When the twins were two months old Emily and Jack had arranged for them to be dedicated at their church and all their family and friends were invited. Amy helped Emily send out the invitations and prepare for the event. After the church service everyone was invited back to the hotel for lunch. A buzz of excitement was in the air as the staff organised the lunch and Emily had a celebration buffet for the staff for all their work. She appreciated that they had a team of committed people working for them and she liked them to know it. Jack was glad Emily seemed more like her old self again and she had a happy contented glow about her that he loved.

"Jack I'm so excited about the twins dedication and everyone being together again."

He laughed at her. "Emily you seem to have gotten your strength back and it's good to see you spark again."

"Jack I know I feel a lot better when I'm doing something. Mum telephoned to say that her son and his wife and her daughter Ellen are all coming over. It will be good to meet them. Just think I have other family I haven't met yet, it feels strange and exciting at the same time."

"I know I'm thinking that when everyone finally comes together we will be one big family circle."

Emily frowned. "Oh Jack I've just thought of something. Your mum, she is going to be looking around at everyone and missing Steven. I think we need to be looking out for her. She wouldn't say anything even if she was feeling miserable but I think we need to be sensitive to her and your dad."

Jack smiled. "You think of everything and everyone. Thank you for being concerned. I know mum appreciates you. I hope she can see that Victoria has moved on and she is happy from she moved here. My mother loved Steven as a son but we all know he wasn't always a good husband to Victoria."

"I think your parents are glad she is making a new life for herself and Chloe. I look at her sometimes and she has a sparkle about her that used to be sadly lacking. The most important decision she ever made was surrendering her life to God. She is at peace with her life and planning for her future, a year ago she was in so much pain and her life was lonely."

"It's good that when we obey God he gives us newness in our lives and hope that we never had before. I've seen marvellous changes in Victoria and I think it's great she has begun to paint again. Who knows what God has in store for her?"

The week of the dedication was a busy one as family and friends began to arrive. Renee White was coming over and she was excited about the twins and being able to meet Emily's birth mother and family.

"Emily how many are coming from the children's home?"

"Iris Boyd will be there and some of the children are singing a song at the service. I've arranged a party for all of the children at the home and I've told Iris we will bring the twins over there."

"What about Amanda?"

"She is doing fine. The day that I had a talk with her seems to have worked and she has settled now. Iris tells me she is doing well with her school work and making friends with the other children."

"Those children are really important to you."

"Yes every one of them. I am really grateful to God for all he is doing in my life but Jack I remember the time when I was in care and felt so alone. If I can help them get a better start in life then I believe God would have me do it."

The morning of the special day Emily woke early and slipped into the nursery. The babies were still asleep and she sat in the rocking chair and smiled at their beautiful faces. She was aware of God's presence in her spirit and she felt bathed in his love and she praised him with a thankful heart.

"Father, you have brought me to a place in my life were I realise that relationship with you is the foundation of everything I ever do. You have taught me how to make the right choices and you have blest me because you are a wonderful God who loves to bless his children. I know from experience what it is like to live my life without having a relationship with you but because of your grace and mercy you gently led me back to you. Today for the first time our families and friends will meet to celebrate the birth of Hannah and Peter but it means more than that to me. I celebrate you today and the children you have given to Jack and I and I thank you for the blessing of having my mother there too. Today we will praise you in church together and that is a miracle. Father, my life has been like a sequence of events that have formed a chain with you being the one who forges the links together.

With you the chain is strong and it is your love for me that has brought people into my life when you saw my need and you answered the cry of my heart. I surrender the rest of my life to you today and I know that the chain will never be completed until the day when I bow before you and see you face to face. Thank you for my life and the husband you have given me, for my family and friends and the work that you have called us to do. Father may I honour you with all I have within me and thank you that our lives are secure in your care."

Emily felt her heart so full of God's love that she desired less of her and more of him. She stood over each of her children and thanked God for them and for the day ahead.

"Emily I know the plans I have for you. Plans for your future, your health, plans to prosper you and give you peace. Always draw near to me for I am near to you and I rejoice over you with singing. Listen to my voice, you will hear me say, this is the way, walk in it. Never allow distractions to side track you from me. Stay close, I am your peace. I have loved you with an everlasting love; I am your Lord, your Redeemer and a mighty God who saves."

Everyone gathered at the church and Emily and Jack came in with the twins and Rosa and Nathan by their side. As a family they stood before God and the congregation, Jack smiled over at Emily and his spirit was overwhelmed by the love God had placed in his heart. The pastor prayed for them as a couple and as parents and then the children's choir sang a song that Emily once sang as a child, Jesus Loves Me. A hush settled on the congregation while the children sang, even the twins slept peacefully and Emily knew in her heart that Jesus truly loved her.

At the celebration lunch afterwards Jack stood up to thank everyone for coming to share their special day. Emily looked around the room of people and smiled as she thought of how God had brought them together and that he would always be at work in their lives.

When the day was over she and Jack kissed their children good night and went into their bedroom. Jack put his arms around her and she rested her head on his shoulder. "Emily when we met all those years ago I never could have imagined what God had in store for us. We are so blessed."

"I know and I'm very happy and very tired."

"Time for bed, you need your rest. I love you Emily."

"I love you Jack and our four children."

As Emily drifted into sleep she was thankful for the wonderful day they had shared with so many and she felt special to God.

She had entrusted her future to him and she was assured that he would perfect all that concerned her and those she loved. The chain of events that had led up to today was simply another link forged by the one who held her life in his hands and there was no safer place to be.

From Me To You

I hope you have enjoyed reading As The Tide Turns, as much as I enjoyed writing it. As the story began to unfold I found myself becoming involved with the characters and the situations they found themselves in.

I have discovered that God can work through any circumstances. There is nothing too hard for Him and nothing impossible for Him. All we have to do is trust Him and we will never be disappointed. We all experience good times in our lives and also difficult times but it is how we respond to our circumstances that makes a difference. We can choose to have a relationship with God or we can try and muddle through on our own. In my experience I find it much easier to trust God than myself! I'm assured through His Word that His plans for my life are for my benefit so why should I muddle through?

If you are a Christian then I hope you found that your faith has been encouraged in reading the story and I hope you enjoyed discovering how God moved in the circumstances the characters had to face.

To those of you who that have read the story and have not made a commitment to Him then let me assure you that Jesus is only a prayer away. Maybe you once walked in relationship with Him but at present He is not high on your list of priorities. Whatever the reason, God knows you and the needs in your life and He is very near you. He may not thunder from heaven in order to get your attention, instead He could speak in a still small voice. Jesus died for you and He paid the price for sin so if you realise that you need a Saviour then all you have to do is open your heart and invite Him in.

Like the characters in the story there were difficult circumstances they had to go through and in reality we all face times in our lives that are painful. God understands and He is longing to carry you through whatever situation you are in. Sometimes we feel that no one can change things for us, maybe we have messed up a lot and life looks bleak. Remember in the story the example of the potter and the clay was mentioned. I love Jeremiah 18 where we read about the potter taking a pot that was marred in his hands so he shaped it into another pot as seemed best to him. God only gives the best and His plans for our lives are to bless us and never to harm us.

As The Tide Turns demonstrates that no matter if your life is sailing calmly through still waters or if you are experiencing rough seas there is a God who loves you and will bring you to the place where your heart will be filled with joy as you praise the One who knows you better than you know yourself.

May His grace and blessings be abundant in each of your lives.

Christine Holmes